Duncan's arms tightened around Serena, drawing her hard against his body. His mouth fit hers perfectly, and nothing existed but Duncan devouring her. He uttered a harsh, raw sound as her tongue came to meet his, tightening his arms around her and burying one hand in her hair.

Like a fast-acting drug, the kiss spread seductive heat through her bloodstream, making Serena totally forget where they were. And why. She vaguely realized that he held her upper arms to steady her as he stepped away. Dazed, she stared up at him, rendered speechless.

"We'll finish this later," he murmured thickly, touching her chin, before turning around and walking away.

ALSO BY CHERRY ADAIR

Hot Ice
On Thin Ice
Out of Sight
In Too Deep
Hide and Seek
Kiss and Tell
Edge of Danger
Edge of Fear

EDGE
of
DARKNESS

A Novel

CHERRY
ADAIR

BALLANTINE BOOKS • NEW YORK

A Ballantine Books Mass Market Original

Copyright © 2006 by Cherry Adair

Published in the United States by Ballantine Books, an imprint of The Random House Publishing Group, a division of Random House, Inc., New York.

BALLANTINE and colophon are registered trademarks of Random House, Inc.

ISBN 0-345-48522-X

Printed in the United States of America

www.ballantinebooks.com

OPM 9 8 7 6 5 4 3 2 1

To the incredible team at Levy Home Entertainment. Howard Reese, John Lindsay, Mike Hesselbach, Pam Nelson, Emily Hixon, and Kate Mirsky and to the wonderful readers who joined us, for making me feel at home among friends during the fabulous Authors at Sea Cruise. It was an experience I'll never forget. Next round of drinks by the pool on me! Until then we'll have the memory of that special, unforgettable table number ██████ to keep us entertained until we sail again.

And to Carla Neggers
who makes me laugh.

Duty o'er love was the choice you did make
My love you did spurn, my heart you did break

Your penance to pay, no pride you shall gain
Three sons on three sons find nothing but pain

I gift you my powers in memory of me
The joy of love no son shall ever see

When a Lifemate is chosen by the heart of a son
No protection can be given, again I have won

His pain will be deep, her death will be swift,
Inside his heart a terrible rift

Only freely given will this curse be done
To break the spell, three must work as one

CHAPTER ONE

MONTANA

Zzzft. Thud!

A flash of orange lightning lit the room, followed by the sudden materialization of a man, dumped unceremoniously in the middle of the conference room table. He was soaking wet. Water runneled on the wood surface around him, then started to pour over the sides.

Duncan Edge merely raised a brow as he shifted his chair out of the way. The other five T-FLAC/psi operatives taking the meeting jumped to their feet at the unexpected interruption, grabbing up computers, paper, and assorted crap before everything was saturated.

"What the hell . . . ?"

"Hey!"

"Holy shit!"

"Jay-zus!"

"Who the f—"

Shaking his head, Duncan prevented the water from cascading into his lap, or onto the floor, with a swift telekinetic thought. He knew the who and the why.

Serena Brightman.

One of her strongest powers was her mastery over water. Clearly she hadn't changed. She still had a bad temper, still couldn't control it. And still had to have the last damned word.

The woman was a menace.

"This is personal," he told the others. "Take five."

"Hell, take ten. Color me intrigued," Connor Jordan told him affably, closing his computer and setting it on the credenza nearby. There were general murmurs of agreement from the others.

Great. Duncan had never allowed his personal life, such as it was, to filter into his professional life. But of course he'd never tried to help Serena before. No good deed goes unpunished. Now he had five freaking witnesses to his folly. Crap.

He waited patiently as his man gasped for air like a beached whale, trying to regain use of his lungs. Understandable, since the guy had hit the solid wood of the table hard and fast. While he waited, Duncan retrieved the note pinned to Chang's crumpled shirt.

"*'I believe this belongs to you,'*" he read the curlicue handwriting out loud. Oh, yeah. He knew the who. Absently he touched the scar bisecting his left eyebrow. Damn woman had lost her temper that time, too. He'd almost been blinded by a flying pencil. "You gonna make it, buddy?" he asked the young half-wizard.

"S-she made me," Chang managed, gray-faced and still spread-eagle in the middle of the polished koa wood table. He'd had the air knocked out of him. His pride, too, if Duncan knew Serena.

"Yeah. Figured that one out for myself," he said dryly. "Told you she was sharp." Too damn sharp, Duncan thought with a stab of irritation. He'd sent Chang, Jensen, and Prost in to watch her back. Serena had been a stubborn pain in Duncan's ass since wizard grade school. But for some annoying reason he always needed to know where she was and what the hell she was doing.

Apparently time and maturity hadn't improved her temper or her stubbornness one iota. He hadn't seen her in what—five? Six years? Not since some charity fund-raiser for the Foundation he'd been dragged to by a date whose name he now couldn't remember. Odd, since he remembered with photographic clarity the backless emerald gown Serena had worn that night.

The glittering material had clung to every curvaceous inch of her body, but had left the upper swell of her creamy breasts and one long, *long* leg exposed. The leg men attending the black-tie function that night had salivated when they'd looked at her, the breast men had their tongues hanging out, and every straight man with a pulse had wanted her.

That was Serena.

Help her echoed in his head like a stuck record. He recognized Henry Morgan's voice, weak though it was. His old mentor was not only Head of the Wizard Council, he also worked in some scientific capacity for the Campbell Foundation that Serena now ran. He'd been "calling" Duncan for the past three days.

"Help her."

The only "her" he and Henry had in common was Serena.

Serena was Henry Morgan's goddaughter, and the old man loved and treated her as his own. Which had sometimes made his and Duncan's friendship difficult.

"Help her. Stop her."

A running litany with growing telepathic urgency but no clear explanation. Why didn't the guy just pick up the damned phone? Henry was one of the few people who had Duncan's private cell number. He knew he was impossible to reach, but Henry could have left a voice mail. He would have returned the call as soon as he was able.

God only knew, he'd tried to call Henry after the first mental SOS. Henry must be off doing Council business and unavailable. Telepathic communication, however iffy it may be, must've been Henry's only way of getting through to him.

While Duncan waited to hear directly from his friend, he'd gone ahead and sent a few guys to see what Serena was up to.

Henry's insistence that he help her, and Chang's untimely return, were indicative of something. *What*, he had no idea. Now he realized it was time to pay both Henry and Serena a visit. If nothing else, it would be amusing to see if he could get a civil answer out of her. Probably not.

He'd contact both of them later this evening when he returned to London, he decided. See what was what. Helping Chang off the table, he noticed that the guy's stick-straight black hair was covered with sand, as if he'd rolled around on a beach. Interesting.

Albert Chang ran a shaky hand over his jaw, his eyes still a little glassy, his breathing ragged. His triangular face flushed with embarrassment as he saw the other wizards in the room. "I can t-try again."

"Don't sweat it." Duncan crumpled Serena's note and lobbed it into the trash can in the corner. He could almost feel her animosity radiating off the light orange-colored, flowery-scented paper. "The others will keep tabs on her."

"Man, I'm sorry, Edg—"

Duncan sent the kid home.

The men picked up their scattered papers and resumed their seats. "That was interesting," Jordan said mildly, reaching for his pen. "Are you using Halves as minions these days?"

"Half" was the term for someone with muted wizard powers. Their claim to fame was that they couldn't be detected by full-blooded wizards, which was why Duncan had sent the three to watch over Serena. They had a few powers of their own, but nothing major. They were neither fish nor fowl. Not fully integrated in the wizard world, but not part of the non-wizard world either.

"Just a little side job," Duncan told them. Prost and Jensen had more experience working side jobs for him than Chang. Serena wasn't going to know *they* were around.

Satisfied that he still had the Serena problem covered, Duncan glanced around. "Where were we?"

Zzzft. Orange lightning fizzled and blinked. "Ah, shit," he muttered, shimmering all the shit off the table before it got soaked.

A saturated Eric Prost, swearing a blue streak, crashed into the spot in the middle of the table that Chang had just vacated. The coral Post-it note protruding from the top of his shirt pocket was dry, and read: *And this!*

Duncan got rid of the puddles and crushed the note in his fist. This was just bullshit, not to mention a serious waste of his time. "Get *anything*?"

"Other than she's drop-dead gorgeous with a temper to match that red hair?" Gingerly, Prost swung himself off the table. "No."

Duncan rubbed a hand over his jaw. "See anything suspicious? Dangerous? Out of place?"

"Not in the forty-eight hours I was tailing her. Just so you know, Mongolia is having an unseasonably hot January, and it's one hundred and nine in the Gobi desert right now."

Duncan was feeling a lot hotter. "Miss Brightman returned Chang as well," he said through gritted teeth.

"You mean Mrs. *Campbell*? Yeah," Prost said with a grimace. "She let me know in no uncertain terms that my presence was far from welcome. That woman can yell without raising her voice. Scary, that. Want me to go back in?"

Campbell. Right. As if he could damn well forget. She'd married. And buried Ian Campbell last year. "No. Jensen's still th—"

Zzft.

"God damn it!"

It was the weakest of the three lightning flashes; Serena sucked at creating fire. Tom Jensen landed on all fours, just shy of the table, tucked and rolled, then sprayed water in all directions like a dog after a swim. He staggered to his feet and handed Duncan his note. It had been attached to his shirt with what looked like a diaper pin.

"I'm trying to *help* her," Duncan said more to himself than the others. He glanced at the note: *And this one as well!* "What the hell is she doing sending you guys *back*?"

"Says, and I quote—she doesn't need your freaking watchdogs following her around, and not to send any more. She'll send all of us back to you, and she won't be nice about it." Prost caught Jensen's eye before both men turned back to Duncan. "Think she pretty much means it, boss."

"I gotta tell you, Duncan," Jensen grimaced, tucking his shirt into his shorts and looking both embarrassed and annoyed. "That woman scares the shit outta me."

Both men had clearly been out in the desert sun. Even in the few days they'd been wherever Serena was—the *Gobi* for Christ's sake?—their skin was already painfully red and peeling.

"Nobody's gonna hurt that one, *believe* me," Jensen muttered. "She'd flay their skin open with that tongue of hers before anyone could draw a weapon."

"But she was *real* sweet to everyone else." Prost picked at the red skin flaking on his nose. "Man, that woman can sure switch moods on a dime."

Yeah. Duncan knew that only too well. "Thanks for your help, guys. You did good." *All things considered*. These half-wizards weren't employed by T-FLAC, they weren't trained in covert ops. They'd done as he'd asked. Kept a low profile, stayed invisible, and watched over Serena. Doing what, he wasn't sure.

"Where can I send you?" Each man told him where they wanted to be teleported, and Duncan sent them on their way. The sizable deposits in their bank accounts would come from his own pocket.

"What'cha do?" Brown asked curiously, tapping out a beat with his pen on the table. "Send those yahoo Halves to observe a female tango?"

Worse than a female tango. "Serena Brightman Campbell." The name said it all.

"Ah. The bimbo who married that multimillionaire old guy, Ian Campbell?" Chapman asked curiously. "He died last year, didn't he?"

"Yeah." They'd been married all of two years. It had made Duncan's flesh crawl, seeing the front-page pictures in all the newspapers. Thirty-year-old Serena and that old fart arm-in-arm at her white—*white* for Christ's sake!—wedding three years ago. There was only one reason a beautiful young woman married a guy like Campbell. Duncan figured not even the combo of Serena and a blue pill was going to get a rise out of the seventy-nine-year-old groom.

Still, they'd both been grinning like besotted fools in the pictures. Duncan knew that forcing himself to look at every one of the pictures was like holding his tongue to dry ice. Stupid. Unproductive and painful.

Serena Brightman Campbell had gotten the lion's share of the estate when her doddering old husband had reached his expiration date. Word out there was that Campbell's two sons, older than Serena by a good thirty years, were gunning for blood. Their pretty young stepmother's blood. *All of it*.

By calling out to him telepathically, Henry Morgan had made Serena's problem *Duncan's* problem.

"She's an old friend," Duncan said, figuring discretion was the better part of valor. "I hired a few guys to watch her back."

"You gonna send more Halves to keep an eye on your 'friend,' Edge?" Noah Hart asked curiously. "I've seen pictures. She's *beautiful*. Shitloads of *drachmas* as well. Too plum an assignment for a Half. Beauty, bucks, and she's a full wizard to boot. You've got some downtime coming. Maybe this requires your personal attention."

"Not interested." One freaking Curse on his head was enough. "Let's finish this up so we can get out of here. Landis?"

"Assignments," Gary Landis brought them back to business. "It's not *that* far off course, but I'll look into the new trajectory of that North Korean satellite."

"Do that," Duncan said absently, forcibly dragging his thoughts away from Serena and back to the task at hand. "If Lark brought up the slight shift as an anomaly, then you can count on there being something fishy going on. Chapman, work with him, see what you can discover."

Another critical situation on the table was the brutal murders of two high-level wizards. The entire wizard community, small as it was, was in an uproar about the killings. "Let's get to the murders," Duncan said grimly. It was rare, if not unheard of, for a wizard to be murdered. Unless he was old, sick, or had somehow lost his powers. But in this case, both men had been in their prime.

"Whoever this son of a bitch is, he's fucking powerful. Either the killer stripped them of their powers before he got the drop on them, or he was more powerful than they were, and took them. Despite their strength. Either scenario is serious, and chilling."

The men started discussing various hypothetical scenarios, taking into account the powers of the two wizards murdered.

Duncan sat back in his chair to listen. The loss of his own powers was his Achilles' heel. Even though he came from five centuries of wizards, he wasn't sure if/how/when those powers could be, or would be, stripped from him. The Edge family had received their powers through an ancient Curse, and had only been wizards for five hundred years.

I gift you my powers in memory of me, the witch Nairne had told his ancestor Magnus Edridge when she'd cursed him and his descendants.

The whole thing went: *Duty o'er love was the choice you did make/My love you did spurn, my heart you did break/Your penance to pay, no pride you shall gain/Three sons on three sons find nothing but pain/ I gift you my powers in memory of me/ The joy of love no son shall ever see/When a Lifemate is chosen by the heart of a son/No protection can be given, again I have won/His pain will be deep, her death will be swift/Inside his heart a terrible rift/Only freely given will this curse be done/To break the spell, three must work as one.*

Since he and his brothers had long ago agreed that the Curse would end with them, the threats were immaterial as far as Duncan was concerned. But somewhere in the back of his mind had always been the concern that if, somehow, the Curse were ever broken, the three of them would be stripped of their powers.

His brothers might not give a shit if they remained wizards or not.

But magic was who Duncan was.

Since he'd never do anything to jeopardize that, he straightened and refocused on the conversation.

"While the appropriate people been notified," he told the others flatly, "the Psi branch is directly responsible for apprehending the killer. And make no mistake. He *will* be caught."

The alliance forged between the wizards and the counterterrorist agency was crucial. The psychic phenomena branch of T-FLAC, known as T-FLAC/psi, had been started some twenty years ago. It was in everyone's best interests to catch the killer sooner rather than later.

"Jordan, Brown, Hart, and I will investigate the murders." Duncan picked up the communication Lark had sent minutes before Chang's untimely appearance. "We'd better hope we catch this guy before he strikes again."

"Amen to that." Noah Hart closed his notebook computer and stuffed it into a black case before getting to his feet. "Whoever this guy is, he has some kind of plan. But *I* sure as shit can't see any pattern here. Other than that he's snuffing wizards."

Jordan rose and shoved his chair under the table. "I'll head to South America. Hart, you want to take Asia? See what we can find there? Edge, aren't you a friend of Trey Culver? That dickh—guy's a social animal. Plenty of time on his hands. Seems to know everyone that's everyone in the wizard community. Might be worth contacting him to check out what he's heard."

"Yeah. Trey's on my list."

"Friend" wasn't exactly the term. Duncan thought of them more as friendly competitors. He'd gone to school way back when with Trey. And Serena. If he *had* to choose which one to take with him into a dark alley, he'd choose Trey. At least he was predictable. But if it was a dark bedroom, Serena was the hands-down winner.

Not that he'd ever do anything that stupid. Or dangerous.

All that fire and sensuality wasted on a husband three years older than dirt. He didn't get it.

"Are you going to have time to chase this killer?" Landis demanded. "Rumor is, you're running for Head of Council."

He snapped his errant thoughts back into place. He had every intention of *winning* the post as Head of the Wizard Council. He knew he had enough votes for a nomination, all he needed to do now was win the various Tests. Winning two Tests out of the four was all it would take. Piece of cake.

"I haven't thrown my hat in the ring yet," he lied easily. It wasn't to his advantage to have the general population of wizards know that he was going to be in Test mode in a week. Jealousies, politics, and just plain shittiness from a wizard faction might screw with the outcome.

"Not what I've heard." Landis gave him a pointed glance.

Duncan shrugged. "Let me know what you discover on that satellite." After arranging a meeting later in the week to exchange intel, he teleported from T-FLAC headquarters in Montana to his seldom used flat in London.

NEW YORK CITY

Serena teleported directly from the desert into her New York apartment bathroom. Dirty, tired, and still seriously pissed off, she turned on the shower, then yanked off her boots and socks. She could magically become clean, lotioned, and ready for bed in seconds, but this situation warranted a real-time shower.

Stripping off her sweat-stained, sand-encrusted shorts and tank top, she kicked the pile aside. She still wasn't sure if she'd been antsy all week because she somehow sensed she was being watched. Or if it was a presentiment of impending—*what*? She had no idea. Things at the Foundation had been copacetic. Much-needed financial support had poured in from the last fund-raiser, and Ian's two adult sons had been ominously quiet.

Which was almost more disconcerting than when they were harassing her with their latest attempt to vacate the terms of Ian's will. Maybe someday the greedy bastards would understand that their father had left almost everything to her for a reason. Ian had known long before he'd married Serena that his sons didn't share his humanitarian leanings. And that she'd use the very last breath in her body to make sure Ian's wishes were followed to the letter.

A year of motions, depositions, and mandatory court appearances was getting old. Had Duncan Edge somehow gotten involved with Paul and Hugh Campbell? It seemed doubtful. But anything was possible.

This, however, wasn't the hour to worry about it. Right now she was going to take a lovely hot shower, slather herself in scented lotion, and crawl between her one-thousand-thread-count sheets. After a good night's sleep she'd look into Duncan's intrusion. She shivered just thinking about Duncan joining forces with Ian's greed-driven sons. Hell, she shivered just thinking about Duncan period.

Giving herself a shake, Serena pulled off the baseball cap she'd worn to keep her long hair out of the way. Then enjoyed the glide of her long hair down her bare back. Tonight was for her.

Used to extreme temperatures in the places she visited for the Foundation, Serena was rarely fazed by weather. Hot or cold, it was a given that each location she and her team visited would be poor and rural, the temperature just one more difficulty they'd face. She was used to sleeping on the ground wrapped in a blanket, used to not looking too closely at what she was eating, used to primitive facilities—assuming there were any facilities at all. Which was why she relished her infrequent visits home. She could hike the jungles with the best of them, but that didn't mean she wasn't a girl who appreciated the indulgence and sanctuary of her perfectly appointed penthouse.

Like the rest of the apartment, her bathroom was spacious, and opulently luxurious. Creamy, peach veined marble, twenty-four-carat gold fixtures, and plush carpeting the color of ripe apricots. They were her favorite colors, and knowing exactly what she loved was just one of the many things her husband, Ian, had been good at. He'd spoiled her, and loved her, and known her, sometimes better than she knew herself.

Her heart squeezed painfully. God she missed him. Missed his dry sense of humor. Missed the love he'd lavished unstintingly on her. Missed his counsel and his wisdom.

The fact that he'd given her almost everything her heart could desire, and countless things she hadn't even known she'd needed or wanted, was immaterial. Those had only been *things*. Lovely things to be sure, but just things.

She missed him every day. And at night, when she lay in their vast empty bed, she missed the comfort of his arms around her.

Neither of them had cared what people said. Their world was complete. They'd had each other, and they'd had the Foundation. And knowing intellectually that her husband would die decades before she did, hadn't changed the heart-wrenching emotional blow she'd felt when he'd closed his eyes that night a year ago and never woken up. How stupid to think that just because she'd anticipated being a widow, Ian's death wouldn't have a devastating emotional impact on her.

Their luxurious home wasn't home anymore. The apartment, which overlooked Central Park, was much too big for just her. She'd sell it eventually. Find something smaller. But not now. It was too soon. Too complicated. Too painful.

Ian would have known how to deal with Duncan. Henry, too, would know what needed to be done. She couldn't even think about Henry lying in a hospital bed, so pale and lifeless. Did everyone she love have to die?

Oh, for goodness sake, she thought, annoyed with herself. "Get a grip. Stop being so damned melodramatic," she said out loud. "*Henry's* not dead." As for Duncan Edge—"Damn that interfering son of a bitch. What's he up to?"

The mirror over the sink bounced against the wall and three bottles of scented lotion on the counter skittered across the marble in response to her inner turmoil. Closing her eyes, she willed herself calm, forcibly reining in her temper. Only Duncan Edge had this infuriating effect on her telekinesis skills. Another annoying thing she could lay at his door. His *revolving* door.

Playboy jerk.

The last bottle fell to the floor. Damn, damn! *That's* what he did to her. Made her curse and lose her temper. She'd always had a problem containing her telekinetic power, and Duncan made that control snap like no one else. And even after all these years, all her hard work to channel the power constructively, just the *thought* of him made it go haywire.

Her reaction to him hadn't changed a bit, from fourth grade all the way to twelfth. Serena scratched an insect bite on her arm as the large bathroom started filling with steam. The mirror stopped moving as she regained control of her temper.

Duncan had always mocked her lack of emotional control.

Her temper was *perfectly* controlled, thank you very much. Unless *he* was anywhere in her vicinity. And now, apparently, even when he wasn't in close physical proximity. Just thinking about the man made Serena's blood pressure soar. The large antique mirror scraped the wall as if in warning.

The mirror started dancing, and her favorite perfume bottle crashed to the floor, filling the room with the fragrance of jasmine.

Had Duncan had *more* than three of his minions watching her? It was pure fluke that she'd managed to catch the men at all. They'd been Halves. Clever of Duncan, since she hadn't sensed their presence. She'd never have known they were there if they hadn't been so stupid. The Halves hadn't bothered to check before levitating food and water to their hiding spot behind a sand dune.

She opened the wide, clear glass shower door and stepped inside the enormous steam-filled stall. The water was hot and plentiful. Bliss. Lord, she needed this, she thought with a happy sigh. Her parched skin almost sucked up the liquid before she could soap up. It had been an unofficial visit to Mongolia. *Unofficial* meaning she'd teleported in and out instead of using the Foundation's private plane.

Her team there was doing a terrific job as always. The two-room schoolhouse/medical center was almost ready for occupancy. The village was already using the basic latrines they'd built for them, and the people had enough food, medicine, and livestock to sustain them until the new cattle bred, and the newly planted crops came in. Serena had "discovered" an underground water source while she was there. She'd left the villagers and her team celebrating their good fortune.

She was a little embarrassed and a lot irritated that she'd dispatched Duncan's men back to him with more force than necessary. It wasn't their fault that she had unresolved issues with their boss. Still, none of his men had cooperated with her when she'd demanded to know what they were doing in a small village on the outskirts of nowhere Mongolia.

Had they even *known* why they'd been sent to the Gobi to spy on her? Probably not. Duncan liked to play things close to the chest.

She hadn't had any sort of meaningful conversation with him in five years, seven months, and three days. Not that she was counting, she thought with irritation as she reached for the soap. It flew off the soap dish, missed her shoulder by an inch, and thunked—hard—into the glass door before shooting upward to hit the ceiling. The scented bar skimmed the marble tile, and crashed down again, hitting the showerhead before breaking in half.

"Oh, for—" She made a grab for the long-handled back scrubber as it flew around the inside of the stall in counterpoint to the two bits of soap.

Deep breath. Hold it. Hold it. Hold it. Breathe out.

She caught the pieces of soap and the back scrubber's handle before they hit her. She hadn't lost her temper in years. Five years, seven months, and three days to be exact. Even the evil step adults and their neverending legal maneuvers didn't make her this nuts. Duncan brought out the absolute worst in her.

What possible reason could he have for sending people to spy on her? *None.* Their paths had no reason to cross. They didn't stay in touch, they rarely saw one another. They'd had an adversarial, highly competitive "relationship" for want of a better word, in wizard school. These days they occasionally bumped into each other at some fund-raiser or charity event.

Pouring a generous amount of fragrant shampoo into her palm, Serena started washing her hair. It was long and thick and she rarely wore it down. Wearing her hair pinned up in a classic, if old-fashioned, chignon suited her perfectly. When it was short, her hair curled like little Orphan Annie's, and made her look and feel . . . out of control.

Duncan preferred cool blondes.

She'd spotted him with a gorgeous Nordic model at the Met a few months ago, but he hadn't seen her. She remembered how damned handsome he'd looked in a stark black tux, his dark hair curling against his collar, that single dimple in his cheek flashing as he spoke intimately to his companion.

It hadn't been her fault that an urn had toppled to the floor, or that a pile of programs had gone flying like projectiles all over the lobby. Could have been a gust of wind from an open door. Or not. Serena dug her fingers into her scalp and scrubbed her—

She felt a sudden tingle, and blinked. "Holy shit!"

She'd been teleported from her lovely hot shower to a chilly, ultra modern kitchen. She knew only one man who'd have a stark black-and-silver kitchen. One man rude enough, and confident enough, to do this without permission.

"Hello, Serena." Duncan's dark blue eyes scanned her naked, dripping body. "You've lost some weight. Been working out?"

CHAPTER TWO

Furious, she met his cool expression. "I'm going to kill you for this!"

Indolently he leaned a hip against the counter, one large bare foot crossed over the other, his arms folded over his broad chest. He, of course, was fully dressed, except for his feet. He looked perfectly at home, unbearably sexy, and completely at ease. Until one noticed the glitter in his blue eyes, which turned from ice blue to the hot blue of a flame as he watched a blob of shampoo plop onto her bare shoulder.

His sexy mouth twitched, causing the single long dimple in his right cheek to flash. "Tsk, tsk, Fury. There goes that temper again."

Serena's blood pressure thumped behind her eyes. The heat flooding her body should have made the sudsy trail of water down her back sizzle. But her nudity took a backseat to her struggle to prevent an emotional outburst. She was now embarrassed and furious, and unable to do anything to rectify either emotion at the moment.

She couldn't materialize clothes when she was struggling to control a physical manifestation of her anger. And damn him, Duncan *knew* it.

Think calm—Calm. Calm. Calm.

"This is an abuse of your powers." How could such an arrogant man be so damned appealing? A rush of heat went through her as his gaze swept her body in a slow visual scan that felt like a physical touch. She felt as though she'd just run a seven-minute mile. Her heart was pounding, her breath was rapid, and her entire body was suddenly . . . *hot.*

One dark eyebrow—the one, she noticed with satisfaction, with a familiar little scar bisecting it—lifted. "Is that so?"

His tall, lean body was clothed in jeans and a black, close-fitting T-shirt. His dark hair, thick, lustrous, and with a hint of curl, brushed his broad shoulders. He'd been the class hunk even back in sixth grade. Handsome, smart, funny, charming, and athletic. He'd been slavishly adored by all the girls, and admired by the boys.

He'd goofed off in class, but he'd still managed straight As, while she'd worked her ass off for Bs.

They'd both lost their parents too young. Serena had thought that their circumstances would forge some sort of bond between them. Too bad neither of them ever wanted to talk about the past. Too bad he was an Edge. Still, she'd desperately wanted to be part of his charmed circle. Just not desperately enough to let him know it. The simple reason was that she hadn't wanted to be just one more member of the gaggle of girls vying for his attention. The complicated reason was—more complicated.

The only times she hadn't passed beneath Duncan's radar was when they competed against one another.

They were both fiercely competitive. If he wouldn't be her friend, then she was more than willing to beat his ass in everything from telekinesis to tennis.

She might have fantasized about being naked with Duncan at sixteen, but at thirty-three she was just pissed off that he was seeing her body this way. And annoyed was exactly how she wanted to appear when her telekinetic powers went berserk around him. She'd hate him to know that it wasn't just anger, but also attraction that made her lose control.

She observed the movement of his lashes as he visually tracked the white foam now gliding slowly down the upper swell of her *naked* breast.

"We need to talk." Duncan's voice was deeper than she remembered as he languidly raised his lids to look at her face.

She met that dark blue gaze unflinchingly, but wondered if anyone had ever died of embarrassment. Probably not. Perhaps she'd be the first. The copper pots in an overhead rack started clinking together as she just stood there, totally and literally exposed, dripping on a silver metal floor, while trying to rein in her temper. Duncan would enjoy it if she lost it. He always did.

She wasn't going to give him the satisfaction. "Next time use a phone," she told him, keeping her voice low, calm, and rational, which would have been great if her inner turmoil wasn't making the pots rattle faster and faster as her temper rose.

She tried to override it and materialize something, *anything* to cover herself. She was too agitated for her magic to work, which made her anger that much hotter. "Besides a total misuse of teleportation, this is an invasion of my privacy. And damn rude. Even for you." She tried, she really did, to use her most reasonable tone. Hard to do when her blood was on fire and her heart was racing and those *damned* pots were doing a samba.

Her fight-or-flight response whenever she was around this man was in the stratosphere. But she couldn't do a damn thing until she got her emotions under control. Her temper, the bane of her life, screwed up her abilities to use any of her other powers.

The black lacquered cabinet doors started slamming. Open. Shut. Open. Shut. Slamslamslam. The pots clanged against each other in a cacophony of noise that made Duncan's lips twitch. If he laughed at her loss of control she was going to—

Damn it. No she *wasn't. He* was the one who used his might to control situations. *She* was the one who'd taught herself, and it hadn't been easy, that a rational conversation was always the best course of action. Far more effective than his Neanderthal approach to everything. Of course, no lesson in self-control covered standing naked in this man's home. She bit her tongue and utilized her relaxing breathing technique until the pots and doors slowed down a little. Duncan's amused gaze was still locked on her face.

"If you've looked your fill, please give me something to put on." There was nothing within reach, and she still hadn't quite harnessed her powers.

Smoky eyes swept her body. "What if I haven't?"

Skin hot with embarrassment and fury, Serena blinked. Damn it, she couldn't *think* with the pots and pans crashing against one another and his freaking cabinet doors slamming. "Haven't what?" she demanded.

"Looked my fill," he said in an even tone, not a hint of what was going on in his devious mind showing on his lean, handsome face. Even his eyes were now opaque.

She'd just started to control her inner turmoil when he added, "Different having a man your own age looking at you instead of one fifty years older, isn't it, Fury?"

The spice bottles in the rack beside the stove flew across the room. Laughing, Duncan ducked as one by one, they sailed by his head. The bottles spun and twirled, forming a vortex over the center island. He grabbed a copper saucepan lid and held it up as a shield even though the bottles were a good six feet away from his hard skull. "Temper, temper."

Sorely tempted to douse his ego with water, Serena's jaw ached from clenching her teeth. That was how she used to retaliate. Not anymore. The fact that he could still reduce her to responding like a twelve-year-old made the bottles spin faster. "Give me a towel. Please."

"So polite. But speaking civilly doesn't seem to help that temper of yours, does it?"

She shot him a murderous look, realized what she'd done, and stared down at the puddle she was standing in. She couldn't leave until she'd calmed down. She couldn't calm down, damn it, standing in Duncan's kitchen. Naked. With him looking at her with hot eyes and a smile disappearing from his mouth as his gaze trailed across her body. It felt as if he was actually touching her.

The refrigerator door sprang open behind her, smacking her on the butt and almost sending her straight into Duncan's arms. She grabbed the counter and held on. Closing her eyes she took a deep breath. Visualized a field of cool, green grass. Breathe. Blue sky. Breathe. Fluffy white clouds. Breathe. Slow. Deep. In. Out. In. Out.

When the noise of the chaos in his kitchen abated, finally, Serena opened her eyes.

"Wow. That was impressive." He materialized a black *hand* towel and extended it between two fingers.

She gave him a cool, narrow-eyed look. "Don't be an ass, Duncan. You wanted me here. Unless you turned into a complete moron, you know how annoyed I am. Give me some cl—" She was suddenly wearing a simple, honey-colored silk charmeuse robe. And she was dry.

"Now that I have your undivided attention, and I'm no longer wet and naked," she said, tightening the belt around her waist, "why *did* you bring me here? And what right did you have sending those men to watch my every move?"

He kept his place as cold as a meat locker, but she wasn't going to attempt any magic until she was sure she had her emotions in check. Instead of a wool sweater, she might end up wearing the damned sheep.

"Henry's worried about you, and asked me to make sure you were okay. Are you?"

"God, Duncan. Don't—" Henry was her godfather. Duncan had been one of his students when he'd taught a series of lectures at wizard school. He worked, *had* worked, for Ian at the Foundation and had brought Serena in fourteen years ago. The rest, as they said, was history. And even though Duncan and Henry had remained friends over the years, it didn't explain why Duncan was pretending that Henry had asked him for help. "You know he couldn't have called you. It's impossible." Über wizard should have known that.

"Yeah. He did. He asked me to help you. Tell me what it is you need help *with*, I'll do what I can, then get out of your hair."

Just thinking about him in her hair made Serena's scalp tingle. Before he could distract her again, she materialized jeans, a burnt orange cashmere sweater, thick socks, and tennis shoes. Dressed—as in *armored*—she felt considerably better. "When last did you speak with him?"

"Spoilsport," he said, giving a disappointed glance at her fully dressed form. "Henry first contacted me a week ago."

She shook her head. "Nice try. He had a stroke *ten days ago*. He can't move. And he certainly can't *speak*. Which you would know if you bothered to return phone messages."

"You didn't call me."

"My assistant did."

"Too busy to pick up a phone?"

To call you? You bet. "I've been busy."

"Yeah. I know. In the last six months you've been to Mongolia, Darfur, Burundi, Somalia, and Schpotistan. Five times."

"How do you know where I've been?"

"If anyone wanted to find you, for God's sake, all they have to do is pick up a newspaper. You aren't exactly low profile, Mrs. Campbell."

"Is there a point in there somewhere?" she asked, dropping a dash of acid sarcasm into her voice. Even from where she was standing, even as uncomfortable and embarrassed, and pissed off as she was, Serena could *smell* him. Nothing artificial. No cologne. Not even the smell of soap. Just a scent that was uniquely Duncan's. It reminded her of secrets and dark, sensual promises, and—

Her heart was thumping like crazy. *God!* she thought, furious with herself, *get a grip.* Stop romanticizing the man.

Hold your breath if you have to. Remember who you're dealing with here.

"I've been getting mental-grams from Henry—he's asking me to help stop you."

"Really?" She arched a brow. "He said, 'Stop Serena, Duncan'?"

"He said, and I quote, '*Stop her. Help her.*' You are the only *her* we have in common. And since I didn't know what, specifically, he meant, I sent a few of my men to protect you."

"I'm a humanitarian, I don't *need* protecting. Butt out of my life, Duncan. If that's all you have to say, I'd like to get back to my shower." The image of Duncan, naked, in that shower *with* her made her skin feel hot and tight, and her heartbeat pick up speed like a jungle beat.

Something smoldering and primal flared in Duncan's eyes as if he, too, had had the same thought, but it was quickly masked as if it had never been.

"Henry has never been an alarmist. He sounds scared. You have to stop what you're doing, Serena."

"Stop building latrines in Mongolia? Stop planting crops in Africa? Building schools? Feeding starving children? I don't think so."

"I do. Henry's concerned about you."

A lump formed in her throat, and it was a few seconds before she could speak. "I'll go and see him again." She'd been there yesterday, and all she could do was hold his hand. He was completely unresponsive, and it broke her heart to see him that way.

"I'll go with you." He put up a hand when she started to protest. "Like it or not, Henry wants me involved. If not, he would have communicated his concerns to you. He didn't. Suck it up." She smelled like soap. Something intoxicating and floral. Jasmine, he thought.

A jasmine-covered arbor, planted by Martha Morgan years ago, was still growing in Henry's front yard today. Did Serena remember the night he'd kissed her beneath it?

He wanted to reach out his hand to touch her. To see if her skin felt as soft as it looked.

She'd probably retaliate by raining on him.

Might be worth it, he thought, almost—*almost* tempted.

"We don't have to go together." Emotion danced across her expressive features as her gray eyes flashed. Duncan could see the effort it took for her not to lose it again. He braced for shit to go flying, but this time she managed to rein in her temper.

"I'm trying to figure out why my accompanying you to see Henry makes you nervous."

Up went the chin. "Don't be ridiculous."

"Then it's not going to Germany together that has your pulse pounding, it's me."

Her lovely eyes widened. "Oh, please. We've known each other for most of our lives, when have you ever made me nervous?"

"I can think of at least half a dozen times, as a matter of fact." The night he'd kissed her outside Henry and Martha's house, for one. Innocence had never tasted so perfect.

"If it makes you feel macho, then by all means— keep believing that b.s." She stared at him for a long challenging moment. "Then put your ego away and remember that you make me furious. Not nervous."

She got furious when she was nervous. He smiled. Fury was all grown up. She was all life, passion, and vitality. And vividly, achingly . . . *Technicolor*. She made everything around her recede into blacks and grays. And he didn't mean his black-and-chrome kitchen.

"You're smiling like that to annoy me," she said crossly. "It won't work."

His smile widened. Yeah, it already had. As a kid he'd intentionally grinned at her to make her lose her temper. He'd enjoyed the hell out of seeing shit go flying in the classroom. Or on the playground. Or at a party. But as they'd both gotten older, he'd recognized that he teased Serena for that brief, one-on-one, interaction with her.

His heart beat too fast as they stared at one another. The smile slipped from his mouth. He wanted her, and there was nothing rational or civilized about it. The intensity of his need made a mockery of his self-control.

Serena was the most gloriously, unabashedly *alive* woman he'd ever met. Interestingly enough, she was sublimely indifferent to her allure. Yet she'd always drawn attention. Even when she'd been a scrawny little kid with freckles and that incredible, eye-catching hair. It truly was the color of flames. Fire orange, it licked and curled past her shoulders and halfway down her slender back. Maybe that's what had first caught his attention, at the ripe old age of eleven.

Fire was his power to call, and Serena embodied everything about it. Hot. Dangerous. Seductive.

Or perhaps it had been her eyes, a cool misty gray, as clear as water. The sadness was gone from them now. And she no longer sported braces and scabbed knees. These days she was tall and slender with small, perfect breasts and a narrow waist and legs that went on forever. She'd figured prominently in Duncan's fantasies for as long as he could remember. Band-Aids or breasts, it didn't matter. Apparently Serena Br—Campbell possessed something that always made him sit up and take notice.

Seeing her naked was going to take those fantasies to a whole new level. Fortunately his tongue had, eventually, come unglued from the roof of his mouth. Serena fully dressed was a thing of beauty. Serena *naked* . . . Holy hell.

How in God's name was he ever going to erase *that* image from his brain? Because erase it he must. He had to resist the lure of her beauty and vitality, resist the . . . *want*.

Wanting wasn't getting.

Like the pact he'd made with his brothers years ago, the vow that the ancient family Curse would end with them, Duncan had also made a promise to himself. To stay away from Serena Brightman.

He'd known, the second he'd taken his first look at her, that she was going to be to him what kryptonite had been to Superman. Too close proximity was going to be detrimental to his health. Mental health, that was.

A man could never be too careful.

He had plans for his future and Serena didn't figure into them. Worse when those plans included taking her godfather's position on the Council. He wasn't sure how she was going to feel about that. Serena adored Henry. He was like a father to her, and she'd always been very protective of him. Henry's stroke must have scared her to death.

He'd offer sympathy, but Serena wouldn't accept it. The woman might look soft and silky, but she had a steel bar strapped to her spine.

"Fine. Don't believe me? Then come with me if you insist," she told him with clear reluctance. "He's in a hospital in Germany."

"In a coma?" He didn't doubt her. Serena was nothing if not brutally honest. "Damn. Hard to believe. I had dinner with him last month when he came to London—looking for a power source for something he was working on. He seemed fighting fit then." When he'd been a kid his instructor had seemed ancient. But the twenty-six-year age difference didn't seem as vast now. Henry was only fifty-nine, far too damn young to remain in a comatose state. The man was not only Master Wizard and as such Head of the Wizard Council, he was also a brilliant scientist and Duncan considered him a good friend. "Can you tell me what happened?"

For a second he saw the fear in her eyes, and he wanted to protect her from the pain of losing someone else she loved. He didn't know the whole story about her parents' deaths, she never talked about it, but he knew how attached she was to Henry. If he died, Serena would be devastated. Christ. If Henry died, *he'd* be devastated.

The small chink of vulnerability slammed shut; Serena was good at masking her pain and she did so now. "He collapsed while he was working."

Though clearly excited, his friend had been strangely cagey about the project he was working on for the Foundation. Had been for the last three years or so. Usually when they got together, Duncan had to listen to an hour-long soliloquy of how amazingly wonderful Serena was, before he got caught up with what Henry was working on in his capacity as head of scientific research and development for Serena's foundation.

At their last meeting, in between hearing about Serena ad nauseam, Henry mentioned his current project only in the most cursory terms. He'd even been closemouthed about the *location* of his latest project, which was unusual. "Where was this?"

"Schpotistan. His assistant, Joanna Rossiter, was with him when he suffered a massive stroke. Fortunately, the Foundation has a medical team on-site; they kept him breathing until the medevac got there. He was immediately airlifted to Germany."

"And the prognosis?"

"Guardedly optimistic to too soon to tell—depending on who you ask." Their eyes met, for once perfectly attuned. They both cared, they were both worried, and they both felt helpless.

"I just have to make a quick call, then we can go."

She stiffened. "I'll meet you there."

"Business, Fury, business." Duncan took his phone out of his back pocket and shot her a grin. "I'm not calling a lady friend, don't worry."

"A: You're the last man in the solar system I'd ever worry about. For *any* reason. B: I don't give a flying fig *who* you call. Just hurry up! I have better things to do than hang around waiting for you."

The phone vibrated in his hand before he could dial. "Hi beautiful," he greeted Lark Orela, one of T-FLAC/psi's controls. It was unusual for her to call unless they were working together. They weren't at the moment. "What can I do for you?"

Serena rolled her eyes, then crossed the kitchen to pick up the flotsam and jetsam her temper had scattered.

"Heads up, Hot Edge. The Council wants you in Chambers in five minutes. Bring Serena."

"How the hell did you kno—" He was talking to dead air. "Change of plans," he told Serena, admiring her heart-shaped ass in those tight jeans as she bent down to retrieve a sauté pan. His heart picked up a little speed. The Council was convening the first Test meeting—

He frowned. Maybe not. There was no reason for them to invite Serena to sit in.

Or was there?

She straightened and turned to face him, brandishing the small pan like a club. "Take her flowers."

"Lark?"

"Is that your girlfriend's name?" She opened a lower cabinet and tossed the pan inside, using her foot to close it. "Wasn't the last one something you'd name a cat? Miffy or Fluffy?"

His last marginally serious relationship, with Marta Jorgensen, had ended five, six years ago. Right after he'd seen Serena and her then boss, Ian Campbell, at the Met. Although the two incidents had nothing whatsoever to do with each other. "No cat. Dixie was my dog."

"It's okay for you to call your girlfriend a bitch in front of me," she said sweetly.

He smiled. "Jealous?"

"That would imply that I care. I don't."

"And on that subject," he said, completely changing it, "why does the Council want to see you?"

"Me? They don't."

"Yeah. They do." He glanced at his watch. "In four minutes."

"Another psychic flash like the one you claim you got from Henry?"

He held up the small phone he was still holding. "Call from my office."

Serena shook her head, clearly not believing it was a business call. "Are you coming to see Henry or not?"

"Absolutely. After we see what the Council wants."

"Someone's pulling your leg. They never warn us when they want to see us, you know that. They teleport whoever they want when they want them. And no one is seeing them for the next ten days because of the Tests . . . What—Oh, don't tell me—*You're* running for Head of Council? *You?*"

Her surprise and incredulity stung, but there was no point prevaricating. Once the three contestants were announced, everyone would know he'd thrown his hat into the ring. "Yeah. Got a problem with it?"

"Actually—no. I don't. You'd make an excellent Head. You're cool and calm under pressure, you're fair, you're intelligent. You tend to make quick, smart choices."

"Why do I hear a giant 'but' in there?"

"You resolve matters with your fists."

Serena didn't know he worked for T-FLAC. The incident she was referring to had happened when they'd been in their early twenties. A party they'd both attended in New York. "The guy," Duncan said mildly, keeping an eye on the time, and remembering just how damn many people he'd had to bribe and coerce to get an *invite* to that particular party, "was stinking drunk, and grabbed my date's breast in public." The guy had tried a lot more than grabbing—what had been her name? Mandy? Megan? Monica? Something like that.

The guy'd almost succeeded in raping her in the bathroom. He'd cut her with his pocket knife, and bitten her hard enough for her to require plastic surgery on the nipple. Duncan had no regrets that he'd teleported her to the hospital and then returned the same way to beat the shit out of the little prick.

"What was I supposed to do? Ask him nicely to cease and desist?"

"I wasn't referring to Denise's party—where, by the way, you beat the crap out of some poor drunk idiot, and threw him out of a window on the *second* floor for a minor infraction. Especially since Moira was wearing a dress cut to her navel advertising her very expensive silicone breasts. I'm referring to the time you were arrested in that Hong Kong nightclub three years ago, and the time you ended up in the hospital because for once some other guy beat the crap out of you. Or that time some guy broke your nose—"

"You should've seen the other guy." *Henry.* That's how she knew this stuff. His friend was bound by secrecy not to discuss Duncan's line of work. Apparently that didn't keep his old mentor from sharing Duncan's assorted bumps, bruises, and worse. Henry had obviously shared his worry with Serena, who took it as just another reason to dislike him. Hell.

Duncan glanced across at her and cocked a brow, realizing that she remembered the name of a casual date he'd had more than ten years ago. A cabinet door slammed. Then slammed again. "What?"

She closed her eyes briefly. "I'm sorry. Damn it, Duncan, you bring out the absolute worst in me, you know that? It wasn't the way Moira was dressed, or *her* fault that some idiot grabbed her. That was just stupid of me to say." She pressed coral-tipped fingers against her temples.

"Having said that, you were at fault for getting into a one-sided fight with a drunk. And all—the other times—" Serena's voice trailed off as she suddenly found herself in a new, albeit familiar, location.

The Council Chambers.

She felt exactly the same dizzy disorientation she'd experienced the first time she'd been summoned here, the day after her parents died. She'd been eight. Petrified. Lost. Confused.

She'd been to the Council on several occasions since. And every time her palms sweated, her heart thudded, and she was suddenly a terrified child again. It didn't matter that she'd seen Henry in his ratty bathrobe and slippers at home; here he'd been Head of Council, and a force to be reckoned with. Here there were no favorites, no favors, no second chances.

With an aching heart, Serena wished that Henry was sitting in that seat behind the big table where he belonged. It was inconceivable to be here and not see him in his black-and-silver robe, his silvered hair brushed back, his blue eyes serious.

Why had they summoned her?

"You rang?" Duncan stood tall and straight beside her. He must be totally freaking fearless to joke with the Council. She desperately wanted to grab his hand and hold on tightly. She didn't, of course; he'd probably flick her off like he'd done on the playground when they'd been ten or so, as if she had cooties.

"Please be seated, Serena. Duncan. We are awaiting our third contestant."

Serena sank into a hard leather chair fifteen feet from the table. Contestant? Since she wasn't running for Head of Council, she hadn't a clue what she was doing here.

Once in a while they asked her to arbitrate a conflict. Perhaps that was it. She shot Duncan, seated a few feet away, a worried glance. God. Had he beaten up a fellow wizard? Or worse?

He didn't look in the least bit concerned. Leaning back, wrists dangling off the arms of his chair, one ankle crossed over the opposite knee, he looked the picture of patience and calm. Maybe an ad for some kind of expensive whiskey. All he needed was a blonde draped over him and a bright red convertible.

Lord, her mouth was dry. Silence throbbed in the vast room. The light was always so damned bright in here, she thought. Would it be considered bad form to materialize sunglasses? Probably. She crossed her legs, and tried not to jiggle her foot.

The Council Chambers looked like the offices of a prosperous law firm. Plush burgundy carpeting, mahogany paneling, lots of leather furniture, and a desk the size of her bed. No one was sitting behind the desk. But in a semicircle behind it, on a raised dais, sat seven men and women all but hidden in shadow. Seeing them shrouded in darkness, while she was in a spotlight, always made Serena shiver. Of course there was nothing the least bit scary about the individuals who ran the Council. They were mostly married, with children and grandchildren. Having spent time with many of them socially, Serena knew that off the dais they appeared to be nothing more than regular business people.

On the platform, and collectively, they just happened to be powerful enough to control most of the

world's wizards. Getting the Head of Council position wasn't easy. The Tests were secret and many
contenders had failed over the years. Not that that
mattered to her.

She wanted to teleport to Germany to see Henry,
then she was due in Schpotistan to see what progress
Joanna was making. The thought made her heart
leap with excitement. They were getting very close
to putting this project into operation.

A slight squeak indicated that someone was now
seated in the chair to her left. Duncan's latest victim,
she presumed. Serena cast a sideways glance at the
man seated beside her, and smiled.

Ah. Trey Culver.

She, Duncan, and Trey had been classmates.

Trey was almost as tall as Duncan, his hair was a
well-groomed, dark, ashy blonde, his bedroom eyes
a sleepy brown. He always dressed beautifully, and
was sexy in his own right. She and Trey had had
some fun times together over the years.

"Please rise," a deep voice intoned.

Allen McKenna, Serena recognized his voice. She
stood.

"You came here today to receive instructions for
your first Test. On the desk are three envelopes. Please
take the one with your name on it."

A second earlier there'd been nothing on the desk
but a high sheen. *Test?* Oh, Lord no. Serena rose
with Duncan and Trey, but hung back as they picked
up their envelopes. "Excuse me, but *I'm* not running
for Head of Council."

"You withdraw your application?"

"I never put *in* an application."

"Two people nominated you," the voice said mildly.

She frowned, flattered, but totally bewildered. "Who? Oh, right. You can't say. I—"

"Serena's humanitarian work is too important to be put on hold for seven years," Duncan inserted smoothly. "It would be unconscionable to take her away from the important strides she's making feeding the world. I'm sure we have a third—"

"*Excuse* me?" Serena turned to glare at him. What right did he have to jump in and make her excuses? What right did he have to do whatever sneaky thing he was trying to do? Why couldn't she do both? The Foundation was a well-oiled machine. If she wanted to, she could do both jobs. Henry had.

"I've changed my mind. I'd be honored to run for the position. Not only do I have the experience to run the Council, but I also have leadership experience. And while the seven-year term is quite a commitment, I'm adept at delegating. And, unlike some people," she paused significantly, "I have a level head, and the patience to arbitrate anything brought before me."

Duncan sent her a warning look, his dark blue eyes glittering under the brilliant overhead lights. "You'll lose your temper—"

"At least *I* don't use my fists . . ."

Trey laughed, grabbing Duncan around the neck and slinging his other arm around Serena's shoulders. He dropped a kiss to the top of her head. "Just like old times. Trey, Fury, and Duncan. Let the good times roll."

Serena shifted out of his hold. For whatever reason, the combination of Duncan, Trey, and herself had never turned out well. She hoped the Council knew what they were doing pitting the three of them against each other.

CHAPTER THREE

He shouldn't have goaded her, Duncan thought, returning to his seat with the envelope. The paper-like material glowed, felt warm to the touch, and pulsed in his hand like a faint heartbeat.

He squinted against the bright, white light of the Council Chambers, not able to make out the features of the shadowy forms behind the empty table. Where Henry usually sat.

He sensed no danger here, despite the power. Their collective strength was tempered with benevolence and profound wisdom. The smell of beeswax candles and some sort of herb lightly perfumed the air, but he saw no candles burning anywhere.

The room was preternaturally quiet, though he was acutely aware of each breath Serena took. The rhythm was uneven and a little rapid. Was she excited by the prospect of running the Council? Or was it the challenge of besting him?

He'd always known that provoking Serena was a way to keep her close, without revealing his attraction to her. An attraction that was completely out of the question. So he'd challenged her to best him at tennis, or levitation, or any number of skills they both excelled at. Sometimes he'd won, and sometimes she'd won. He'd enjoyed the interaction with her more than he'd ever let on. It had become a habit. They'd become friends.

Friends in combat for most of their formative years, Duncan thought with amusement.

Hell, he'd rather spar with Serena than make love to any other woman.

What was Serena's reason for always rising to his bait? A habit after all this time? Absently, he touched the small scar and felt a certain comfort as he struggled not to smile. He could still see Serena's face, bleached white, when she realized that the pencil was imbedded so close to his eye.

That was the first time he'd experienced her unguarded power unleashed along with her temper. While the other students were horrified as blood trickled down his face, Duncan had been . . . *impressed*. And amused as hell.

Over time, she'd sent other things flying in his direction, only now he knew enough to duck, roll, or shimmer out of the way.

Surely she wasn't still pissed over the prom thing? Yes, they'd been in an exclusive, private school for wizards only. They were intelligent and quick. But they were still teenagers and prone to small blips of stupidity and large doses of hormones. Three days before the prom, when he'd spotted her in the quad chatting with Trey, he'd seen it as the perfect opportunity to ask her to the annual event.

A: He'd forgotten that girls took last-minute invites as an insult. B: He didn't know Trey had already asked her. And C: He had no clue that her response would be to send him flying across the grassy court-yard, slamming him into the brick wall.

Duncan had taken someone else, and watched the blossoming of Serena's relationship with Trey. He felt a stab of discomfort in his gut as he remembered that shortly after that, Trey and Serena had become an item, which totally screwed up the triangle of their friendship. Their whole history was a succession of competitions. Serena besting Trey and Duncan on an essay; Duncan kicking ass in levitating inani-mate objects—he still held the school record; and Trey? He had to be the only guy in the upper grades to never get a demerit.

Wizards could do some crazy stuff. Pranks could be anything from moving a teacher's books off their desk while their backs were turned to shimmering to the top of the flagpole.

They each had a different style when challenged. Serena used nonconfrontational methods, logic. Duncan tended to use force, fists, and brute strength, and Trey oozed, and used, charm.

Duncan knew that he and Trey were physically fairly evenly matched. Their powers were on a par as well, and sometimes the two would just spar for the hell of it. Trey, like Duncan, never seemed to take the black eye or bloody nose personally.

Serena was a whole different story. She was always willing to forgive Trey any transgression, but not him. No, Duncan was usually held accountable for any behavior she deemed inappropriate and/or violent.

So, setting her hair on fire hadn't been his finest moment. But all that was years ago and they were adults now. Surely it was time for them to bury the hatchet. Preferably not in the center of his head, he thought with an inner grin.

Something told him that a truce between them was unlikely to happen. Especially if they were now going to compete for Head of Council.

It would be interesting, given their differing views of the world. She'd probably keel over if she had even an inkling of what he did now. There was evil in the world. Evil that needed to be eradicated— expediently. T-FLAC was the perfect place for him. He liked meting out the kind of justice that courts and international tribunals were unable or prohibited from so much as considering. Terrorists didn't care who or how many innocents they killed or maimed.

But Serena wouldn't understand their myopic disregard for human life. No, she'd probably suggest he sit them all down at the table and try to reason with them. Like you could reason with terrorists.

A heavily carved wooden chest materialized suddenly and soundlessly in the center of the desk. Pulled from the past, Duncan's mouth went dry. Although he couldn't see beneath the heavy lid, although he'd never laid eyes on the ancient wooden box before now, he knew with every hard beat of his heart what was inside: the ancient Wizard Medallion.

Passed down from Council Head to Council Head for centuries.

He barely heard Serena's faint gasp beside him. His entire focus was glued to the box as if drawn by a powerful magnet. *He* wanted to be seated behind that dais wearing the antique Medallion of Office, the head of those shadowy forms lined up behind him.

He wanted it more than his next heartbeat.

He'd waited his entire life for this. He'd wanted to be Master Wizard since he was twelve and been summoned here for the first time over some minor infraction.

The minute he'd materialized in this chamber, Duncan had known that *this* was his destiny. Not the pomp and ceremony. But the quiet certainty of his place in the world. Because of the Curse, he'd never have love. Marriage. Family. Or a woman to share his life with. But this, this had become his El Dorado.

He wanted this. And by God he was going to get it.

It seemed fitting that Serena be here participating, too.

Actually, Serena would make an excellent Head of Council. She was intelligent, compassionate, and logical, and Duncan could easily see her sitting behind the big table, wearing the black-and-silver robes. The heavy silver chain draped around her slender neck, the Medallion between her breasts.

Still, he believed that his strength, ability to deal with the scum of the earth, and his instincts would serve the Council better. And if the strength of sheer desire would cause him to win—he had that in spades.

Duncan couldn't imagine Trey in the position. As likable as he was, Trey wasn't a team player.

The only time Duncan had felt less than affable toward Trey was a few years ago, when Henry had

told him Serena was dating him again. The knowledge had filled Durcan with intense *something*. He
didn't like himself for being such a dog in the manger
and begrudging Serena and Trey the very thing he
couldn't have.

Which was why, when he'd seen the intimate smile
she'd bestowed on Culver when he'd shimmered in,
Duncan had spoken without his usual filter. Ridiculous
really. *He'd* never dated Serena, and hadn't sought out
either Trey or Serena since they'd all graduated from
high school some fifteen years ago, other than a few
brief, enjoyable conversations with Trey at various
social events over the years.

Serena was a whole other story. Every time they
crossed paths, he experienced more pull, more attraction, more desire, more.

Hell, didn't matter. Even without factoring in the
family Curse, he'd sabotaged himself with his thought-
less words.

Fury had a stubborn streak a mile wide, and she
was almost as competitive as he and Trey were.
Damn stupid of him. She didn't want the job, he
knew that instinctively. If she had, she would have
jumped at the chance instead of refusing initially.
Now, she'd go through the vigorous testing process,
just to show him she *could*.

The irony was that they were both hot-tempered.
Always had been. The difference was, Duncan easily
controlled his emotions. Serena had a hard time har-
nessing that power. She was glorious in a temper.

"If we may have your attention?"

Duncan recognized Lark's husky voice with surprise. If she was here, then she was a member of

the Council. But she'd never given any indication that she was part of the governing body of wizards. He'd taken meetings here several times over the years, arbitrated a couple of disputes, but her name had never been mentioned. And she certainly never mentioned it in any T-FLAC/psi briefings. Interesting.

Still, Lark was one of the smartest, most intuitive women Duncan knew. If anyone could talk sense and logic into Serena, Lark would be the one.

"You will be summoned without notice," she told them, shrouded in darkness. "There will be four Tests to perform within the next ten days. You will be permitted to use only the powers allocated to you. No one is permitted to assist you, and you are not allowed to aid each other. Doing so will cause you to forfeit that Test. Due to the nature of the Tests, there is the possibility of death or grave injury. Be sure to put your affairs in order before you begin. The first individual to pass two challenges wins. Good luck."

Serena rose from her chair. "Could we just discu—Crud, I hate when they do that."

The three of them had been summarily dismissed, and returned to Duncan's London flat before she'd finished the sentence. In fact, he and Serena were standing in exactly the same positions they'd been in before they'd been teleported. But this time Trey was standing between them.

"Hello, my darling Fury. Beautiful as ever." Trey pulled her close. At the last minute Serena turned her head so his lips kissed her cheek.

She spread her palm on his chest and gave him a

little shove. "Behave yourself, Trey Culver. That ship sailed a long time ago."

Good to know, Duncan thought with surprising savagery. "Drinks?" he asked, pushing between them to get to the bar at the end of the kitchen. He could conjure the drinks, but there were some mundane civilities he liked to uphold.

"I'll have a beer," Trey answered with his eyes still fixed on Serena. Unapologetically, he added, "Can't blame a guy for trying."

"You're both *very* trying," she said sweetly, materializing what looked like a cola in a short squat glass. She took a large sip.

"Shit," Trey muttered. "Lost my—do you guys have your envelopes?"

"We'll get them back when we're called for the first challenge," Serena told him, clearly still mulling over how she'd been nominated for a position she didn't want.

Trey took the beer stein from Duncan with an easy smile. "This should be an interesting race." He raised his foaming glass.

"Interesting as in death or dismemberment?" Serena asked dryly. "That possibility certainly puts an interesting spin on things."

"Scared?" Duncan asked.

She gave him a steady look. "I'd be a fool not to be."

"So you're in?"

"I'm in."

"May the best man," Trey shot Serena a grin, "or woman win."

"We haven't had a female Master Wizard in several

hundred years, have we?" Serena's eyes sparkled over the rim of her glass. "I'm *so* going to enjoy arbitrating your cases."

Duncan set his glass on the countertop, then rubbed his scarred brow. "Would that be before or after you dig all the writing implements out of the walls and ceiling the first time someone pisses you off?"

Trey laughed. "I *remember* that. Shit that was funny."

"Only because you weren't on the receiving end of a newly sharpened pencil point," Duncan said dryly. He'd made her lose her temper on purpose, just to see crap fly like shrapnel around the classroom. The entertainment value had been high, but he was lucky she hadn't put his eye out by accident.

"You're like a damned elephant," Serena told Duncan mildly, making her glass vanish as she pushed away from the counter. "As entertaining as this hasn't been, gotta go."

Duncan found he didn't want her to leave. Damn. His well-honed sense of preservation didn't come into play with Serena. He better dig it out before he made a big fucking mistake. He ran a hand across the back of his neck, while he thought how he could spend a few more minutes with her without appearing to want to. "I thought we were going to see Henry?"

"That was," she checked her watch, "three hours ago."

Among its many other powers, the Council controlled time during an on-site summons. Duncan had always envied them, and his brother Caleb, that cool power. When he became Head of Council he, too, would have the power of manipulating time, as well as assimilating every unique talent available to a wizard. *All* of them, which would be invaluable in his fight to end terrorism.

"I'll meet you in Germany in the mor—"

"I have something I have to do in the morning," she cut him off. "I might be able to make it in the afternoon sometime. Why don't you go ahead and see Henry without me?"

"Old Henry Morgan?" Trey asked, looking interested. "What's he been up to lately?"

Serena pushed a long, glossy strand of hair over her shoulder, her eyes shadowed. "He had a debilitating stroke almost two weeks ago. He's been in a coma ever since."

"Damn, that's a shame. If you and Duncan are going to see him, maybe I'll tag along."

"He's noncommunicative," Serena told him. She materialized a business card. "But I'd like to believe that he'll know you're there. Here's the doctor's card with the address of the hospital, maybe I'll bump into you guys there." She left the card on the glossy black countertop, then vanished.

Back to her shower, Duncan thought, staring at the empty space she'd occupied. Naked. Hell. Being anywhere near Fury made him feel like a randy sixteen-year-old.

"Man, that woman is *hot*. Can you imagine that old fart Ian Campbell crawling all over that sexy body?"

Duncan had tried very hard not to over the years. "Maybe it was a true love." Something, thanks to the Edge Curse, he'd never experience.

"Oh, come on," Trey scoffed, lifting his glass to his mouth. "You don't believe that for a second, do you? *Nobody* believed it was a real marriage. She exchanged a couple of years of her youth for a cool fifty million dollars and control of Campbell's Foundation. They both got what they paid for."

Duncan tamped down his annoyance. Trey had dated Serena for several months—*twice*. Once when they were all in high school, and then again for a couple of months about five years, four months, and ten days ago. Yeah. He knew to the day how long ago, and the duration. Stupid, but unavoidable.

He'd always kept track of her. While he'd tried his damnedest to *avoid* her, he always knew where she was, and what she was up to. Being friends with Henry had been an unexpected bonus.

"You know Serena better than that. Fury wouldn't marry a man for his money." Although for all intents and purposes it sure as shit had *looked* that way. "I know for a fact that despite their age differences, Serena and Campbell had a genuine marriage." Henry had told him so in no uncertain terms.

"We always did compete for everything, didn't we?" Trey smiled. "Fries you that I got to her first, doesn't it?"

"Absolutely," Duncan said with honesty, and because he knew it was what Trey expected to hear. "You knew I liked her."

"Liked?" Trey's lazy chuckle would have fooled anyone who didn't know him. "Yeah, you liked her all right. Lusted after her, watched her, panted after her. Maybe if you'd told her how you felt she would have chosen you instead of me. You acted indifferent."

That first burgeoning feeling of forbidden love at fourteen had thrown Duncan for a loop. He'd believed, even at that age, that love would never be in the cards for him. Yet the intensity of his feeling for Serena had snuck up, slamming into him like a bolt of lightning. He'd managed, barely, to hide it from her, but he hadn't done as good a job as he'd thought hiding it from Trey.

"I didn't have your suave way with women," he told Trey dryly as he rounded the counter and pulled out a bar stool. Sitting down, he materialized a refill on his beer. What the hell. He'd like to think that his friend had used a Charm spell on Serena, but he knew that wasn't true. Serena had just liked Trey better than she'd liked him.

Except the night of Trey's sixteenth birthday.

Serena had kissed *Duncan* that night.

Water under the bridge. Best forgotten. "Yeah, well, I got over the crush and moved on."

Good fucking thing he didn't see her that often. Every time he *did* lay eyes on her he also wanted to lay his hands, lips, and body on her. Each time his knee-jerk reaction was twice as bad, twice as strong as the time before. Once he resolved this thing with Henry, once the Tests were over, he wouldn't have to see her again. Not even in passing.

Yeah. That would be better for his raging libido.

"Interesting to ignite that old rivalry again, huh?" Trey's eyes glowed devilishly. "Here we are again, and damned if she's not right back in the middle. We were always like two dogs with a bone, with Fury as the prize."

The prize had never been *his* to take, Duncan

thought grimly, keeping his fingers loose around the glass with effort.

Even back when he'd been young and stupid, he'd known on some instinctive gut level that she was off limits. *Way* off limits. He'd done whatever he could to keep an emotional distance between them.

Safer that way. Safer for both of them.

The threats and consequences of Nairne's Curse were never far from his mind. The Curse was as much a part of him as his DNA.

"I'm not in the running, never was. The field's wide open." *And if you touch her I'll*—He cut off the thought. If Serena wanted Trey's hands on her, then who the hell was he to protest?

"Is it? I think you're still jealous of the connection she and I share," Trey said cheerfully, finishing his beer in one last draw. "You always tried to score points off me. Admit it. You've always wanted to beat me at everything. Serena was the one game you couldn't win."

It had been the other way around. If Duncan had it, Trey wanted it. And fought damn hard to get it. "Can't be good at everything," Duncan agreed mildly. Trey had always kept a running tally of the points. Be it grades, football, or women. Duncan accepted that he was as competitive as the next man. But Serena had never been a game to *him*.

"Anyway, I didn't see that one coming, did you? Serena marrying a man almost fifty years her senior? Jesus, that's gross."

"Campbell and Serena shared a passion for aiding and comforting the masses," Duncan said neutrally, wishing Trey would get lost. He was already on Serena overload, God damn it.

"The sons are going after her, you know. Campbell funneled all his money into his Foundation. The grieving widow runs said Foundation, ergo she controls the purse strings."

"Ergo?" Duncan shook his head. He already felt feral on Serena's behalf. Campbell's sons were constantly taking her to court to contest their father's will or nullify their marriage. They'd generated a lot of press, and the day after a court appearance there'd be another salacious headline painting Serena as a money-grabbing opportunist.

Trey shrugged. "They live to give her shit. Take her to court every chance they get."

And took great pleasure in spilling their guts publicly. Bastards, Duncan thought, sipping his beer. He considered paying the Campbell brothers a visit, but it was none of his business. And knowing Serena, she'd just be pissed at him for interfering with her life. Dismissing his displaced anger, he turned his attention back to the Council situation.

"Do you really want this Council position, Trey? Or is this just another game for you?"

His friend raised a brow. "Will you Test any differently one way or the other?"

"I'll Test to win."

"What about Serena?" Trey's smile didn't reach his eyes. Duncan had seen that look before. Many times. On the soccer field. On the rink, over a tennis net— When Trey and Serena had strolled hand in hand into Duncan's favorite Italian restaurant in Florence. Sometimes, it really was all about the win.

"What about her?" Duncan asked, swirling the foot of his glass into the ring of condensation on his black marble countertop. It repulsed him a hell of a lot more to think of Trey crawling all over Serena's "sexy body," than the idea of her eighty-something-year-old husband doing the same thing.

"She didn't back out," he told the other man. "Now it's too late. She's in, just as we are. There can only be one winner."

"Then I repeat. May the best man win."

"What about best woman?"

"Don't be obtuse, Edge. She was nominated as a placeholder. The Council's gotta have three contestants. This is between you and me, pal. You and me."

Serena shivered as she walked quickly down the long corridor in a building that, in America, would have been condemned ten years ago, hell, probably twenty years ago. Even though she was inside, she was dressed in a thick down parka, insulated pants, and heavy gloves. She was *still* cold. So cold her nose was numb and the plume of her breath preceded her.

The group of top scientists who comprised the Foundation's think tank both lived and worked in this old abandoned aluminum factory in the tiny country of Schpotistan, at the northern tip of Siberia. The three-story building had been shored up as best the Foundation's engineers could manage. Still, Serena had used magic to *ensure* that the ceilings stayed up, the floors remained intact, and the walls didn't collapse. She had in fact gone above and beyond to make sure that her people were as comfortable, and safe, as she could make them in this inhospitable climate and temporary location—without revealing her wizard skills.

She'd moved the entire think tank team to this facility in one of the coldest places on earth for a reason. If this project was viable in Siberia, it would be viable *anywhere*. She'd pulled people off other assignments to expedite this one. Not that anyone was complaining. Despite the cold, and the isolation of their location, everyone was in a fever to see this innovative and potentially life-altering experiment work.

She pushed through the last set of double doors, and was welcomed by a blast of warm air. "Joanna?"

It might be icy in the corridors, but the work areas were nice and toasty, thanks to propane heaters. When they'd first arrived, they'd had generators outside. But even out here in the middle of nowhere, the expensive equipment had been stolen the first night.

How anyone could drive off with six half-ton generators out here without attracting notice was still a mystery. Due to the project's top-secret status, Serena hadn't wanted to attract undue attention by contacting authorities or making a fuss. It was easier to beef up security, use a makeshift heating system, and cast a protective spell, even though it was a day late and a dollar short.

Getting no reply, she assumed Joanna was in a meeting in the conference room on the second floor.

Serena checked to make sure she was alone, then teleported to the second-floor landing. It was just too damned cold to wander around the corridors if she didn't have to. Other than Joanna and a few other Halves, the Foundation's team members weren't wizards and didn't even know of their existence. As it should be.

As far as anyone knew, Serena lived among them here at this temporary facility whenever she was visiting. The fact that she was head of the Foundation allowed her to spend as much time as she needed "on the phone" or "working alone" in her rooms, which meant she could teleport wherever she needed to be without arousing suspicion. For normal transportation, they had the Foundation helicopter, carefully protected from the elements, on the roof.

She could hear voices and laughter from the conference room. A good sign, she thought with satisfaction, speeding up her pace and shivering. Duncan, with his power of heat and flame, would be able to warm this derelict building up better than their two dozen space heaters. Serena's lips twitched. And he'd probably burn the place down—no, he wouldn't. Duncan was many annoying things, but she had to grant that he was accomplished at controlling his powers.

Better than she was, which rankled.

Fire. He had it at his command. She wondered if that was what the project needed—Duncan's ability to call fire. If she didn't think he'd ask too many questions and butt in, she would consider, for a nanosecond, asking him to come and give her a hand both with heating the factory and with expediting the biggest project in the history of the Foundation.

Lord that was tempting . . .

He was tempting.

Standing in his ultramodern kitchen before they'd been summoned to the Wizard Council, Serena had had the most ridiculous urge to reach up and kiss him. Of course, that wasn't a new urge. She'd wanted to taste Duncan Edge since that fateful day in sixth grade when he'd set her hair alight and she'd retaliated by dousing him with water. He'd laughed.

Her heart had turned over. She had never met anyone who had such an enormous capacity for—*joy*. He'd been fun, and funny, and popular and confident. She'd been scared, shy, and unsure of just where she belonged. Like every other girl in the school, Serena had wanted to bask in the warmth of that smile, that laughter.

She'd fallen for him before she realized that he was an *Edge*.

She'd be wise to remember that when she was wondering how his hands would feel skimming her bare breasts. Or how his mouth would feel opening against hers. Or how his tall, hard body would feel sliding—naked—over hers.

Yep. Duncan Edge the man was just a bigger, badder version of Duncan Edge the boy who'd been the bane of her existence all through school. He should have a giant warning sign tattooed across his handsome face. *THIS MAN IS CURSED.*

As for Trey Culver—Serena shook her head. Why couldn't she be more attracted to *him*? She'd tried, she really had. Twice. He and Duncan looked physically like two sides of the same coin. They were both tall and good looking, but while Duncan's looks seemed somehow more intense, Trey's looks were storybook fabulous. He had thick, dark blond hair, soulful brown eyes, and a charming smile. He was wealthy, old money, and he was ridiculously charming. Seemingly without effort.

The problem with Trey was when she was with him she enjoyed his company. But when she didn't see him she didn't think about him. In fact, on those rare occasions that she did think about Trey, she wondered why she'd gone out with him at all. There was no chemistry, no spark.

She was out of her mind for agreeing to run for Head of Council with them. Out of her freaking mind. Duncan and Trey had competitive streaks a mile wide. Neither one of them liked losing. Not that Serena was all that fond of it either, but she was better able to put failure behind her and move on. Use it as a learning experience.

She didn't *want* to be Head of the Wizard Council, she thought crossly, glancing at the huge posters of tropical beaches that lined the crumbling walls of the freezing cold corridor, and wishing she were there, sipping a pineapple drink and feeling the heat of the sun on her face.

She had enough problems with controlling the powers she had now. God only knew what would happen if she was gifted with *all* powers. She shuddered to think.

In fact, she wasn't quite sure *how* her agreement to run had come about. Even with Duncan's taunts she hadn't been motivated to run. Yet, somehow, she'd heard herself jumping right in to accept the challenge. Hadn't she learned a long time ago that she had nothing to prove to him? Or to Trey, or to the Council for that matter.

She liked her life; liked the purpose and results of the things she was involved in. And while Head of Council wasn't that big a time suck, it was still another responsibility and her "to do" list was already full. Thanks in no small part to her petty stepsons and their unrelenting pursuit of the Campbell fortune.

Dismissing her family troubles for now, she really wanted to know who the two people were who had nominated her. Would have been nice of them to ask *her* before tossing her name into the cauldron, as it were.

Damn. She didn't have time for another job. She was already running, 24/7. And there was nothing that would convince her to abandon the stewardship of the Foundation that Ian had entrusted to her.

She needed some time to think this through. Withdrawing now was out of the question. Once voted in, the contestants were *in*. And, for her, losing intentionally was out of the question. Once she was committed, Serena was fully invested. If she competed, it was to win.

She frowned, feeling manipulated, but not sure by whom or why.

She opened the door to the common room, and was greeted enthusiastically by the twelve men and three women seated around a cozy grouping of plush easy chairs. These people represented the brightest minds in fields Henry and Ian had considered necessary for increasing the world's food supplies.

Each led their own specialty unit of the team, and had come here together for what they all hoped was the holy grail: a way to produce crops in one of the most barren areas on the planet. If they could make this project work here, the device could be used anywhere. Crops would flourish, and food would be not only plentiful, but cheap. This was Nobel Prize caliber stuff. And once they got the thermal blanket up and running, Serena would happily celebrate as the group earned a litany of scientific prizes and accolades.

The coffee table in the center of the circle of chairs was littered with empty insulated paper cups, and crumbs from what might have been a chocolate cake. Joanna liked to bake when she was stressed. There was also a pile of crumpled potato chip bags. Her team had the eating habits of a bunch of frat boys. And they'd been at it a while.

"Mom's home from Outer Mongolia." Steve Pool, their twenty-three-year-old climatologist, shot her a smile as he rose. "Coffee's fresh. Want me to get you some?"

"Please," she said with feeling as she walked across the room, greeting everyone as she went. She removed her gloves and coat, tucking the gloves inside a pocket before hanging the coat over the high back of the only empty chair.

She looked from face to face. "Well?"

"Let us put it this way, boss," Joanna, an atmospheric scientist and temporary head of the Foundation's think tank, began with barely restrained excitement. "We've gone from hopeful, but skeptical," she said, "to guardedly optimistic."

Joanna was forty-three, to Serena's thirty-three. But she looked considerably older than that. Her short, no-nonsense hair was prematurely graying, her skin had seen too many drastic climate changes without moisturizer, and she didn't seem to give a damn about what she wore beyond its functionality for a particular task.

She'd had a tragically brief marriage, only four years. Twelve-year-old Casey was in an English boarding school. Over the years, he'd come to various job sites on his school holidays and Joanna's demeanor instantly changed. She clearly adored her only child.

Serena felt a twinge of envy. Not that she was in any hurry to listen to her biological clock, but there were only so many times she'd be able to hit the snooze button.

Serena liked Joanna a great deal. She might be brisk and standoffish when it came to her work, but she had a wicked, dry sense of humor, and a way of speaking her mind that didn't ruffle feathers. The Foundation, and Serena, were damned lucky and grateful that Joanna had been willing and qualified to step into Henry's shoes after his sudden stroke.

Joanna sounded excited—well, as excited as Joanna ever sounded—but Serena noticed the other woman's eyes were shadowed. She looked as though she'd lost weight in the two weeks since Serena had last seen her. She knew Joanna had refused to take the one-week vacation that the others took every month. Instead, she opted to bank her vacation days for those times when Casey had a school holiday.

Her excitement explained why Joanna hadn't wanted to leave the project right now. Things were starting to click together. Serena shot a glance at Sal Pedskya. He and his team had successfully sequenced the complete rice genome last year, something that could be used to improve the quality and size of crops. They were now working frantically to apply what they knew to wheat. They were making incredible scientific breakthroughs.

Sixty-year-old Sal grinned, exposing three missing teeth in his broad, flat face. He'd forgotten his bridge again. "This damn thing is going to work, Serena," he said in his nasally Russian accent. He shoved up the sleeves of his ancient khaki sweater. He had another one just like it. His wife, who'd died of cancer twenty years ago, had knitted them for him. He wore one every day, and carried her picture in his wallet. "Damn thing it is going to *work*."

Her heart leapt. She'd always been sure it would. A giant "heating blanket" that would heat the ground, melt the permafrost, and turn frozen tundra into crop-producing farmland. My God. They were going to actually *do* this amazing thing. It could eventually eradicate world hunger.

She resisted jumping up and down with excitement. "What about a power source?" she asked Stuart Menzies, their electrical engineer. He was in his late seventies, a stick of a man with a shock of creamy white-blond hair and almost invisible eyebrows over deeply-set rheumy brown eyes. Stuart survived on not much more than coffee, canned tuna, and some weird, thick green drink that he consumed three times a day and which smelled like cow manure and looked worse. Absentminded, totally brilliant, and Serena made sure she never stood upwind of him for at least an hour after he'd consumed his liquid "supplement."

"Working on it," he said, not looking up as he scribbled schematics on the pad propped on his bent knees. He had both feet braced on the coffee table, one shoe embedded in his slice of Joanna's chocolate cake.

"How close? Denny?" She glanced at Dennis Cole, a fifty-something, giant bear of a man with shaggy dark hair and soulful eyes. Which, when not focused on his work, were usually watching Joanna.

Denny shook his head. Ian had "stolen" Denny from NASA's jet propulsion lab the year before he died. "I'm working on it as well."

Disappointed, Serena leaned back in her seat. "Too bad we can't just plug it in."

"Plug what in?" Duncan Edge asked, strolling into the room.

CHAPTER FOUR

Duncan wanted to ignore this resurgence of the attraction he'd felt for her for years. But it was proving to be damn well impossible. Couldn't do it. Worse, it seemed to be more powerful, *more* compelling each time he saw her. Which was precisely the fucking reason he'd gone out of his way *not* to encounter Serena whenever humanly possible.

His self-control was such that he could want her with an urgency that shocked him, yet he could remain motionless as he watched her move to the door with a fluid grace, despite her bulky clothing. He couldn't, however, control the fantasy playing out behind his cool gaze. Christ, Duncan thought, reluctantly amused at his own insanity, if Serena had a clue how she turned his body into rock-hard knots, he'd never hear the end of it.

"What are you *doing* here?" Serena whispered, cheeks flushed with temper as she slammed the bedroom door behind her. She'd wasted no time grabbing her coat and pushing him out into the hall before teleporting them to her room on the third floor.

She'd missed the interior of the room by a good three feet, and they'd ended up outside in the refrigerated corridor. Fury's aim had always been a bit off when teleporting.

"Still directionally challenged, I see," he said quietly. She shoved open the door and marched inside.

He followed her in.

"And why are we whispering?" he whispered back, going for amusement because the alternative was to grab hold of her and kiss away her annoyance. And maybe not stop for a week or two. Now that he knew she had about five thousand freckles sprinkled all over her creamy body, he'd like to peel off her clothes and kiss each one.

"Because if I wasn't whispering I'd be *screaming*. Damn it, Duncan," she said in her normal, albeit annoyed tone. "Joanna and I don't *do* magic in front of the others."

Apparently he annoyed her whether she was dressed or naked. He much preferred her naked. In fact, the image of her pale, gloriously freckled body was permanently engraved into his synapses. And if he'd ever had the faint hope that she was a woman he could forget, that illusion was long gone after he'd seen her naked. His greedy eyes took in her flushed cheeks, and the rapid rise and fall of her breasts beneath the coat she'd thrown on when she'd hauled him out of the meeting downstairs.

"They didn't seem that surprised that I'd flown in. With the wind howling outside it would have been hard to hear a chopper landing anyway. I think they were more interested in who I am rather than how I got here."

"Lying to them wouldn't have been necessary if you hadn't showed up unannounced. And as soon as you leave I'll go downstairs and correct their obvious assumptions that you're a boyfriend."

"Not a boy. No."

He shot out a flattened hand onto a nearby framed print before her temper got the better of her. Her pretty lips tightened when she realized that he was hanging on to the picture to prevent it from going flying.

She shook her head, clearly mentally counting to ten as she took off her parka. "Now I'm sorry I sent those Halves back to you," she told him ungraciously, tossing the apricot-colored coat onto a nearby brown sofa. The kind of oversized, overstuffed furniture that was great to snuggle in on a cold winter's night with a cold beer and a hot woman, Duncan thought, glancing around. All the comforts of home. She was planning on being here for a while.

The room wasn't that large—perhaps twenty by thirty, but it was furnished comfortably with well-worn furniture and decorated in warm browns and a variety of shades of her favorite color, orange. There was nothing luxurious about it.

Clearly she used the space to both entertain and sleep. Duncan could just see the corner of a bed behind a japanned screen. He cast her a glance, dragging his mind away from the image of Serena spread across that coyly hidden bed, her amazing hair fanned out around her. One of his stronger powers was the ability to call fire, but nothing he could produce could possibly match the fire of her hair.

"I hate to ask," he said, enjoying the way her hips, snugged into skintight ski pants, swayed as she paced. "Why?"

"Because now you're like a damn salesman with his foot in the door. I can't seem to get rid of you. What do you want, Duncan?"

She was wearing a close-fitting orangey-red sweater that should have clashed with her hair but didn't. It had a row of tiny gold buttons down the front. The top three were undone, and he could count the hard thuds of her pulse at the base of her pale throat.

He unzipped his heavy black parka. Nice and warm in here. With her. "We were going to see Henry today, remember?" He removed his coat, tossing it on top of hers. Both coats slid to the floor in a heap.

Glancing around he noticed that pretty much every flat surface in the room was covered with framed pictures, most of them of groups of children grinning from ear to ear. But one picture in particular caught his eye. This one was of Henry, a man he guessed from his vibrant red hair as Serena's father, and Ian Campbell on a fishing trip.

"I gave you the name and address of the hospital." Her lips tightened. Shoving up the sleeves of her sweater, she gave him a wide berth to reach a chair. "Fly free."

He'd take a bet that she wouldn't sit down. She was too agitated. The temptation to reach over and wrap her in his arms was almost overwhelming. Almost. He resisted.

"Aren't you even going to offer me a cup of coffee?"

"You won't be here long enough to drink it," she told him firmly as she stood there glaring at him. "Ah, geez, don't sit d—Damn it, Duncan! Why are you suddenly so in my face? We haven't seen each other in years—Do *not* put those filthy boots on my coffee table!"

Resting his arms along the back cushions of the plush sofa, he crossed his ankles on the scarred trunk. "What are you doing up here?"

"Trying to get rid of you."

"Not up here in your quarters. Up here near the damned Arctic Circle, Serena."

"I'm sorry. I didn't get the memo that I had to run Foundation projects through you. Must have got lost in the mail. I'll lodge a complaint with the Postal Service. Thanks for the heads up. Bye."

"Know what's an inch away on any local map?"

"Man's inch or woman's inch?"

"The Russians are trying to pump oil out of the ground. They're pretty inept, and it's taking awhile, there are a lot of people very interested in what they're trying to do and the progress they may or may not be making."

"And I care about this—why?"

"Because there's a faction of Russian tangos, called the—What?"

She was scowling at him. "A faction of Russian *dancers* is interested in oil exploration?"

"Not *dancers*. *Terrorists*. The group called Red Mantis is extremely interested, and just waiting to gobble up whoever gets in its way."

"Send all *those* people a memo. Better send that one registered—sounds too important to chance it getting lost, too. I'm not interested in oil. And by the way, there are also gold and diamonds an 'inch away on the map.' I'm not interested in those, either."

"What *are* you interested in then? Why do you have a mechanical engineer, a jet propulsion engineer, a Nobel Prize–winning microbiologist, a climatologist, and God only knows who else, gathered out here in the middle of nowhere Gofuckistan? If it's not oil you're after, what the hell is it?"

"Food for millions of starving people. *Crops.*"

Duncan raised his pencil-scarred brow. "In the *permafrost?*"

"Yes."

He stared at her. "Yes?"

"That's a complete answer."

"Not to me it isn't." He dropped his feet to the floor and sat forward, elbows on his knees. "The security in this place sucks. Whatever you people are doing here will eventually arouse the suspicion of the local equivalent of the Mafia."

"Been there, done that. After they helped themselves to my generators I agreed to pay both the Dolgopruadnanskaya and the Solntsevskaya to leave us alone."

"Jesus, Serena—"

"Foreign companies here pay up to twenty percent of their profits to the Russian Mafia," she cut him off. "That's the price of doing business in Russia. Ignoring shakedown threats would've just invited something *worse* than them swiping my generators. I need to get back downstairs. Tell Henry I'll be there tonight to visit him."

"You people need to close shop, and get the hell

out of this place," he told her, not mincing words. "It's too damn volatile and dangerous for civilians."

"You people?" Her hair seemed to crackle with electricity. He simply looked at her. Glaring eyes at ten paces. An orange silk pillow jettisoned off the sofa and flew across the room, and a framed painting vibrated against the brick wall.

"What business is it of yours, Duncan?" she said through her teeth as she stood, feet spread in a fighter's stance, fist stuck in the side pocket of her black ski pants. "What damn right do you have to follow me here and disrupt my life's work?"

For some reason that got a rise out of him. "The Campbell Foundation was your *husband's* life work."

"And mine," she told him quietly. "I care that people all over the world are starving to death when they shouldn't have to. I care. And I can make a difference. Go away, Duncan."

"Why did you marry him?" He walked toward her, feeling agitated and primitive enough to toss her over his shoulder and carry her behind the screen to that bed hidden back there. He wanted to fill his hands with her breasts, and feast on her mouth. He wasn't going to do either. But if he didn't at least touch her soon he was going to explode.

Her lashes flickered, but other than that she didn't move, although he was still walking toward her. She'd never backed down as long as he'd known her. "I know you well enough to know you didn't marry him for his money."

He was close enough now to count the golden freckles across her nose, and count the rapid beats of her heart visible at the base of her throat. He wanted to put his mouth there and feel her vibrancy on his tongue. "But he was almost fifty years your senior. Old enough to be your grandfather."

"I loved him."

"As a parental figure."

"I loved him as a *wife*. Not that my marriage has anything to do with you. And news flash. You don't know me at all."

He was now close enough to inhale the faint hint of jasmine-scented soap on her skin. Duncan's mouth watered. "We've known each other for almost twenty plus years," he drawled, picking up a long strand of her hair, which lay across her shoulder like a skein of copper silk.

"Wh—" She narrowed her eyes as she looked up at him. "What are you doing?" A world of awareness filled that question.

Yeah. What the hell *was* he doing? "Seeing if your hair is as hot as it looks." It wasn't. It was smooth and cool to the touch and curled around his fingers as he savored the texture. Touching her fried his judgment and made the endorphins flood his brain. She tried to move out of reach. But she wasn't trying too hard, and she only moved a foot, still well within touching distance.

"Don't be ridiculous. The only time my hair was hot was when you set it on fire. Let go."

Duncan curved his palm around her stubborn jaw in a light, possessive grip. He traced her lips with his thumb. "Why do we always seem to strike sparks off one another, hmm?" If his synapses were short-circuiting, it was only fair to do the same to hers.

Her pupils dilated. "I don't want to get water on this area rug. I just got it."

He laughed, drawing her closer by sliding his hand down her throat and around to her nape. "Don't rain on my parade, Fury." He felt her warm, coffee-scented breath on his mouth, "I'm just going to kiss you."

She tilted her face and whispered hoarsely, "Bad idea."

"God. Don't I know it."

The sensation of Duncan's hard fingers closing gently on the back of her neck was as shocking as a sudden jolt of pure electricity. Euphoria made her head swim, and she had to grab his upper arms as her knees buckled. She closed her eyes as he drew her into his arms. The heat of his body was like a furnace against her. He was big and solid and smelled of icy air and—*Duncan*. A fragrance that was unique to him, and one she could easily recognize blindfolded.

"I . . ."

His firm lips touched hers, effectively stopping even that half-hearted-sort-of protest. She'd always wondered—God—always—if the adult Duncan would taste as intoxicating as the teenage boy who'd given her her first real kiss. She'd shuddered under his mouth then. But that had been nothing like this.

This was—devastating. Consuming. More darkly sensual than anything she could have imagined. Her lips clung to his as an electrical thrill zinged along her nerve endings like the tail of a Roman candle.

The tip of his tongue, warm and slick, traced the

seam of her lips until they parted. She felt rather than heard the deep sound he made as her mouth opened for his exploration. The taste and feel of him filled Serena's senses, making the blood pulsing rapidly through her body feel like thick, warm honey. His tongue stroked hers at the same time he caressed the tender skin on the back of her neck with the callused pad of his thumb. As rough as a cat's tongue, the sensation made chills race up and down her back.

He kept up a slow, mesmerizing rhythm with his mouth on hers and his fingers stroking her skin. The combination made her body come alive, and her nerves jump.

Her breasts felt full and heavy, her nipples painfully aroused. Serena pressed her body against his. She never wanted this kiss to end.

Her heart pounded as the kiss deepened, and she made a soft, helpless sound in the back of her throat. Vaguely afraid of the intensity of her reaction to him, Serena started to lift her arms around his neck, giving in to the storm that was Duncan.

He lifted his head. "Enough." His voice was thick, his eyes dark as he placed a large hand on her upper arm and moved away, leaving her body cold. And confused.

Enough? Not even close, damn him.

Thoughts more than a little scattered, she somehow managed to collect herself enough to move out of his reach. And that was only by shimmering. She wasn't sure she could make her legs work right then if she'd attempted to walk away.

"That was interesting," she managed coolly while her insides were still somersaulting. "But uncalled for. We don't have that kind of relationship."

He raised a dark brow sardonically. "Really? What kind of relationship do we have?"

She blinked, baffled by how he could kiss her like that, hot and intense, and still remain unaffected. Emotionally anyway. His body had left little doubt that he was fully engaged in the kiss. Annoying man.

"The kind," Serena shot back, "where we don't see one another for years at a time, and are fine with it." She wasn't fine with it. Not anymore. She had no idea what he'd intended when he'd so casually kissed her. But the kiss had opened a Pandora's box of memories and feelings that she would have preferred remain in the dark. Like butterflies, the snippets of their history flittered about her mind, colorful reminders that she wasn't immune to him. Never had been.

The taste, feel, and scent of Duncan still filled her senses. He'd stopped when she'd been starving for more. More fool her. Watching his lean, handsome face, she didn't see so much as a flicker of expression now. Had she imagined the heat in those blue eyes that were now watching her in that remote, impersonal way?

"Did you just use Charm on me?"

He laughed with real amusement. "I have all the charm I need without having to resort to magic."

"Swear to me."

He shrugged. "I swear."

Damn. So what she'd felt in his arms was real? That was bad news. She rubbed her upper arms through the soft cashmere sweater. When she was around him she always felt slightly drunk. With lust. With longing. With—God. Insanity. There was no way on God's Green Earth that she could become involved with an Edge.

"Trey has Charm."

"Trey is suave and sophisticated and has bucket-loads of *charisma*. He doesn't need to use magic on women."

"Neither do I."

"Stop believing your own hype," she snapped, stunned, *stunned* that he could stand there so calmly when her entire world had been turned upside down by a simple kiss. "And stop wasting my time. If you have a valid reason for this visit, then spit it out. I have to get back to my meeting."

"I really did come to get you to join me when I go to see Henry, but now that I know where you are, I'm concerned."

He wasn't concerned; that would require that he actually gave a hoot about her. No, he wasn't concerned, he was interfering. Why, she had no idea. "No need. I told you, I have the Russian Mafia situation under control."

"They'll just keep coming back for more. You know that."

"I explained that we work for a nonprofit organization, and that we have nothing to give them. They took what I offered." *And six generators, and a truck. And I have a protective spell around us now.*

"Probably because you're way the hell and gone out here surrounded by nothing but frozen tundra.

That protective spell you used was a good idea, though. Anyone else knocked on your door asking if you plan on drilling up here?"

"Of course not," Serena said with exasperation. She could still taste him on her mouth. She wanted more. She wished he'd leave. Being around him this much, this close, was a very dangerous thing indeed. "Because we're not. We're working on a thermal blanket so we can expand our crop locations. That's it. Anyone with half a brain," she said pointedly, "can see that we aren't here trying to dig through fifty feet of permafrost to get a trickle of oil."

"Any wizards on this project?"

"Henry, of course, Joanna's a Half—Why?"

"Weird shit is going down. We're looking into it."

"We who? And what is it exactly you're looking into? Because it sure as hell isn't here!"

"I work for the paranormal branch of a counter-terrorist operation called T-FLAC."

"Ah."

"Ah?"

"That's a convenient outlet, and a legal one, I presume, to get out all the violent tendencies you have."

"Jesus. I don't have 'violent tendencies.' I do my *job*. Violence is frequently part of it, yes, but a very small part."

"Well, I agree with what Gandhi said on the subject. 'I object to violence because when it appears to do good, the good is only temporary. The evil it does is permanent.'"

"I'll be sure to send out a memo to the world's terrorist population," Duncan said dryly. "Gandhi also said: 'Better to be violent if there is violence in our hearts than to put on a cloak of nonviolence to cover impotence.'"

"There's always a nonviolent way to achieve the same results," she told him, knowing as she said it that while true, her delivery was of the stick-up-her-butt variety. "You just have to use your brain instead of your brawn. I don't know why we're even having this conversation, because you won't listen to me anyway."

"Keeping the world safe from terrorists is worth fighting for."

Of course it was. It was *Duncan* and his "I am always right" tone that she had a flipping problem with. "If *women* ruled the world we'd sit down over a cup of coffee and work it out without brawling," Serena said, needling him on purpose. She knew it wasn't a simple problem, but Duncan always had to be *right*, and it didn't annoy her any less now that they were adults. If he said black she was always going to say white. It was ridiculously childish she knew, but it had become a comfortable habit.

"If women ruled the world it would be littered with fur balls, broken fingernails, and clumps of hair," Duncan said with an annoying grin.

Serena felt a gurgle of laughter bubble up. "Fur balls?"

He shrugged, still smiling. Damn. He wasn't just sexy, he *could* also be quite charming. He'd always been hard to resist. More so now than ever. But Serena had several good reasons why resisting him was mandatory.

"Let's agree that men and women should work

together. How about that?" She moved away to sit on the arm of the sofa. "Is this group you work for U.S. military?"

"No. It's a privately funded organization."

The news that Duncan was involved in some form of James Bond-y job didn't surprise her at all. He'd always been a very private man, and for all his sophistication he was extremely . . . tempered. And although he had a reputation as a brawler, she realized she'd never seen him actually lose his temper. He was always in control. Even when she'd observed him fighting, it had been chillingly calculated.

Aside from minor acts against her in school, like the hair-burning incident, he'd never actually *hurt* her. In fact, he'd used magic to protect her a couple of times when they'd been kids.

The time she first went to wizard school came to mind. The kids had taunted her about being an orphan, and Duncan had erased their mouths until the math teacher made him undo the spell and he had to write "Freedom of Speech is a right" one hundred times on the blackboard.

So as annoying as he'd been over the years, he'd also been a bit of a white knight to her. Of course, the *annoyance* part of the equation won over any kind of hero worship.

But a counterterrorist operative made a lot of sense.

Serena was intrigued. "How many people are involved? What's your jurisdiction? Do you carry a gun? What kind of—You're not going to tell me, are you?"

"I'd hate to have to kill you."

"Could you?"

"Yes."

A tremor rippled across her skin. Yes. He looked quite capable of killing someone. With just that cool, unemotional look in his eyes. "You didn't come here to do that did you?" she teased.

"If I came here to kill you, Fury, you wouldn't be alive right now."

"Good to know." *Really good to know.* "Now that you're aware that nobody is threatening my project, thanks for stopping by, you can go."

"You know that a couple of wizards were murdered in the last few weeks?"

"I heard about it, yes. Awful. But what's that got to do with me or the Foundation?"

"As far as I know, nothing. I didn't mean to imply that it did. But these murders are a grave concern. As one of T-FLAC's psi operatives, I'm charged with looking into it. I'd like to talk to Dr. Rossiter. You mentioned she was with Henry when he had his stroke."

Still balanced on the broad arm of the sofa, she kicked off her shoes, and lifted both feet to the sofa cushion. "She was. But why do you think the killings have anything to do with his stroke?"

"I'm not sure if the incidents do have anything to do with one another. But until then Henry was in great shape. The German doctors are puzzled as to why he had the stroke. And if *they* put up a red flag, you can bet I'll be checking into it."

"How do you know what Henry's doctors think?"

"I called them and asked."

Of course he had. He and Henry were as thick as

thieves. Duncan was many things, but he had been a good friend of Henry's for years.

"I hope you aren't implying that Joanna had anything to do with this stroke? For God's sake Duncan, just because you deal with bad people in your line of work doesn't mean everyone has to be tarred with that same brush! Henry brought Joanna in two years ago. She's been an asset to the Foundation, and I consider her a friend. Step lightly around her, please."

He picked up a book from a low table without looking at it. "So Dr. Rossiter's in charge until Henry's back on his feet?"

"Yes." And please God that would be *soon*. She felt rudderless without him. Henry and Martha had taken her in when her parents had died. They'd loved her, and taken care of her, and been her family for almost twenty-five years. Scared, Serena tamped down the resurgence of panic she'd been feeling ever since she'd gotten the call from Joanna.

Duncan propped himself against the rough brick wall near the window and stuck his fingers in the front pockets of his jeans. "Who's she sleeping with?"

The big window showed it was dark outside. And it was a given that it was well below freezing. Brutal. Inhospitable, and filled with promise. Serena wanted to get back to the informal meeting downstairs. She wanted to know what new baby steps had been made, and—"What?" she said blankly.

"Joanna is sleeping with . . . ?"

"Joanna? Nobody. As far as I know. Why would you even ask a question like that?" She tucked her cold feet under the sofa cushion.

"Because she had several hickies on her neck she didn't want anyone to see. She tried covering them with makeup, but when that didn't work she wore a turtleneck."

"I'm trying to figure out how my staff's love life, or lack thereof, has anything to do with you."

"Everything has to do with me until this has been resolved."

"And you've decided in your infinite wisdom that because the head of my think tank had a stroke, and his second in command has a couple of marks on her neck, that she's a *terrorist*? Don't you think that's a pretty enormous leap in logic?"

"Yeah. I do. For some reason there are rumblings in the terrorist communities about this location. The question is: Are they interested in one of the Foundation's wunderkinds? What you're doing up here, *you* personally because of your powers? Or none of the above?"

"Well, if you came here to scare me, you've succeeded. Even though you're way off base. Henry's stroke was bad luck, but there was nothing suspicious about it. And if Joanna has found a lover in one of the other scientists, more power to her. I hope he makes her a very happy woman."

"And what about you, Serena?" His smile didn't reach his eyes as he pushed away from the wall. "Are you a happy woman?"

CHAPTER FIVE

Relieved to see him and frantic for news, Dr. Joanna Rossiter flew into her lover's arms the moment he materialized in her room. "Did you find him?" she demanded, welcoming Grant's embrace as he closed his arms tightly around her. She buried her face against his neck. "Please God, tell me you found him."

Grant Cooper was the only one who knew that her son Casey had been kidnapped. The only one she could share her fear with. The only one out there looking for a little boy who must be paralyzed with terror.

The word "terror" didn't even come close to the emotions she'd been experiencing ever since she'd gotten that first call from the kidnappers. Casey was her entire world.

"Not yet, baby," Grant whispered, kissing the top of her head as he gently rocked her. "Not yet. Don't lose faith."

Devastated, her knees buckled and she tightened her grip on the back of his jacket as tears welled. Casey. *Oh God, sweetheart—*

Normally she was so focused on her work she was

barely aware of her surroundings, but Case's kidnapping had turned her world upside down. Everything and everyone had taken on sinister undertones that she was at a loss to deal with. Like the man that had strolled in on the meeting earlier for instance. Who *was* he?

Did *he* have anything to do with her son's kidnapping? She knew she was being paranoid, but couldn't help herself. The kidnappers had taken Casey from his boarding school just outside London. Until their conditions were met, she wouldn't get her son back.

God, oh, God. What they wanted could take months—*years* to complete.

Thank God she had Grant; she'd had to tell *someone*. And who better than a powerful full wizard? If anyone could find her baby it was Grant Cooper. Even his name sounded strong and gave her confidence. The fact that she even *had* a lover was astonishing enough, but a man this powerful, this sexy and handsome, who was in love with *her*, still stunned her. It was as though he'd walked straight out of her fantasies and into her life. But right now she didn't care about Grant's blond good looks, or his sexy smile, all she cared about were his skills.

"Please. Oh, please—"

He touched her hair, his eyes tender. She immediately felt calmer. "I'm sorry. No. Not yet. Shit, baby, don't cry." He folded her into his strong arms. "Don't give up hope. I promised I'd find Casey for you, and I will. I've tried tracking his aura, but I hit a dead end. Look, I've heard stories about a wizard who can go back in time. I'm going to find him and make him help us. I'm sorry, honey. I know the waiting is making you crazy, but no matter how long it takes, I'll get Case back."

Today. Bring him back to me today! She slipped her arms around Grant's waist, holding on to the back of his coat tightly. Dropping her head to his chest, she felt the sting of tears pressing against her eyelids. "It's been three weeks," she said brokenly. "Case is only twelve. Old enough to be terrified. What if—"

"No *what ifs*. I'll bring him back to you safely, I promise." He brushed a tender kiss on her forehead. "Did they contact you today? Show you he was okay?"

Her heart squeezed. "Yes."

As they did every day, the kidnappers sent her a short video of Casey via e-mail. He was being held in a small room. His hair had grown too long, she thought, feeling the familiar pain deep inside her chest. Every day he had a different foreign language newspaper in one hand to show her the date. He always mouthed, "Hi Mom," and waved.

The picture was too grainy to see details, but Joanna knew her baby was scared out of his mind. The e-mail videos never lasted more than a few seconds. Then the screen would go dark. In the center, a military style clock counted off the minutes.

She had to find him. She had to. Soon. *Now,* damn it. Right now!

"I don't want to know what it is you're working on, I know it's top secret," Grant said soothingly. "But are you *close* to being able to give the kidnappers what they want?" He was rubbing her back, and her heart rate started slowing down to normal, and her fears became muted.

She'd never realized just how good it felt just to be held. It had never been like this with Drew, Case's father. They hadn't been married that long before he was diagnosed. He'd died when Case was barely four. Joanna missed Drew, but she'd come to terms with his absence from her life. It was different for Case. He didn't complain, but she knew the other kids often teased him about not having a father. Kids could be so cruel. Things were getting better now. In the months she'd been with Grant, he'd gone out of his way to be nice to her son. Case needed that. He needed a strong, decent male figure in his life. So, she'd discovered, did she.

"No! Yes. Oh, God, I don't *know*."

"Can I give you a power that would help you in your work? Something that could speed things up for you? God, baby. I hate to see you so upset and stressed. Let me help you."

She shook her head. He was so dear to offer to amp up her powers. He'd offered to do anything she needed to help her get this project to completion so she and Case could be reunited as quickly as possible. "I love you for offering again, but thank you, no. It was interesting being able to levitate, but it just made me dizzy, and it was too hard to control. And I have no need of superhuman strength, that just gave me a terrible headache. If I could think of a power that might help me find Casey, I'd be happy to accept it."

Halves had very few powers, and Joanna was fine with that. She was first and foremost a scientist. Trying out different powers was interesting, but one

needed a lifetime to learn how to master them efficiently. Besides, she secretly thought gifting a Half
with full powers would somehow upset the balance
of things. She knew it was strictly forbidden by the
Council, which only proved how very much Grant
cared if he was willing to risk the ire of the Master
Wizard just for her.

Of course Henry was still in a coma and didn't
know anything right now. Her stomach cramped
with fear.

"How *is* the project coming along?"

"We're ahead of schedule by a few weeks, thank
God," Joanna answered. The knot-like pain in her
middle unraveled as it always did at Grant's soothing, matter-of-fact tone. "Serena came back from
the Gobi project today. Whenever she's on-site there's
a nice energy that she always brings with her. I
admire her so much. She's absolutely tireless, and I
want to help her bring this dream of being able to
plant crops anywhere to fruition."

"I know you do, baby. And you will. *Soon.* I have
all the faith in the world in you."

She lifted her head and stroked his beautiful face
with her blunt fingered, no-nonsense hand. What a
ridiculous contrast. Almost beauty and the beast-
ish, she thought painfully. What he saw in her she
had no idea. But she was grateful beyond words that
they'd accidentally bumped into each other in the
bank back home in Chicago three months ago. It
had been love at first sight. Unbelievable that he'd
lived four miles away from her for years without her
being aware of his existence.

They'd discovered mutual friends, they shopped

at the same grocery store, and banked at the same bank, yet they'd never met before that fateful day.

Joanna had been widowed for eight years. Having her son to love had been enough for her since Drew had died of brain cancer. Case and her work consumed her life. And face it, she wasn't exactly Christie Brinkley. She was thirty pounds overweight, hadn't worn makeup since . . . she didn't remember when, and had let her short dark hair go gray without a qualm. Grant loved her just the way she was. Amazing.

Better still, Casey already loved him, and Grant adored her son, and spoiled him terribly. There was something about her lover that filled her with a profound sense of well-being whenever he was around. And knowing that he was diligently searching for Casey made her heart swell with gratitude.

Joanna looped her arms about his neck and kissed his jaw. What a lovely man he was, inside and out. She hated to keep him a secret, but she had to see him every day, and Serena had cautioned all of them to keep a low profile and not invite anyone inside the project until they were ready to show it to the world.

"Oh, some guy showed up earlier," she told him, nibbling his throat.

He stroked her breast until her nipple rose hard and aching in his palm. "Oh?"

"Serena didn't look happy to see him. She introduced him—Duncan Edge? Then hustled him out of the room awfully fast, and disappeared with him. I've never seen her so agitated." Which just proved how right she'd been not to introduce him to her friend. No, Grant could stay her own delicious secret for now. One thing that could no longer remain just *her* secret was Casey's kidnapping. She had to tell Serena about the kidnappers' threats to the project. She'd wanted to tell her boss and friend right from the start—

She suddenly experienced a little buzzing sensation in her brain, and her thoughts became jumbled and unclear. No. The kidnappers had warned her to tell no one. And she wouldn't. Not when her precious son was with them.

Grant kneaded her shoulders. "You're tight. Lie down. I'll give you a nice relaxing massage."

The "nice relaxing massage" would turn into sex. Joanna let him take her hand and lead her to the bed. He was so good to her, she thought, as he tenderly undressed her. So gentle and loving. He was the only thing in her shattered world that made any sense at all.

"I want to see this thing you're working on." Duncan paced around her furniture like a caged lion. Her room was too small for so much freaking activity. She watched him pick up a crude, hand-carved wood statue she'd been given by the children in Zimbabwe last year. After looking at it, he put it down and moved to the bookshelf to scan the titles.

Watching him, she bunched her hair and twisted it at her nape, then looked around for something to hold it there. She didn't remember Duncan taking out the pins, but whatever he'd done with them, she couldn't see them anywhere. Finding a pen on a nearby table, she efficiently anchored the glossy mass out of the way, immediately feeling more in control. "It's good to want things," she told him, heart still skipping beats.

She was shaken by the kiss. Shaken by the intensity of her feelings, and shaken by how much she'd wanted to keep on kissing him.

Duncan Edge of all people. God.

She dismissed out of hand her overwhelming desire to have sex with him. Nothing could come of it. An Edge and the descendant of Nairne, the woman who had cursed his family five hundred years ago. The thought of a physical union between the two of them sent a shiver up Serena's spine.

She, like the three Edge brothers, had been brought up on a steady diet of Nairne's Curse. Duncan had no idea that she'd always known about the Curse. Although for reasons she had never been able to fathom, he'd confided in her about it when they'd been sixteen.

It had been difficult, but she'd managed to keep an ancient family promise. She'd kept her connection to Nairne a closely guarded secret. And she always would.

By now the Curse should have run its course. Surely five hundred years was long enough to prove Nairne's point? Apparently not. But judging by Duncan's proclivity for mayhem and violence, Serena knew this generation of Edge brothers hadn't yet figured out the secret to breaking it.

She knew. But if she told them she'd lose her own powers.

"You're getting fingerprints on my things," she told him crossly as he returned a book to the shelf. "Would you please settle somewhere—preferably London? You're making me dizzy."

"You always did get cranky when you're embarrassed." Duncan rested his hands on the sill behind him, leaned back, and crossed his ankles. "Thinking about the kiss?"

"What ki—Oh, you mean?" She waved vaguely to the spot across the room where the kiss had occurred.

Duncan laughed. "Your heart's beating too fast for you to have forgotten, Fury."

"It wasn't that memorable, I assure you." She didn't want to talk about the kiss, she really didn't. Time to change the subject to the lesser of two evils. "Just as a matter of curiosity, what makes you think that I'd show you what we've been working on?"

"Why not? It's a humanitarian project, right? You raise funds for your projects. Perhaps I'm feeling altruistic and would like to make a sizable contribution."

"Good. I'll hold you to it," she told him, wishing he'd shimmer the hell out of her room and leave her in peace. He'd always . . . bothered her. But now he was bothering her a lot more. She didn't like it. Mostly, she didn't like that she wanted to reach out and touch him.

"The blanket will be in transit from the warehouse where it was constructed the day after tomorrow. I'll let you know when it gets here, and you can come back."

"Let's go now."

"It's the middle of the night." He was relentless. She didn't want to go anywhere with him. Not until she got her galloping hormones in check.

He glanced at the large, matte black watch on his wrist. "It's barely ten."

She didn't mind showing him the thermal blanket. Duncan was many things, but Serena trusted him enough to know he wouldn't do anything to screw up her project. Screw up her good intentions, yes. But once he saw how incredible the design was, how totally, brilliantly simple the thermal blanket was, he'd be impressed as hell. Maybe once he saw how dedicated they all were to the project, and how non-threatening it was, he'd go back to his own freaking business and leave her alone. After he made that generous donation.

"It's in a warehouse on Vladimirskaya Street. Number 18739. I'll meet you there in an hour. I have a few things to clear up first." Like calling her lawyer to see how the motion hearing had gone that morning in New York. She hadn't needed to be there, but she'd bet her new Ferragamo crocodile Avila pumps that both Ian's sons had been perched, like the vultures they were, right in the front row. She could just see Hugh and Paul, their pupils nothing but dollar signs, wearing their collective sense of entitlement on the sleeves of their custom-tailored suits. It was hard for her to fathom that sweet, kind Ian had fathered two such greedy, spoiled sons. But he had, and now they were a major thorn in her side.

"I'd prefer to go now." Duncan zipped up his thick coat. "Together."

Exhaling, she wondered if anyone had ever told him no and meant it. If a quick trip to the warehouse would get rid of him, she'd go. "Fine." She knew she sounded ungracious, but what did he expect? It wasn't as though she'd invited him to butt into her life any old time he felt like it.

She chose to pick her battles. This wasn't one of them. She pulled on her coat, zipped the front, then pulled up the fur-lined hood, snugging it around her face. "Let's do it."

He gave her an amused look. "Unless you give me the exact coordinates, you're going to have to touch me."

Reluctantly, she walked up to him and grabbed his sleeve. "Happy?"

His laughter followed them as they teleported together. She'd never shimmered with anyone before today, and now she'd done it twice. It felt . . . pretty good. Until a rush of ice cold, garbage-scented air greeted them. She'd miscalculated by at least twenty feet, placing them outside instead of inside the nondescript building. Duncan gave her an amused look.

Releasing his sleeve without comment, Serena started walking across the weed-infested gravel parking lot, her breath pluming in front of her in the frigid air.

The cold made her lungs ache. "We're here, aren't we?"

His teeth flashed in the darkness. "A miss is as good as a mile."

Oh, she wanted to make it rain on him, she really did. But he was walking too close, and she was damned if she'd get wet just to punish him. Besides, if she rained on him, it would freeze instantly *and* he'd know he'd gotten to her.

He, she knew, was pinpoint accurate when he teleported. He'd always been top of that class. In fact, he'd pretty much been top of every class, with herself and Trey always vying for second place.

The only thing that made his natural aptitude halfway bearable was the secret she held. Sometimes she wanted to rub the knowledge in his face. But that was petty and childish and beneath her. And against the rules, damn it.

She'd show off the thermal blanket, and wave him good-bye. After the Tests their paths didn't need to cross for any reason whatsoever. With any luck she wouldn't run into him again for twenty or thirty years. And when she became Head of Council, she'd have *all* the powers she could possibly need or want at her disposal. And that included pinpoint accuracy when teleporting.

The small industrial area was several miles out of town, and very quiet at this time of night. The crunch of their boots on the frozen layer of ice grouting the gravel sounded very loud in the still, cold air.

"You need to get that light fixed," he told her. The bulb over the door had been burnt out, or stolen, but it wasn't pitch dark. There was a fairly bright light over the door of the warehouse across the street that did an adequate job of lighting their way. They followed their shadows to a side door, and Serena used her code on a small panel to gain entrance.

Ordinary locks hadn't worked. No matter how secure, they'd all been stolen. The keypad had been integrated into the tungsten steel security door. So far so good. Although every time she came here Serena expected the entire thing to be missing, despite built-in keypad, burglar-proof construction, and a strong protective spell.

She'd be happy when the blanket was loaded onto

the Trans-Siberian railcars the day after tomorrow, and en route to their final destination. If they could figure out an efficient way to keep the blanket heated, or cooled, with an independent power source, they'd be ready for the first tests.

She stepped inside, flipped back her hood and locked the door behind them, then flicked on the overhead lights. They came on in a straight line high above in the rafters, POP, POP, POP, flooding the enormous shadowy space with white light. Metal pallets on wheels filled the room, each holding a roll fifteen feet high, covered in heavy black plastic.

Duncan glanced around. "Looks like a carpet warehouse."

The place did look like a carpet warehouse, which was why she'd be grateful when the rolls shipped out. The locals were already curious about the contents of the warehouse without knowing what it contained. If they thought she was storing carpeting, a highly desirable commodity, they'd try just about anything to get in. "I'll partially unroll one for you to take a look at."

With a wave of her hand she peeled back the thick protective covering, then caused the top of the roll to unfurl onto the floor at their feet.

Duncan crouched down, picking up a corner. "Heavy. Looks like the netting used to string Christmas lights over shrubbery."

"It is based on that, as a matter of fact. Our textile engineer came up with a viable material." Serena crouched down beside him. Their knees touched. She felt a curious zing of electricity pass through her body, but didn't move out of the way.

"The blanket will be rolled out, when it's in place the sections will be connected—"

"What size are we talking about?" He put his hand out to grasp her arm as she started to lose her balance.

His hand remained on her arm. "A football field is about—what?" she said, hoping her start at his touch wasn't obvious in her voice. Damn it. She'd always had a crush on him. But this was ridiculous. This feeling wasn't as simple and innocuous as a crush. This emotion was stronger, fresher, more powerful.

Why him? Why now?

Why not? her mind demanded. Oh, crap. Don't even go there. There were plenty of reasons why not him. The two primary ones being Duncan and Edge.

"Including the end zones and sidelines? A hundred and twenty yards by fifty-three and a third," he said almost absently, watching her mouth.

"*Whatever.*" She imagined she could feel the heat of his large hand, even through the thickness of her down coat. "Each of the sections will make up an area approximately one quarter of that. When they're joined it'll be the size of a football field. An acre of land covered by this thermal blanket. See this?" She draped the heavy, silvery-gray, open weave fabric over her palm.

"The thermal blanket will keep the plants not only warm, but fertilized and watered through microscopic perforations, similar to a garden soaker hose. The crops will grow through the netting."

"Very short, *stubby* crops apparently," he said skeptically. "The ground might be heated, but the air isn't."

"With the correct power source, the team believes

this blanket will warm the air up to seven or eight feet above the ground. An invisible greenhouse, in effect. Everything protected from even the harshest environment." She glanced up and met his eyes. "Amazing, huh?"

He frowned as though something was bothering him and said slowly, "Amazing is one way to put it. Yeah." He rose, reaching out his hand to help her up. The look he was giving her made the little hairs stand up on the back of her neck.

Pretending she hadn't seen his offer, or that hot, predatory gleam in his suddenly dark eyes, Serena got to her feet on her own. "Seen enough?"

"For now. Yeah. Got a bulb?"

She frowned. "You want to plant something?"

"*Light*bulb."

"I'll have one of the men install it tomorrow."

"Now would be better."

She sighed. He was right. But what a guy thing. She strode into the small, dirty office nearby, opened a cabinet, and handed him a four-pack with a lone bulb in it. "Here you go. Then we'd better leave."

She didn't want him helping her. The sooner she put some distance between them, the better. Especially since she was having a hard time keeping her brain and her body from replaying that kiss. She tried to convince herself that her reaction to his mouth on hers was a simple function of biology. She hadn't had sex in almost two years.

The problem was she didn't want sex. She wanted *Duncan.* And that wasn't even a remote possibility. Not with Nairne's Curse wedged between them.

He removed the bulb, tossing the empty container into a nearby trash can. "Come with me."

She relaxed fractionally and smiled. "Scared of the dark?"

"Itch on the back of my neck. Stay close."

"No thanks. It's too cold to go back outside." She arranged her hood over her head, feeling the sensuous brush of the soft fur against her cheeks. Suddenly Serena had a vivid image of herself and Duncan, naked, sprawled on a soft black fur rug— *Don't go there. Do not go there,* she warned herself.

"I'm going back to the facility. You get back to . . . whatever." Annoyed that he'd invaded her imagination and wouldn't leave, she glared at the lightbulb he was holding. "Don't you know how to install it from here?" Filled with a restless longing that wasn't going to be addressed, she felt cranky and out of sorts.

In other words she felt exactly like she always felt when she was around Duncan. Crazy with longing, and cross that she couldn't seem to move beyond wanting him. It wasn't as though they could ever be together. Not in any meaningful way, anyway.

How about in a *non*meaningful way? she asked herself.

No. Not that way either. She'd never been satisfied with half of anything. Nope. Her best bet was to stay as far away from Duncan as possible until these feelings died a natural death.

The fact that the last fifteen years had *intensified,* not diminished, her response to him, was grounds for some concern. But Serena figured as long as Duncan wasn't aware of her feelings, she could work on getting an antidote.

A lust-for-Duncan-Edge antidote. She'd get right on that.

"I want to take a walk around the perimeter."

His dark blue eyes smoldered in reaction to something he must've seen in her face. Serena gave him a cool glance, getting a firm grip on her emotions and controlling her expression, because not to would invite conjecture. She was not going to go there. "You don't have to. My protection spell is solid."

"I don't doubt it." His eyes lit up, as if he knew what she was thinking. Which he didn't. Thank God.

"But I'm going to check anyw—" The cardboard package flew out of the trash can, and almost hit him squarely on the forehead. "Holy shit, Fury," he said with a wide, sexy grin that deepened the dimple near his mouth.

He simply cast a glance at the crumbled cardboard and it flashed into flames, instantly reducing it to a small pile of gray ash at their feet. "Temper, temper."

"Annoyance, annoyance," she mocked his tone. "If I actually lost my temper the entire *building* would fall on you." She stuck her hands in her pockets. Damn it, she hadn't even realized she'd subconsciously attacked him until she'd seen the cardboard go flying. "If you want to be the manly man, go for it. Fly free."

"If you won't come with me, then stay here," Duncan said softly. "Wait for me."

He meant, Serena told herself watching him open the door, wait until I get back inside. But the words sounded like a sensual promise. Ridiculous. She telekinetically rerolled the thermal blanket, rewrapping it in its protective covering. Duncan didn't like her any more than she liked him. So what if the sparks flew when they were in close proximity? Just because there was some sort of pheromone thing going o—

A fusillade of gunfire cut off her thoughts and made her jump. A bullet ricocheted off an outside wall with a high-pitched ping. Her heart leapt into her throat, and she started running for the partially open door, then pulled herself up short. Was she nuts? There were *bullets* flying out there.

"Duncan!"

CHAPTER SIX

Duncan teleported back inside the warehouse just in time to observe Serena racing for the door, screaming his name. Which might have been intriguing if she wasn't running straight out into the barrage of live rounds directed at the door.

He'd find out the who and why later, he thought grimly, keeping his weapon trained on the doorway. Right now he had to get Serena out of the line of fire.

He yelled her name. She kept going. Jesus, the woman had always been focused and intense, but this time it could get her killed. Duncan shimmered directly in front of her, grabbed her arm, and yanked her away from the partially open door just as a bullet ricocheted off the corrugated wall beside them.

Screaming bloody murder, she swung blindly, almost putting his eye out with her fist.

He didn't waste time. Lassoing her struggling body with his arms he teleported them the fuck out of there. She was still fighting him when they arrived in his apartment. The bedroom, to be exact.

Bracing his body against the wall, Serena's back to

his chest, he locked his arms around her waist. "Whoa! You're safe. Stop fighting."

"Let me go, damn it." She wiggled out of his hold.

He put his hands up in the surrender position.

Serena, being Serena, whirled around and punched him in the stomach as soon as she was free. She curled her fist as he'd taught her in seventh grade, and put her whole body into it. Apparently it hurt her a lot more than it hurt him, because she jerked her arm back.

"Ow! Damn it to hell, you son of a bitch. Ow!" She shook out her hand, annihilating him with a glare. "You had a gun with you. You knew those men were going to be there, didn't you?"

"I always carry a weapon, and no, I didn't expect anyone to be there." Not *there* in particular. But he was always prepared. And rarely disappointed. This little jaunt had been no exception.

"Funny how you just attract that kind of excitement, isn't it?" she said furiously. "Nice work. You've progressed from fistfights to bullets. Were you shot?" she demanded through her teeth, scanning his body as if she had X-ray eyes. She'd barely taken a breath.

Probably. There was a smear of blood on his palm. "No. I—"

She punched him again.

"Hey! Stop that before you hurt yourself." He sucked in a breath, thinking it was actually fortunate that his artwork wasn't flying off the walls. He half expected the damned carpet to be yanked out from under his feet and the fire sprinklers to go off, she was so annoyed. This was Serena at her best.

He choked back a laugh. "You sure do a lot of hitting for a pacifist."

"I'd hit harder if you'd just stand still!" Her hair caught the light from the wall sconces, shiny as satin and the color of living flame as it fanned out around her. Fire.

A hectic flush made her skin seem lit from within. Damn she was gorgeous. He kept *that* incendiary thought to himself.

She stepped away from him, her flaming hair settling inside the fur-lined hood of her coat hanging down her back. Rubbing one hand with the other, she narrowed her lovely gray eyes until they glinted like pewter between her long, dark lashes. "Damn it, Duncan! Why is it that whenever you're around, violence erupts? I told you I didn't want to go to the warehouse. Activity invites interest and we're trying to keep a low profile until the blanket is loaded on the train."

He admired her ability to shift blame at the same time as he counted guns from memory. Three of them. Double-action semiautomatic RAP-410s by the sound. "You're blaming your robbery on me?" he asked innocently, wondering what the Russians were doing with South African weapons in a small, nothing town on the edge of Siberia.

No one could have known he'd be there. And Serena, the Humanitarian, didn't *have* any enemies other than her two middle-aged stepsons. And Duncan couldn't see them lurking around an industrial neighborhood in Siberia.

Still, he didn't believe in coincidence either. He put it on his mental checklist. He watched her decide whether retreating from the argument was the better part of valor. "I didn't have anything to do with those guys shooting up the place." He rubbed his palm across his belly because he knew it would give her satisfaction to think she'd hurt him. He'd been hit by harder things than the small fist of a woman.

"Oh, please," she scoffed. "*You* show up and ten minutes later bullets are flying. Of course you're responsible." She suddenly realized where they were. "And what the freaking hell are we doing in someone's *bedroom*?"

"Not *someone's* bedroom. Mine."

She twisted around, taking in the surroundings in one visual sweep. The bed was king-sized, covered with a heavy, scarlet silk, Oriental spread—thing. The furniture was black lacquer. The lighting was low and dim, the wallpaper textured charcoal silk. It was sumptuous, sexy, and masculine. Or that's what the decorator had told him. The jury was still out. Looked like a freaking dark bat cave to him. The only thing that he liked, and he'd had them for years, were a series of black-and-white etchings.

"What do you think?"

"About your décor? The red silk is a little . . . chichi isn't it? How about orange?" She waved a hand and the red silk became a heavy, nubby material the pinkish-yellow of the inside of a Travita orange. She dusted off her hands. "Much better."

The moment she turned to study his artwork, Duncan changed the spread to a navy blue. He didn't much like that either, and tried the soft gray of Serena's eyes. Silk? No, velvet. *That* worked.

"Have you slept with all these women?" she asked, walking across the thick carpet to inspect the twelve nude etchings lined up along one wall, stark in their black frames. There was a large brush-and-ink nude over his bed by the same artist.

He wondered if she'd notice that the model bore a striking resemblance to herself. "I collect them," he told her, watching her face. She didn't see the likeness, which was fine with him. When he'd started collecting the pieces, he'd never imagined that he'd ever have Serena in his bedroom.

"Of course you do."

He knew she wasn't talking about the Hans Esneck etchings, but didn't bother disputing her assumption. She was swaying on her feet. "You look a little pale." An understatement; her paprika-colored freckles were standing out in sharp relief on her chalky skin. "Feel okay?"

"Sure, why would a few bullets flying over my head be a problem?" she snapped sarcastically. "No, Duncan, I'm not okay. I'm a long way from okay."

He frowned when he noticed the slight tremor in her fingers as she brushed a strand of hair from her face. "That's a given," he murmured, concerned. "Stay and have a drink before you go. Some coffee at least."

"No thanks, I—Oh." She sat down quickly on the foot of his bed.

He suddenly had an image of Serena's naked, freckled body, spread pale and supplicant against the gray spread. "You've gone from pale to green."

"I can tell," she said weakly, closing her eyes. "I feel kind of pukey, actually."

Her admission ratcheted his concern up another notch. "Lie down," he told her gently, but his tone was implacable.

Gingerly, she lay down on her back, her feet still on the floor. The fact that she'd obeyed his order, no matter what his tone, without protest brought him to her side immediately.

"I bet you say that to all the girls."

"You're the first woman I've brought into this room." Because he'd only bought the flat six months before, and the decorator had only finished dicking around with fabric and swatches he didn't give a rat's ass about, a week ago.

Her eyes were closed, but her lips curved in a small smile. "Are you telling me you're a virgin? Do I look—What do you think you're doing?"

He was tugging down the long zipper of her coat. "Taking off your coat. This is London, not Siberia." He could easily have stripped off the garment, and anything else he chose, without so much as touching her.

But touching Serena was pure pleasure.

"I don't want you undressing me."

He pulled her left arm out of the sleeve without any resistance at all. "Ah, love words," he teased as her arm fell limply to the bed as soon as it was free. "Don't toy with me, Fury."

"I'm serious, Duncan. I'm not just going to lie here while you undress me. This is a very, very, very, *very* bad idea. Very."

He started to smile. Any other woman, and he'd be thinking she'd finally come to her senses and decided that making love would ease the tension left by the shoot-out. But Serena wasn't any other woman. The amusement disappeared instantly as he started pulling off her other sleeve and saw the blood.

She'd been shot.

A straight line slicing through her down coat showed the path of the bullet across her upper arm. Damn it to fucking hell, he thought, hit with panic and a pain so sharp it could have been his own. Adrenaline was preventing her from feeling it, but any second now she was going to realize she'd taken a hit and then she'd feel it. With a vengeance.

What he'd at first attributed to the dissipation of the adrenaline rush, was instead loss of blood. He swore under his breath. Screw the slow removal of her clothing, he wanted to check her arm *now*. He used magic to strip off the coat, and materialized a glass of Scotch at the same time.

"Hey, Fury." He tapped her cheek with his finger. She was conscious, but just barely. He lifted her head and pressed the glass to her lips. "Take a sip." Unless she'd changed drastically over the intervening years, Serena rarely drank. She had a low—make that *extremely* low—tolerance for alcohol.

Which he'd discovered the night she'd chugged shots of tequila at Trey's sixteenth birthday party. He'd teleported her home to Henry and Martha, making sure to shimmer to the spot where the old oak blocked the front door light.

He'd kissed her, there in the jasmine-scented darkness. She didn't remember their kiss.

He'd never forgotten.

She took a small sip of whiskey, choked, and

made a face, all without opening her eyes. "God. That's disgusting."

Ignoring her dismissal of his prized, very expensive single malt Macallan Scotch, he magically removed both her sweater and the shirt beneath it. Which left her pale, upper body clothed in nothing more than a wisp of a semitransparent bra already stained with her blood. The room was cool, and her nipples peaked beneath the thin cloth.

"Medicine," he told her firmly, looking down at her arm instead of the temptation of her breasts while he held the glass to her mouth. The crease from the bullet wasn't too deep. No muscle damage that he could see, but it was bleeding copiously. The velvet spread beneath her was already darkening.

He couldn't heal her as his brother Caleb could have done, but he materialized the necessary items he'd need to clean, stitch, and bandage the wound. Fortunately he could do what needed to be done without physically holding needle and thread. "Swallow."

"Poisoning m-me?"

Trying to get you to pass out. "Open your mouth and finish this or I'll kiss you." He managed to get another ounce of whiskey into her before she clamped her teeth together. Stubborn.

"I have to treat your arm. It'll hurt like hell if you're not anesthetized in one way or another. Whiskey or pain? Here or a hospital?"

He studied her face as she took a quick inventory of her own body, and gauged the pain. "Whiskey." She shuddered. "Here." She grudgingly allowed him to finish pouring the rest of the amber liquid into her.

"Better get a—get a b-bucket. Know what happens when I drink."

Yeah. He did. He materialized a bucket from under the bathroom sink. If he could still be this attracted to a woman about to hurl he was in serious trouble, he thought, half amused and half terrified as he placed the container within easy reach.

It didn't take long for the Scotch to hit her overloaded system, and before she could puke, she was out like a light. Duncan tended to her arm quickly and efficiently. He'd done the same procedure dozens of times, both on himself and others; it was all part of his T-FLAC training. Cleaning and stitching by rote, he didn't enjoy sticking a needle into Serena's soft flesh.

She was going to hold every single one of the small, evenly spaced stitches over his head like the freaking Sword of Damocles, too.

When her arm was bandaged, he picked her up and carried her to the head of the bed. Mentally stripping back the covers, he gently laid her on the mattress and covered her.

Nine stitches.

Damn those sons of bitches to hell. Who were they? Had the shooters been after the technology for the thermal blanket? Did they even know what the fuck the thermal blanket was? Or were they just willing to kill anyone who got between them and what they thought might be inside that warehouse?

He'd locked the door, and more effectively, strengthened Serena's protective spell, even though the one she'd cast had been excellent. No one was supposed to have been able to get that close to the warehouse. That fucking close to *her*. Didn't make sense.

But he'd find the answer soon enough.

He'd never had the leisure of looking at her this closely before. Her skin was as fine-grained as a child's, the freckles charmingly sprinkled across her pert nose and cheekbones. She'd been such a complete and utter pain in his ass for so damned long that it was strange to allow himself a moment to let down his defenses and just enjoy *looking* at her. His chest filled with an overwhelming surge of desire. Still. After all this time. He'd always had a serious case of the hots for Serena. And as strong as that attraction had been, had been the knowledge that he could never act on it.

Emotional commitment had never been in the cards for him. Duncan had known that from childhood. Known the Curse so well, and so completely, that he never had to think about it. It just—was.

Over the years he'd observed Serena growing from a gangly, engaging little girl to a beautiful young woman. And every year it had become harder to ignore the compelling pull of attraction he felt for her. Even knowing that a relationship between them was ill advised, if not downright dangerous, it had been hard enough to resist Serena's allure when they'd been teenagers.

But now . . .

Resist her he must. Nothing had changed.

But God, he wanted her.

He was dying of thirst, and she was a cool, still well.

Duncan brushed his fingers lightly across her warm cheek. So soft. She was so delicate and yet so damned strong. Seeing the small, feminine outline she made beneath the covers, it was difficult to relate her sleeping form to the larger-than-life persona she was when she was awake. She'd hate knowing just how vulnerable she looked when she was asleep. She'd hate, Duncan thought wryly, shrugging back into his coat, *really* hate, knowing that she snored.

With a grin, he teleported back to Schpotistan, and Vladimirskaya Street, to have a little chat with the bad guys.

CHAPTER SEVEN

Joanna listened with half an ear to the after dinner conversation. *Hurry up, people,* she thought with rising panic. *My son's life depends on us working through this problem. Now!*

Casey must be terrified. *I'm going to give those bastards what they want, sweetheart. Mommy is going to get you home. Soon.*

Please God. Let it be soon.

"Thrust augmentation methods can be used to increase the effectiveness," Dr. Stuart Menzies suggested, shoving his fingers through the pale, flyaway hair over his left ear. The yellow-white strands stuck up in all directions because he was always pulling at it as he talked.

As they did every evening after dinner, the scientists gathered around the junk-food laden coffee table in the common room. Serena had made sure that the meals at this facility were top-notch and plentiful, but the thought of eating when she was this stressed made Joanna's stomach churn. The thought of making idle dinner conversation made it worse, so she'd stayed working at her computer until the dinner bell had sounded, then she'd slipped into the kitchen and baked a cinnamon swirl cake. Her son's favorite.

Despite the frigid weather outside, the lounge was toasty warm with two space heaters going. The aroma of strong coffee and cinnamon hung in the air, but Joanna found no comfort in the familiar scents tonight. She let the sound of the other team members' voices lull her into a feeling of safety and she wondered for the thousandth time if she should tell Serena how badly someone wanted to steal the technology for the thermal blanket.

Her stomach clenched and her heart raced.

No.

She'd *never* risk Casey.

Not for money. Not for anything.

But how long would his kidnappers keep him alive? They, like everyone here in this frigid place, needed a power source for the thermal blanket. The idea was brilliant and truly had the possibility of saving the world. But she just wanted her son back. Joanna was terrified that the only thing keeping him alive was that one last piece of information—who was to say that they'd actually let Casey go, as they'd promised?

Her mind was a maze of terror. She lifted her coffee mug, noting the way her hand shook. But she needed the caffeine, it kept her semi-coherent.

The only respite she had from the debilitating fear was when she was with Grant. He understood her tears, and the reason she had to keep the kidnapping a secret. There was nobody in this world that Joanna loved more than her son. Yet there was something about Grant that allowed her to forget, just for a little while, how scared she was. He gave her a shoulder to cry on, a strong chest to lean against. As always, thoughts of Grant were welcome and brought a warmth the coffee hadn't been able to give. Guilt followed. Casey should be the *only* one on her mind. God. When had she become a lousy mother?

It wasn't that Grant took precedence over her missing baby—but he offered her hope, a light in the darkness of despair. Was it so terrible to take a small amount of comfort in Grant's capable arms?

What if? What if something happened to Casey? *Then what?* Sitting here, surrounded by her peers, Joanna felt the familiar cold wash of unadulterated panic bathe her body inside and out, and she quickly hid her face behind the mug before she cried out loud. She wanted to hold her son. She wanted his lopsided grin smiling at her from across their kitchen table, she wanted to trip over his sneakers in the foyer . . .

Casey consumed every waking, and most of her sleeping, moments. The only time she felt less stressed was when she was with Grant. Anxiety clenched at her heart. She was pinning all of her hopes on the poor man, making Grant a hero for trying to find her son. That wasn't right. God. That was *wrong* in a million ways.

Joanna rubbed a hand across her eyes, sick, scared, confused. Trapped.

Serena was one of the most compassionate people Joanna had ever met. What if she *did* go to Serena . . .

They'd kill Casey.

But how would they *know* she'd told her boss?

Bile rose in her throat. The same way they'd known she'd told Henry.

The Foundation Director could *possibly* have had the stroke anyway. But Joanna wasn't convinced that they hadn't somehow caused it. Henry had been in a coma for almost two weeks, and he might never recover.

Serena was so visible with all the work she did for the Foundation, she'd be an easy target for the people behind the kidnapping.

And damn it, she still wasn't any closer today than she'd been three weeks ago to finding the power source. She'd bloody well given the bastards everything else they needed to know about the thermal blanket on a silver platter. Well, almost everything. There was that one little piece Henry had forgotten to document. The piece she'd been asking him about when he'd collapsed.

As soon as the kidnappers realized that they were missing that piece of the puzzle, they'd run out of patience.

She was running out of time.

Making an effort to pretend she was listening to the spirited conversation around her, Joanna smiled and nodded, wondering if Serena was even in the building. She hadn't seen her all day, but that wasn't unusual. Serena spent hour after hour on the phone trying to raise funds for the Foundation.

She was either upstairs in her room, or maybe she'd teleported somewhere else for a while, checking on another project.

Maybe those horrible stepsons were giving her

grief. Her husband had known what he was doing, putting Serena in charge of the Foundation.

She was good at it, too, Joanna thought, curling her hands around the unwanted cup of lukewarm coffee. Serena was beautiful and smart. People gravitated to her.

Studies had been done proving that tall, attractive people, both male and female, got the best jobs, earned more money, and generally fared better than their Plain Jane counterparts. But she wasn't jealous—she'd come to terms with her forgettable features a long time ago and it didn't bother her. Especially since she'd become involved with Grant. He thought she was beautiful.

Love was definitely blind.

She checked her serviceable watch, trying to keep from screaming. The kidnappers should have sent the video e-mail by now.

There'd been no contact all day, and they usually sent an e-mail before lunch. Her stomach roiled with tension, and a headache throbbed behind her eyes. Setting the mug on the table, she rubbed her temples as she tried to concentrate on what Stuart Menzies was saying.

Please, God. Let this be the breakthrough we need. Please.

"Driving force of a jet engine is the afterburner," Stuart continued, leaning forward, animated and intense. "We could use water-injection, and air bleed-off methods. An afterburner would use the exhaust gases from the engine for additional combustion, which would result in higher compression. However, it *does* consume large amounts of fuel."

He blew out a frustrated breath, although no one had interrupted. "Yes, yes. I know. Not viable in all locations. Injection of *water* into the air-compressor inlet also increases the thrust, but would also be problematic because it can be used only at takeoff and the water consumption would be astronomical. Air bleed-off, the fan augmentation method, also makes more efficient use of air otherwise wasted—" He cut himself off and glanced at the faces of the others. "Not going to fly, is it?"

"What we need is something that doesn't utilize any of the resources of the countries we're trying to aid," Denny said quietly. It was a much-used phrase that none of them needed to have repeated. Dennis kept his verbal contributions brief. If he didn't have anything he considered valid to share he'd just sit there and listen.

He was sitting in the easy chair beside Joanna, and she realized that it wasn't just the fragrance of cake and coffee that should be comforting, but the smell of a surprising sexy cologne from the man sitting beside her.

Edgy, she snapped, "Every power source we've come up with utilizes *something*." Her voice was sharper than she'd intended, her frustration at the kidnappers unraveling her temper. "We can't exactly run the damn things on *corn*."

"Well, in theory we could," Dennis pointed out in his quiet tone. "But taking the very food source we're trying to give them doesn't have any bene-fit."

"What we need is an autonomous in-orbit satellite system. That'll work." Sal slid a generous slice of

Joanna's cinnamon swirl cake onto his napkin, lifted the cake to his mouth, and took a large bite.

Joanna swallowed convulsively and briefly shut her eyes against the thought that Sal was enjoying Casey's cake.

"Sure," Stuart said, just as frustrated as everyone else. "And it would take us ten years at least to get it up and running."

"Perhaps," Denny mused sitting up straighter. "If we had to design it, assess stress analysis, engineer materials, create a prototype and flight test support. But what if we didn't have to do *any* of those things?"

"You got a magic wand, boy?" Sal asked.

"I wish," Denny took no offense at being called a boy. "No. But we *could* piggyback onto an existing, fully operational satellite. We don't need to develop our own lasers and advanced instruments, because we'd find someone who has a satellite doing some of those tasks already. The development of subsystems—propulsion system design, controls systems, and appropriate reliability analysis and quality assurance—will have already been done for us."

Denny had come up with the answer. Joanna had to use all her self-control not to jump into the air and shout for joy. *Thank you, God.*

She half listened to the others as they hashed out the feasibility of piggybacking their need of a power source while she tried not to panic about the meaning of the odd lack of communication from Casey's kidnappers. Terror for her son's safety made every part of her body hurt unbearably. Now she knew that the phrase "a broken heart" was absolutely true. The pain in her heart was a physical reminder that Casey's life was dependent on her. And only her. She wasn't sure she could sustain this level of pain much longer without cracking under the pressure. It was hard to think of anything *but* Casey.

How could anyone survive this? She certainly wouldn't want to live if anything happened to her baby. No, she thought fiercely, *nothing* was going to happen to him. Nothing. Her team had come up with what the kidnappers wanted. She'd give them the information, and find that last little piece of information on the manufacturing of the thermal blanket, and they . . . God.

Would they keep their promise? Logically, she knew the chances were slim that they would return her son to her unharmed.

She was damned if she did, and damned if she didn't.

She wished Grant was more easily accessible. He was the only person who knew the tremendous stress she was under.

"Are you all right?" Denny leaned over to ask quietly.

"Headache." She rose and shrugged into a full-length alpaca coat. "I'm going up. I want to see feasibility studies and satellite data at our lunch meeting tomorrow." Or sooner. Like now. *Immediately.*

Denny rose as she did. "I'll walk you up."

"No. Don't." Done buttoning her coat up to her throat, she pulled on a knit cap over her short hair. Denny reached out and tucked a strand of hair beneath the edge. His touch on her skin made her shiver, but it wasn't from cold. Their eyes met. His were brown, a soft, gentle brown that invited trust.

An emotion she couldn't afford. "It's too cold out there," she said briskly, stepping away from him and pulling on her gloves. "Thanks. I'll be fine. Good night."

She left the room quickly because she felt the unaccustomed prickle of tears behind her eyes. Glancing at the watch sandwiched between the edge of her sleeve and her knit gloves, she walked quickly down the freezing corridor toward the stairs. Grant should be here soon. Any minute. And she had excellent news. With a furtive glance to make sure nobody saw her, Joanna teleported to the third floor.

Materializing in her room, she rushed over to the bed where Grant was lounging as he waited for her.

He frowned at her. "That wasn't very smart, Joanna."

She flushed, pulling off her hat and gloves, shoving them into the pocket of her coat before she unbuttoned the garment and hung it in the closet.

"I made sure no one saw me."

"It's not those brainiacs downstairs I'm worried about," he said, not moving. "What if Serena saw you teleporting?"

Half-wizards like Joanna weren't capable of teleportation. Grant had gifted her with the power. She was very careful to use his gift judiciously. "Serena isn't here." Joanna didn't think so anyway. "I was in a hurry to see you."

He relented and held out his hand. "Were you, darling? Then come and show me how much."

scorching wind caused by the fire eating up the oxygen. "Into *what*?"

"I don't—A *cave*. It's forming into a cave." Automatically he reached for his Sig. "Stay here. I'm going in."

"Stay here? There are three people competing, bud, not just you." She glanced at his drawn weapon. "Are you out of your mind? Yeah, clearly you *are*. Planning to shoot the big bad fire?"

"If the scroll is inside the fire cave I'm going in—alone."

"You and which army? Think again."

"You'll be burned."

"I left my entire bonsai collection to you in my will. Take good care of it if I end up crispy."

"Not funny, Serena. I'm not willing to risk your life."

"*You're* not willing? Excuse me? What suddenly made you the boss of me?"

"This," he said grimly, pulling her into his arms.

She took his warm palm, her troubles evaporating at his nearness. This was what she craved, oblivion for just a few minutes.

"I think we finally have the answer! God, this could be just what you need to get Casey back for me."

He pulled her down beside him, his body hard and strong as he settled her head on his broad shoulder. "Slow down, and tell me about it. You know I want Casey found just as much as you do, baby." He rubbed the back of her neck and the tension headache vanished. "Remember to keep it simple, I don't understand all that scientific mumbo jumbo." He kissed her forehead and she melted a little more.

While she told him about the idea of utilizing a satellite as a power source, they slowly undressed each other.

Trailing kisses down her throat, Grant chuckled. "There's something very erotic about science and sex, don't you—"

He suddenly, and without warning, disappeared.

Serena woke with a headache, a sore arm, and a feeling of having missed something.

Sitting up in Duncan's bed she took stock of her injury. He'd done a good job bandaging the bullet wound, she noticed. A *bullet* wound, for Heaven's sake! Damn that man. He attracted violence like metal filings to a magnet.

He'd poured Scotch down her throat as an anesthetic, knowing how much she hated hospitals. Or, she thought, throwing back the covers, because he didn't want to have to report what happened and explain a gunshot wound to the authorities. The latter made the most sense.

A covered glass of orange juice had been left on the bedside table with two white pills and a note.

Drink the juice. The bigger pill is an antibiotic, the smaller one is a pain pill. Take both and stay put.
D.

His handwriting was as self-assured and autocratic as he was.

Ignoring the pills, Serena chugged down the freshly squeezed juice as she walked over to pick up her ruined shirt from a nearby chair. To her surprise, Duncan had magically returned the shirt to its pristine, pre-bullet-hole condition. The same went for her coat.

Good of him.

But it would have been unnecessary if he hadn't drawn her into his violent world and gotten her shot in the first place.

Glancing at the alarm clock by the bed to see how much time had elapsed, she noticed that almost an entire day had gone by. Damn. She needed to get back to the warehouse and check on the security of the thermal blankets, then back to the Siberian facility to check on any progress they'd made in her absence. She also wanted to have a private talk with Joanna. Something was worrying her. Serena wasn't sure if it was work related, or something to do with Joanna's little boy—the woman didn't appear to have any other family.

Perhaps Joanna needed some quality time with her son. If she didn't want to take the time to leave the program, not when things were so critical, maybe Casey could visit his mother in Siberia?

She'd talk to Joanna in a few minutes and see how she felt about her son coming for an extended visit. Buttoning her white shirt, Serena tucked it neatly into her jeans and looked around for her shoes.

Her cheeks got hot imagining Duncan removing her clothing . . . "Oh, get a grip, Serena!" she said aloud. He'd removed her shoes and shirt. That was *it*. It wasn't as though he'd liquored her up to *seduce* her.

He hadn't taken advantage of her. This time.

Not like that night of Trey's birthday party when Trey had encouraged her to chug down several shots of celebratory tequila. Serena frowned at the memory as she sat on the foot of the bed to draw on her shoes. How was it that Trey could always convince her to do things she knew were wrong? He'd known she couldn't hold alcohol, and yet he'd taunted her into complying.

She'd managed three shots before she'd almost passed out.

Oddly, it had been Duncan who'd teleported her home. She'd been embarrassed and woozy, and terrified that Henry and Martha would find out and be furious with her. Or worse, disappointed.

Duncan had wrapped his arms around her in the darkness of the front yard, holding her gently before lowering his mouth to hers. She'd never let him know that she remembered that kiss.

She'd never told him.

Standing straight up, Serena scowled. Chances

were, Duncan didn't even *remember* the incident anyway.

Okay. He probably did remember what happened right after that kiss. She'd thrown up at his feet.

"Oh, boy," she said ruefully, reaching for her coat. "*There* was a Hallmark mome—Oh, hell—" She was teleported out of Duncan's London flat without warning.

He'd looked around for hours. Duncan stood across the street from the Foundation's warehouse. A dog howled in the distance. A couple of rats, the animal kind, scurried behind him in the darkness. He was alone.

He'd found several casings on the ground outside the building. Chances were he would have been nailed but good if he hadn't teleported back inside to Serena. So, pros for sure. Could be Russian Mafia. But his contacts assured him not. None of the normal players or the locals had been out to the Foundation's warehouse looking for trouble.

Pissed him off that Serena had paid their price to stay away. Trust her to be capable of reasoning with these goons. Reasoning, bribery, whatever. She'd managed to find a way.

It wasn't the Russian Mafia.

They didn't have access to South African weapons. Not unless they did business with Red Mantis.

Why the fuck *would* Red Mantis be interested in Foundation business? Unless they planned to grow their tomatoes in the tundra, Duncan thought, amused at the prospect.

He stood perfectly still in the shadows. Not stamping his feet, or rubbing his arms, even his breath was invisible behind a black face mask. *Damn*, it was cold out here.

He wondered if she'd woken up yet. If she had, he'd bet his flat was torn apart and soaking wet by now. Amused, hoping he could be there to witness Serena waking up sans her shirt, Duncan prepared to teleport back home. He'd put out enough subtle feelers about the earlier shooting. If anyone discovered anything, he'd be contacted immediately.

He imagined sipping his fine single malt Scotch, Serena in his bed—

He was suddenly teleported out of the Siberian night without fanfare.

Hot damn. The Tests had begun.

Hot. Dry. Silent.

Duncan stood dead still in the Stygian darkness, orienting himself. For all he knew he could be a mile underground, or standing on the edge of a thousand-foot drop, or even on another planet.

A pleasurable surge of adrenaline surged through his battle-ready body.

He'd waited for this moment his entire life. He was ready.

Bring it on. He closed his eyes to the darkness, concentrating on the smallest sounds. He could just pick up the almost silent shush of waves gently sliding across fine sand. No crashing surf. No gulls. No footsteps. No foliage rustling in the still air.

He inhaled. No salt-laden ocean air. No source of heat. Yet spatially he sensed he was outside.

Sweat rolled down his temples. It must be upward of ninety degrees, and five seconds ago he'd been suitably dressed for a minus five Siberian night. He ignored the discomfort as he opened his eyes again.

A familiar fragrance teased his senses. "Serena," he said barely above a whisper as he sensed her materializing beside him. She shouldn't be here, he thought, tamping down the combination of annoyance that she was even in the competition, concern for her well-being, and a serious dose of the hots.

"This is creepy," she whispered back. He felt the brush of her coat against his arm as she shifted closer. "Where are we?"

She was looking up at him. He smelled orange juice on her breath. It didn't surprise Duncan that she wasn't clutching his sleeve, or demanding an answer to her question. Serena was pretty damn well fearless. Which she'd have to be. There was a reason a Head of Wizard Council was only chosen every seven years, and the failure rate was astronomical. Henry had been in the position for almost four terms because, in the last twenty-seven years, no one had managed to pass the Tests and usurp his position. If Serena's foster father, and Duncan's mentor, hadn't had the stroke, he'd *still* be in office another year before the Test was opened to the general wizard membership for nominations.

"No clue," he told Serena almost inaudibly. "No. Don't move until I figure it out."

"You're not supposed to help me," she reminded him.

"Exactly. I'm not coming after you if you fall down a hole." He hoped like hell she didn't test that threat. She was another problem he was going to have to deal with soon.

"It's fucking hotter than hell in here." Trey whispered uneasily, fortunately cutting off Duncan's thoughts of Serena and the Curse for another day.

"*In* here? We're inside?"

"Jesus, Serena. I have no idea *where* we are. That was a figure of speech."

Duncan tuned them out, although he could have said to an inch where each of the others stood in the sweltering, inky darkness. This was not the darkness of a moonless night. This was the darkness of hidden secrets. Of things that went bump in the night. This was the first Test. And he was already totally involved and focused. Well, except for that momentary Serena blip, he was good to go.

He felt a mental probe and jolted at the intrusion. Who the fuck . . . ? He managed to block whatever the hell the person was searching his brain for.

Serena? No. This intruder felt male. Strong. Dark. Trey? Possible, but unlikely. Trey wasn't that strong. A member of the Council? Duncan didn't give a shit. Nobody, but *nobody* occupied his brain but himself.

He slammed a mental door, then locked it. *And stay out, dickhead. Whoever the hell you are.*

A barely perceptible beat started in his palm, followed by the phosphorescent light of the Council envelope that suddenly materialized in his hand. Serena and Trey had theirs in hand as well.

Instructions.

"Open your envelopes," Lark's disembodied voice instructed.

Let's get ready to rumble. Lifting the glowing square, Duncan used the faint light to quickly scan the area as a postcard-sized piece of paper rose slowly from inside what had been a sealed envelope, and hovered at exactly the correct distance for him to read it. He had a quick view of Serena's profile, limned against the darkness, before he refocused his eyes to read his own instructions.

> *An ancient scroll is the goal of this quest*
> *Four pieces are torn and that is the test*
> *One fragment protected by fire within*
> *Retrieve the prize and you might win.*

"What do you suppose this mea—Holy crap!" Serena let out a yelp of surprise, jumping backward, as flames, some of them thirty feet high, leaped and danced, shooting red and orange branches of fire against the black sky.

Duncan automatically put out a hand to grab her arm, ready to pull her out of harm's way. Then forced himself not to touch her. He dropped his hand.

She was right. He *wasn't* allowed to help her.

Stripping off his coat, he tossed it aside. Fire was his power to call. Piece of cake. He hoped Serena, and Trey, used extreme caution, and didn't try any histrionics.

The wall of dancing flames was a hundred feet wide and at least thirty feet high. He had no idea how deep it went.

Now, all he had to do was figure out where the scroll was hidden.

The conflagration danced and swayed, arcs of shifting shapes soared into the night sky beckoning them closer.

"I'm going round back," Trey announced, a split second before he disappeared.

Beside him, Serena shrugged off her heavy coat, her white shirt taking on an orange cast in the shooting flames. She looked like a pagan goddess with her wild mane of hair flowing down her back and her hands raised. "I'm going to win this one. Fight fire with water."

Duncan chuckled. "Fight fire with *fire*."

They aimed their powers at the same time. Serena dumped hundreds of gallons of water directly over the inferno.

Hissssssssssss

Nothing but a plume of steam.

Duncan amped up his power, shooting a powerful shaft of white-hot flames directly into the blue center of the blaze.

Fire met firestorm in an explosion of twenty-foot-high sparks and lightning-like shards of crimson fire.

Serena glared at him. "You *did* something."

"Yeah. And it didn't work." He focused on the left-hand side and sent a barrage of fire directly at the base. Damn it! He wanted to tell her to get lost. He really did. She was going to get badly hurt. There was no way she could win this one. He kept up the assault, still without any apparent results. No way.

Fire was his.

But by the same token he didn't want her out of his sight in this strange and magical situation where he wasn't quite sure if what they were seeing and experiencing was real.

The heat of the flames certainly *felt* real. But this was a *Test*. Who knew? Until he was told differently, he'd consider everything in the Test environment the real deal.

The question was: Why wasn't his power extinguishing the flames as it normally would have done? He'd fought forest fires, and hellacious oil field fires, and in every case he'd successfully put them out in short order.

Not so this one.

What was the source of this fire?

He smelled no accelerant, saw no gas jets.

"Why the hell couldn't you have taken up . . . knitting or something?"

A deluge, centered directly over the flames, drowned out the last part of the sentence, but she heard him anyway, and shot him a startled glance. "Why? You want a sweater? *Buy* yourself one."

"You shouldn't be he—"

She redirected part of the torrential downpour—just a three-foot square of it—directly over his head.

"That feels great," he said, swiping water out of his eyes. "But save your water for the fire."

She turned it off. "Look! I think it worked."

"No," he said through his teeth as he automatically dried himself as he'd done with her water nonsense for years. "It *didn't* work. The fire is just reformatting itself."

Her long hair was glued to the sweat glistening on her face and neck, and the thin silk of her shirt clung to her skin as the heat billowed toward them in a

CHAPTER EIGHT

He moved so fast she barely had time to suck in a gasp of air before his arms tightened around her, drawing her hard against his body. He was fully aroused. The hot hungry look in his eyes immobilized her seconds before he crushed his mouth down on hers. No gentle exploration. No warm-up. His mouth fit hers perfectly, and he went from zero to sixty without a mother may I? and straight into an intense, juicy French kiss that had Serena's bones turning molten.

Nothing existed but the slick glide of his warm tongue devouring her mouth. He uttered a harsh, raw sound as her tongue came to meet his, tightening his arms around her, and burying one hand in her hair.

She should put a stop to this, she thought vaguely. *Now.* She stood on her toes to get closer. God. He tasted delicious, and he *smelled* so good. Coffee, soap, hot skin, and a scent uniquely his own. His jaw was prickly, rough against her face, his chest broad and hard with muscle as he crushed her to him. His fingers gripped her hair as he explored her mouth with teeth and tongue. More. More. More.

It was as if Serena had been holding her breath, waiting twenty years for exactly *this* kiss.

A lifetime.

Like a fast-acting drug, the kiss spread seductive heat through her bloodstream.

Seductive bastard was melting the flesh right off her bones, reducing her good intentions to ashes, and making her totally forget where they were. And why. She vaguely realized that he held her upper arms to steady her as he stepped away. Dazed, she stared up at him, rendered speechless.

"We'll finish this later," he murmured thickly, flickering firelight reflected in his eyes. Touching her chin, he turned and walked away.

Walked away!

Frustration burnt her cheeks. "There's nothing to finish!" she shouted after him.

Damn him. She shut her eyes and counted to ten, acutely aware of her nipples rubbing inside her bra, and her wet silk blouse brushing her skin as she struggled to draw in a normal breath without losing any more of her control.

Lungs locked, heartbeat in the stratosphere, Serena pressed her fingers against her damp lips as she watched him retreat. Skin hot, mouth swollen, she was getting damned tired of Duncan kissing her and then just walking away whenever he felt like it. Their entire relationship—not that they actually *had* a relationship—always seemed as though they were an inch away from something . . . *big*.

Dangerous big. Forbidden big. Lifemate big.

When they'd been sixteen, he'd told her about the Curse. Serena had wanted to tell him she already knew, and that she'd always believed that *she* was his Lifemate. He'd never picked up on that vibe, and since she knew the entire Curse, and the way to break it, she'd been forced to stay away, keeping him at arm's length with water tricks and sarcasm.

She opened her eyes, watching Duncan's arrogant stride with a mix of longing and frustration. She had to put the brakes on this dangerous infatuation she had for him before it got out of hand. It couldn't go anywhere, and the more time she spent with him, the deeper she seemed to be falling. Stupid. Unlike Duncan's usual flirts, she knew ahead of time that getting emotionally entangled with him was not only a dead-end proposition, it would also be one-sided.

She figured Duncan's fear of messing with the Curse had kept him away from real relationships all his life. Which, to her dismay, had made her feel marginally better when she'd been a teen, but wasn't working quite as well now that she was an adult.

Back then she'd rationalized that it was just a little pride thing. If she couldn't have him, no one else would either.

He had Nairne's powerful Curse hanging over his head. He had no intention of ever getting romantically serious with anyone. She knew *that* for a cold hard fact. He'd told her flat out the night he'd told her about the Curse.

He'd also admitted that he wasn't interested in breaking the five-hundred-year-old Curse. *"I gift you my powers in memory of me,"* was what Nairne had told Magnus five hundred years ago. Duncan had always been afraid of the potential consequences in the vague passage of the Curse.

Over time, she'd seen that he hadn't changed that much, and his powers still defined him. He probably still thought that breaking the Curse meant losing the powers he held so dear.

Which pretty much meant that Serena had always known better than to waste time wanting something she could never have.

Calmer now, she sighed. Her knowledge of the Curse, and the ancient family secret of how it could be broken, only strengthened her belief that she and Duncan didn't have a snowball's chance in hell of ever having anything close to a relationship. Like him, she was in no hurry to relinquish her powers.

She'd have to strongly discourage him from kissing her again, Serena decided, admiring his tight ass as he strode away from her toward the blaze. The man looked *damn* good in jeans.

Getting kissed by Duncan was like giving a diabetic a Twinkie. One taste made her head spin and her heart pound, and made her crave more.

That was the last freaking time he grabbed her for a drive-by kiss. Next time he put his mouth on her, she was going to make damn sure he didn't go anywhere.

This wasn't the time for him to kiss her anyway, blast him. The Council was probably somewhere watching their every move.

Test. Right.

Where had Trey disappeared to? She glanced at her watch to see how long he'd been gone. No help there. The damn thing had stopped. She narrowed her eyes against the heat. Had he already found the article? Since only one of them could win, probably not. She presumed when one of them had the scroll, they would be teleported back to where they'd come from.

In her case—Duncan's bedroom.

Damn.

Test. Right.

Duncan was now a black silhouette striding toward the fire. Not an ounce of hesitation as he approached the wall of jumping, living flame, headed directly for what looked like the mouth of a cave or the gaping opening into a blast furnace.

Serena's heart pumped hard with every step he took. Like Duncan, she believed the fragment of the scroll was inside that flame cave. But unlike Duncan she had no control over fire. Her power to call was water, and dumping God only knew how many gallons of it directly over the fire minutes ago hadn't made a jot of difference.

Still, she didn't think the Council would skew a Test in one person's favor. Would they?

She could feel the heat of the fire from where she stood some hundred feet away. Walking forward slowly, she wrapped her hair in a knot at her nape to keep it out of the way as she looked around for anything she might use. A weapon? A fire extinguisher? A canary? she thought drolly. The ground was hard packed, no vegetation, no animal, no mineral that she could see. The heat made her blink rapidly to keep her eyes lubricated.

How on earth could Duncan be so close and not burn to a crisp?

Cupping her hands, she summoned cold, sweet water, then lifted them to her mouth to drink, keeping her eyes fixed on Duncan's dark form. The chilled water quenched her thirst for the moment, and she splashed the rest on her warm cheeks. She almost called water for Duncan too, but knew she wasn't allowed to help him. Not even by relieving what she was sure would by now be a powerful thirst.

Since the Test was clearly in Duncan's favor, she needed a plan to get into that flame cave. A good plan. She hadn't tried hail, or sleet, but if a powerful deluge of water hadn't worked, she doubted if the hard stuff would either.

Maybe Trey had had the right idea and found another, safer, way inside.

"Guess not," she said out loud as Trey suddenly materialized beside Duncan. There was no other way into the cave but from here. If there had been, Trey would have been long gone. Clearly he was willing to throw his lot in with Duncan—at least until they were both inside.

Suddenly a flame-covered form jumped out of the fire and engulfed Trey; they tumbled to the ground, rolling and twisting, sparks shooting white and gold into the air. Duncan half turned, but another figure jettisoned out of the inferno and surrounded him with flames.

He—it—Lord, *whatever* it was—grabbed Duncan, lifting him off his feet, holding him ten feet above the ground, twirling him in arms of pure fire.

Serena sucked in a scream, paralyzed with fear as flaming hands danced and jumped across Duncan's rotating body.

She could almost make out the outline of a man—

head, broad shoulders, impossibly long arms and legs, a flame-thin torso. But it was no man who held him. Duncan was high in the air and there was nothing but fire in a human form manipulating his body.

Screw the Test!

Summoning a tropical downpour directly over Duncan, Serena ran toward him. But almost before it hit, the water instantly turned to steam as it encountered the flames supporting Duncan's twisting form. God. Oh God. An exploding cloud of white vapor obliterated Duncan from view.

Once again trying to put out the fire with her water hadn't made a damn bit of difference. Narrowing her eyes, she caused a hailstorm with one-inch balls of ice bombarding the Fire Ghoul. They melted and turned instantly to a thick fog.

"Duncan!" Frantic, she magically dispersed the haze just in time to see his body slammed down to the hard packed earth like a broken rag doll. Serena's body jerked with the impact of the drop. God, he must have broken every bone in his body.

Duncan. She couldn't push his name through her dry lips. *Oh, God. Duncan . . .*

He leapt to his feet. Thank God. He was okay— What the—Damn idiot was trying to fight the fire man with his fists! Like *that* was going to do any freaking good!

When would he learn that violence never solved anything?

She spared a quick glance to check on Trey. He was still on the ground, surrounded by half a dozen terrifying Fire Ghouls kicking and punching the crap out of him.

Serena stopped running toward them before she ran straight into the same problems the two men were experiencing. She didn't know what the heck to do. She wanted to help both of them, but if *they* couldn't defend themselves, what did she think *she* could possibly do?

As far as she knew there was only one way to prevent both men being killed in the next few minutes.

The Council had to pull the plug on this Test. *Now.*

"Stop this!" she shouted, her temper and fear making small whirlwinds whip up, swirling dust and sand around her. She reined in her temper until the fine grains sifted back to the ground. "Stop it now," she shouted at the spark-filled black sky. "Can't you see you're killing hi—them."

Lark had told them they could die during one of the Tests.

Duncan and Trey were in grave peril—

Was that what this was about? They wanted her to win Henry's seat? The egotistical thought horrified and appalled her. Were they willing to kill a powerful wizard like Duncan to ensure *she* got the job? And if so, *why*? Oh, God.

"I don't want your damn job. Do you hear me? I don't want the job. I abdicate. I resign. Oh, shit. Whatever it is. I *do* it."

If anyone was listening to her running around, screaming at the top of her lungs like a madwoman, they weren't speaking up. Frantically she looked around again for something to use as a weapon. A rock. A branch . . . Like either of those would work, she thought with disgust. There was nothing but dark dirt, black sky, and every shade of red, orange, yellow, and blue inside the greedy inferno. They might as well be on the face of the sun.

Trey's lungs were on fire. The heat was unbearable, the power of the blows and the high temperature of the superheated air had robbed him of air. Whatever the fuck was kicking him had on steel-toed boots, and they weren't giving him a moment's respite to catch his breath. Drenched in sweat, he attempted to roll out of the way, but the flaming images were all around him. Jabbing, shoving, kicking, punching. The attack was fierce and unrelenting. He rolled into a ball to protect his body as best he could.

Goddamned wasn't fair. Fire, for Christ's sake. That was Duncan's power. How the fuck was *he* expected to fight it? He couldn't Charm a quick-start log!

His clothes weren't burning, but he could feel intense, dry heat stinging his skin through the fabric and real or imagined, he smelled the sweet, sickly, stink of burning flesh.

He remembered Lark's warning that one of them could die during Testing. It wouldn't fucking well *wouldn't* be *him*.

"Duncan. God. Help me. Help me!" If Duncan came to help, these creatures would turn on *him*. Trey put every ounce of terror in his voice. Duncan could handle it. Fire was his power after all.

He squeezed his burning, dry eyes closed and tried to find a way into Duncan's mind. He'd tried a little illegal mind entry earlier. To discover what Duncan's greatest fear was. Just to level the playing field. But like every other effort Trey had made to gain a little insight into his friend over the years, Duncan had firmly slammed the door to his probing.

But Duncan did have an Achilles' heel and her name was Serena. Now that was something Trey could definitely use to his advantage.

"We've been friends all our lives. Don't let us die like this. Save us, Duncan. Save Serena and me."

The Fire Ghouls were strong, determined, and not human. Duncan, blocking a blow to the head with a raised arm, found there was nothing solid inside the leaping, dancing flames attacking him with such intensity. Nothing to connect with when he lashed out. Which was apparently a one-way street, because when these suckers connected, it sure as shit felt like being hit by a semi.

Trey was screaming, begging for help. Duncan tried to get closer to him, but a ghoul blocked his path, scarlet eyes spewing streams of flame. Narrowly avoiding a direct hit to the face, he covered his face with a bent arm and zigzagged, changing direction. The too-close encounter of superheat burned along his nerve endings. Jesus, that was close.

Fuck the rules. If he could have reached Trey, Duncan would've done what he could to help him. Thank God Serena was well back out of the way. His extensive T-FLAC training wasn't worth a damn bit of good here. Even his powers didn't hold any weight with these creatures.

His exposed skin felt as though someone were

holding a blow torch to it. All the oxygen was being sucked out of his burning lungs. He willed away the pain, and forced himself not to think about Serena facing these flaming monsters with superhuman strength and no substance.

Serena realized that until one of them retrieved that scroll, they would all have to continue fighting the fire. And the Fire Ghouls. The only way for this to stop was to find and retrieve the artifact. She had to slip past the Seventh Level Fire Ghouls, nasty creatures she'd thought a myth, something her father had told her as a bedtime story. She teased the long-ago memory to the surface, her lips barely moving as she whispered in a singsong five-year-old's voice,

> To trick a ghoul, stay nice and cool.
> Show your measure, snatch the treasure.
> To kill him dead, bash his head.

She ran back and picked up the thick fur-lined coat she'd been wearing. Serena knew she was probably going to die a hideous, agonizing death, but she had to try *something*. Duncan and Trey were in battles to the death. They weren't capable of going anywhere near the fire cave while under attack.

If she didn't do something quickly, getting the scroll would no longer be an option. They'd all be dead.

Before putting on the coat, she doused it, and herself, with water. The cool liquid felt fantastic on her too-hot skin. Envisioning ice cold Atlantic ocean water, she shoved her arms into the sodden sleeves and drew the hood up to cover her soaking hair, letting it fall forward to cover most of her face.

Generating her own personal rain cloud with a perpetual supply of large, fast-forming drops, Serena engulfed herself in water, then pulled the cloud around herself, covering her entire body. Girding herself for an extra second, wondering if she'd lost her mind relying on a half-remembered nursery rhyme, she teleported inside the cave. And into the center of Hell itself.

The heat was like nothing she'd ever felt before, yet she stood in the middle of the flames without being burnt to a cinder. Her personal rain cloud blanket was working overtime to keep her wet. She might not be getting burned, but it was hard to draw a breath, and the heat was almost unbearable.

Cocooned inside the living flames, she looked around. If the scroll had survived intact she saw no sign of it. "Okay. Where are you? Show my measure, steal the treasure." She shut her eyes. Brilliant color flicked, ebbing and flowing behind her lids.

"Ancient scroll come to me, let this end, so mote it be—"

She was back in London, standing in the middle of Duncan's flashy bedroom, holding a rolled scroll and dripping water on his carpet. "Holy crap! Ask and ye shall receive."

"Thanks. I'll take that." Lark Orela was seated at the foot of Duncan's bed. She rose in a lacy swirl of purple-and-black skirts and plucked the scroll from Serena's lax hand. "Good job, knew you'd win that one," she said with satisfaction.

She was the most extraordinary looking woman,

Serena thought. The younger woman's hair was fuchsia and black, she had the body of a center-fold, a mind like a computer, and dressed like a Goth princess—piercings, tattoos, and all. On the few occasions that Serena had met her at Council meetings, Lark dressed as a cross between a rocker and a top fashion model. Not one or the other, but both fashion statements together. On her it worked.

She was a member of the Council, and from all accounts she and Duncan had some sort of relationship, but Serena wasn't sure exactly what that entailed. She tamped down a bite of jealousy.

"We work for the same organization," Lark answered the unasked question, amusement in her husky voice. "There's nothing romantic between myself and Hot Edge."

Hot Edge? Now that was an apropos name for him. Serena quickly put up her mind shields, having momentarily forgotten that Lark was clairvoyant. "I couldn't care less. How come I didn't have to bash a ghoul over the head?"

"Great visuals. Really, I commend your imagination."

"Thanks," Serena said, feeling out of sorts.

"You've won the first Test, Serena. You thought outside the box. Instead of reacting physically, you drew your strength from something you knew. A rhyme. What will you do if you win the seat?"

She guessed that they hadn't heard her shout her-self out of the running when she'd been so scared. "Run the Council as best I can."

"What about Duncan?"

"What about him? He has just as much of a shot at this as I do."

"Which of you would be the better Head?"

"Duncan," Serena answered automatically. "*Me*," she switched immediately. "Honestly, I think I would be better in many ways. I'm more logical than he is, I'm better dealing with the minutiae of everyday problems, more reasonable in disputes because I empathize with both sides." She felt compelled to be fair. "But Duncan makes faster decisions. He's stronger physically, too. Where I would allow disputes to run their course, Duncan would intervene and force the sides to resolve the problem more quickly."

"Duncan solves his problems with violence?"

Blocking her thoughts, Serena frowned and said cautiously, "It appears so, yeah." It didn't *appear* so. It *was* so. Duncan used his fists instead of his wits every time.

"And you believe there is no instance where violence should be used?"

"Reasoning always works best." She was certain.

"Are you going to allow him to break the Curse?"

Serena's head shot up at the change of subject. "There's no reason to." It didn't surprise her that Lark knew about Nairne's Curse. Lark seemed to know a lot about everything.

"Scared?"

"Down to my bones," Serena admitted with a small shudder. "Fortunately I don't have to do anything. Duncan doesn't want the Curse broken."

Lark's ring-pierced brow rose. "He told you so?"

Serena shrugged. "He told me he never wanted to

get married. And I *know* he doesn't want to risk losing his powers."

"He told you he'd never marry when you were both sixteen," Lark said dryly. "Things have probably changed since then."

"I sincerely doubt it. The *Curse* is still in effect. I've watched him over the years. He doesn't get emotionally entangled, so he does everything else he does whole hog. Duncan isn't a man who does things half-assed, you know that. He would never risk loving a woman who he knew beforehand was destined to die. And I think that he feels that giving up one thing to keep the other is worth it.

"He and his brothers made a promise to each other years ago. Duncan takes that promise very seriously."

Lark cocked her head. "What promise was that?"

"That the Curse would end with the three of them."

The other woman raised a multiple pierced brow. "*Duncan* told you this?"

Serena half laughed. "No, actually. It was Gabriel."

"Is that so? And why would Duncan's overprotective older brother warn you off?"

"He wasn't warning me off. He was just— Hmm—I'm not sure why he told me."

"Maybe he saw the way you watched Duncan."

Serena stared at her. "How do you know how, or even if, I watched him?"

"I don't. But you were a teenage girl, and he must have been hot, even back then."

"One smoking hot Edge," Serena agreed. "Even if Duncan ever did go back on his promise to his brothers, he'd *never* risk breaking the Curse and losing his powers."

"Even you don't know if breaking the Curse *would* cause the Edge brothers to lose their powers."

"True. The important thing is that *Duncan* believes it."

"Nothing ventured, nothing gained," Lark said enigmatically, before disappearing.

"Thank you," Serena muttered to the empty room. "That was really enlightening. *Not.* I think I would have preferred a handshake and a gold star for my win."

She wasn't sure what she'd expected when she won a round, but it sure as hell wasn't standing alone in Duncan's bedroom. She caught a peek at her image and grimaced. She looked like something the cat had dragged in. Glancing at her watch, which was now working perfectly fine, she groaned. She had exactly one hour to pull herself together both physically and mentally before she presented herself to the courts in Ian's sons' ongoing battle to gain control over the Foundation and all the money.

If Serena had anything to do with it, they would spend the rest of their greedy little lives working soup kitchens and homeless shelters. Ian had good reason to exclude those spoiled bastards from involvement with the Foundation. And it wasn't as if her late husband had left them penniless. They'd each received a million, but apparently, that wasn't enough. Well, if Paul and Hugh wanted a fight, she'd give it to them. Then maybe for fun she'd turn them both into toads.

* * *

Invisible, Duncan leaned against the wall of the New York city courtroom a few feet away from Serena and her attorney.

Wearing a stylish amber-colored suit, her vibrant hair twisted up in a knot that left her vulnerable nape bare, Serena sat with both white-knuckled hands clasped on the table in front of her. Her makeup was subtle, but her color was high.

Duncan quickly cast a restraining spell around her before shit began to go flying. Not that he wouldn't enjoy seeing the judge's gavel knock some sense into Serena's two middle-aged stepsons, but she had enough things to deal with right now without that.

Fifteen minutes into it and the plaintiffs' attorney still droned on and on in a too-long, myopic opening statement. Christ. What an asshole. How could anyone believe the bullshit the attorney was sprouting about Serena? Duncan presumed they were hoping that some of the shit would stick if they threw enough. He gritted his teeth as he listened to the short, bald attorney with the pricey suit tell the judge how the defendant was nothing more than the gold-digging second wife of an ailing old man who had married him only to get her hands on his vast fortune.

The attorney omitted all the good Serena had done, and was still doing, with the Foundation. He conveniently left out that she'd raised matching funds from various fund-raisers throughout the years. Both before and after she was married to Ian Campbell. And that she could squeeze money out of donors like nobody's business.

Campbell's smug, useless sons sat calmly at the

plaintiff's table, listening as their highly paid tiger shark bloodied Serena's character and motives. He explained to the court that after Mrs. Campbell's parents were killed in a boating accident, she was taken into the home of Henry Morgan, who worked for Ian Campbell at his Foundation. The attorney carefully suggested that Serena and Henry had had an "unnatural" relationship.

Thank God for the restraining spell. The shit that *should* have gone flying around the courtroom stayed put. Barely. Serena casually pressed the flat of her hand on her attorney's briefcase, which was wobbling on the table while her attorney shot up and protested. The judge agreed, sending the sons' attorney a scathing warning.

By the time their attorney was finished, Serena was white-faced and rigid in her seat.

Duncan wanted to pummel the useless bastards. The judge called for Rhonda Butler to stand. Concerned as hell that the petite blond lawyer might not have enough muscle to go toe-to-toe with Ian's sons' attorney, he pushed away from the wall. He wasn't sure what he thought he could do in this situation, but if her attorney couldn't stand for Serena, *he* sure as hell would.

Fortunately, the minute Serena's attorney opened her mouth, Duncan's opinion began to change. For a small woman, she had a commanding, pleasant voice. She was assertive, but low key. And if the sons' lawyer was a tiger shark, Ms. Butler was a great white.

Tugging at the hem of her tailored navy suit jacket, she politely greeted the judge. "I'd like to make some additions and," she paused and sent a withering glare over her shoulder to opposing counsel, "corrections to the plaintiffs' recitation of the underlying facts that are the basis for this motion."

Kind blue eyes turned to steel. "Actually, the only part of the plaintiffs' argument based in fact is the fifty-year age difference between my client and her late husband. Mrs. Campbell worked for the Foundation, but contrary to plaintiffs' claims, she was not overambitious, she was committed to the causes supported by the Foundation. In fact, referring you to defendant's Exhibits A through K, Your Honor will see that during her late husband's illness, death, and to this day, Mrs. Campbell has raised more than seventeen million dollars in funds for the Campbell Foundation."

"Objection!" The sons' attorney practically leapt out of his chair.

"Basis?" the judge demanded, clearly annoyed with the interruption.

"Defendant's exhibits show donations to date. They do not attribute said donations to Mrs. Campbell."

Serena's attorney smiled. "Apologies to the court," she said. "May I approach?"

The judge motioned the two attorneys forward.

Butler carried a two-inch-thick stack of papers. "At this time, defendant wishes to enter these notarized letters from the donors in question attesting to the circumstances of their contributions to the Foundation." The judge scanned the papers. "As you can see," Serena's attorney said smoothly, "all the letters confirm Mrs. Campbell solicited the donations and all monies were properly deposited in the Foundation's accounts."

"Objection overruled," the judge motioned them back to their seats. "Continue, Ms. Butler."

"Respectfully, Your Honor, defendant requests that you dismiss the motion with prejudice on two grounds. The first being, plaintiffs have failed to meet their burden. They have offered no evidence to prove Mrs. Campbell is unfit to run the Foundation. Secondly, the plaintiffs in this action had ample time to file objections to the will in probate court. Since no fraud has been proven, we respectfully request that this court remand this matter to Probate Division. In addition, defendant requests that based on the complete lack of evidence offered by the plaintiffs in this matter, plaintiffs be ordered to pay all costs and reasonable attorney's fees to the defendant."

"Absolutely not!" Hugh Campbell shouted as he and his brother both shot to their feet. "Our father worked his entire life for that money. We're not giving it up to his whore!"

The judge banged his gavel. "Control your clients."

Duncan flicked his finger, causing each man to have chest pains. It wouldn't kill them, but they didn't know that. Ashen, they fell back into their seats, identical expressions of terror on their faces. Duncan eased off, and they straightened cautiously in their seats, their faces shiny with nervous sweat.

They were going to be doing a shitload more sweating. He wasn't finished with them. Not by a long shot.

The judge cleared his voice, then rendered his decision. "Plaintiffs have failed to prove that Mrs. Campbell's marriage was void. Further, there is no evidence to suggest that she coerced her husband in any way." He leaned back against his high-backed leather chair and steepled his fingers.

"Further, the claims made by the plaintiffs that Mrs. Campbell manipulated her late husband with sex are both unfounded and bordering on defamation. It is therefore the order of this court that the motion be denied and the plaintiffs are hereby ordered to pay court costs as well as the defendant's reasonable attorney's fees."

Their attorney frowned, buttoning his jacket as he rose. "Motion to reconsider, Judge?"

"Denied," the judge replied, clearly exasperated. "This is a probate matter and as such, I'm remanding all future issues in this case to probate court." He turned to look at Serena and her attorney. "Ms. Butler?"

"Yes?"

"File your fees with this court within ten days, and don't pad the bill. Court dismissed."

A nanosecond after the judge disappeared into chambers, both sons shoved back their chairs, shooting venomous glares at Serena. Paul, his face red with rage, jabbed a finger at her. "This isn't over, you opportunistic little bitch."

Duncan sent a lightning bolt up the guy's ass.

CHAPTER NINE

Serena filled the coffee carafe with water, grateful to have something to do, no matter how mundane the task. She would have preferred to be alone. Feeling battered, angry, and worst of all—embarrassed, she wished Duncan hadn't insisted on accompanying her home.

Sunlight poured through the ceiling-to-floor windows overlooking Central Park, and the room was filled with the delicate fragrance of the fresh roses that were arranged in half a dozen vases and scattered throughout the apartment. Usually the soothing colors and textures of her home were a balm to her frazzled nerves. But not today. Not with Duncan there.

He had the unexpected effect of making her feel as if all the secret, lonely corners of her life were filled. Which was ridiculous. He was nothing more to her than a minor annoyance.

Right, she thought, frazzled. *I'll just keep telling myself that. Maybe someday I'll believe it.*

She'd removed her suit's jacket, but still wore the silk blouse and pencil-slim skirt with the high heels and discreet jewelry she'd hastily put on early this morning. She'd be considerably more comfortable in the jeans or shorts she usually wore. But on occasion she could out-chic the best of them. For reasons she didn't bother analyzing, she didn't want to go into the bedroom to change while Duncan was there. The fact that he'd seen her naked was immaterial. Naked and Duncan were two words that should not be used in the same sentence.

She hadn't wanted to hear all that garbage in the courtroom about herself. She most certainly hadn't wanted *Duncan* to hear it, she thought, as she spooned coffee into the filter and closed the basket. It didn't matter that it was all lies and wishful thinking on the part of Ian's sons. Paul and Hugh, and their thousand-dollar-an-hour attorney, had come to court today locked and loaded, and Serena was afraid that some of the mud might stick despite her attorney's quick objections and ardent arguments to the court.

"Your attorney seems to know her stuff," Duncan called from the other room. She could see him through the breezeway between the kitchen and living room as he wandering around like a bull in a china shop for heaven's sake, looking at her things.

The enormous living room/dining room was tastefully decorated in shades of white and soft apricot, a sophisticated backdrop for Ian's extensive art collection. Her husband had been a passionate patron of the arts, but what Serena loved most was all the crude artwork made for her personally by people who had nothing else to give in appreciation for the work she'd done through the Foundation.

Mingled with Ian's million-dollar paintings were

the hundreds of framed photographs she'd taken in the field. The men, women, and children who had touched Serena's heart and enriched her life over the years.

"Rhonda's terrific," she agreed, bracing herself for Duncan to start asking if any of the nonsense he'd heard earlier was true. Ian must be rolling in his grave, *spinning*, Serena thought, trying to see the humor in the situation.

"It's inconceivable to me that Ian, who was a kind, generous, warmhearted man, produced two sons so unlike himself," she told him. "And from what he told me about his first wife, whom he was married to for thirty-five years, the sons' behavior didn't come from Rita's side either."

The brothers, now in their late fifties, had begrudged their father the amount of time and money he'd poured into the Foundation.

"I'm guessing they didn't hassle Ian like that."

"No way. They were too subversive to openly challenge their father." But they'd made life as unpleasant as possible for his new young bride behind his back.

Now with their father gone, Hugh and Paul were determined to void Ian's will. Ian's posthumous, generous endowment to the Foundation had given her a life, and his sons fifty million reasons to screw with it.

Leaning back against the counter, she absently kept an eye on Duncan as he moved around the living room. It was strange to have a young, handsome, virile man in her home. She'd loved Ian in a quiet, peaceful way. She supposed loving a man so much older than herself had been a way to avoid the pain of losing someone else she loved without warning.

She'd known going in that she'd outlive him. Foolishly she'd thought his loss would be bearable because she'd anticipated it.

She'd been wrong.

She'd loved Ian dearly, and still missed him, but she was a healthy, sexual woman. Duncan's presence here made her realize how much she missed the closeness of human contact. Hell, she missed *sex*.

Serena shook her head at the direction her healthy libido was taking her. Duncan was *nothing* like Ian. The only thing the two men shared was their gender.

She'd better drag her healthy libido away from the one man she couldn't have.

Cowardly as it was, Serena took her time getting out mugs, sugar, and a tray to delay going into the other room and hearing Duncan's opinion of the morning's events. Her cheeks stung with embarrassment.

She'd sensed him the second he'd teleported inside that courtroom. Preternaturally aware of exactly how close he stood by the sudden racing of her heart, and her ultra awareness of his presence, she hadn't been happy knowing he was hearing every vitriolic word and accusation. Even though all of it was lies.

She still wasn't sure why Duncan had suddenly shown up in New York, and at the courthouse of all places. Although she was happy to note he hadn't been burnt to a crisp and seemed to be whole and hearty, not to mention disgustingly cheerful after surviving the first Test.

Having won made her want to do the very undignified Snoopy dance. Serena refrained. Standing in her kitchen waiting for the coffee to finish dripping, she watched him prowl around her apartment, much as she'd watched Lark walk around his this morning. He was like a caged tiger as he stalked about, picking up various objects before putting them down again. What was it with him and touching her things? she thought crossly. He'd done the same thing in her room in Schpotistan.

She jerked her attention off his elegant hands as he ran his fingers lightly over the curve of the soapstone woman's hip. She'd recently bought the statue in Namibia because she, too, liked the subtle curves. It took a second for Serena to realize that her breasts ached in response to his sensual touch on a piece of stone. She had to stop this. She really did.

His footsteps were silent on the plush carpeting as he strolled to the Oriental display cabinet and looked inside. Without permission her gaze wandered over his body. He wore beautifully tailored dark slacks and a pink—*pink!*—dress shirt, open at the throat. Only Duncan could get away with wearing pastel pink and still look achingly masculine.

There was a tightly leashed strength beneath the sophisticated, civilized clothing he wore so well. And a faint sense that he wasn't nearly as relaxed as he appeared. Eventually she was going to have to go out there. But in the meantime Duncan was too busy checking out her possessions to demand to know what the hell she was doing hiding in the kitchen.

No, not hiding, Serena thought, annoyed by a conversation that was taking place solely in her head. She wasn't *hiding*, she was making the damned coffee he'd asked for. She watched him with decidedly mixed feelings. She couldn't help her physical reaction to him, it was some pheromone thing she was helpless to prevent and which she found annoying as hell. But the high lust factor was tempered by regret. Because wanting wasn't getting. And Duncan wasn't available.

"*Remember* that."

He turned his head, a faint smile curving his sexy mouth as his eyes met hers. "Remember what?" he asked, as if he could read her mind. Which he couldn't, because she always blocked him.

"Just thinking aloud."

"Hmm," he stared at her for another moment, his blue eyes almost black, the smile leaving his face. "What's taking so long? Waiting for Juan Valdez to deliver the coffee beans?"

"If you're in such a hurry, materialize your own damn coffee, or go down to the Starbucks on the corner." Serena put a bite in the words because if she didn't, she'd tell him flat out how appealing he was to her. How badly she wanted to rip off that pink shirt to check out his chest to see if it was smooth or covered with black hair. How hungry she was for him to kiss her again. How badly she wanted to touch him and learn his body.

Ack! Blast the man. He made her crazy.

"Get up on the wrong side of my bed this morning, Fury?"

Serena put a hand on top of a teetering canister as her temper spiked. This response to him was more normal, and so much better. "I couldn't find a comment card," she told him sweetly. "The mattress was too hard, and all that black is depressingly like waking up in a vampire's coffin."

"Lark likes it."

So he *had* slept with her, the bastard. "Goodie for her. I changed the color of your chichi bedspread. I hope she likes orange."

"She likes the black. Not the feel of the bed," he finished, not bothering to acknowledge her comment.

It was almost *worse* imagining Duncan doing it on the floor. Or, God help her, on that black granite kitchen counter.

"I've never slept with Lark. And no, I've never made love to her either," he added.

Could he read her mind? Damn it. What was taking the coffee so damned long? "Tell someone who cares about your serial love life, Hot Edge." She had forgotten to press the "on" button. *Oh, for—*She stabbed it so hard she almost broke the coffee pot.

He grinned and she wanted to hit him instead of kiss him, which made her feel considerably better.

"How's *your* love life lately, Fury?"

"I'm still in mourning."

He raised his bisected eyebrow. "After thirteen months?"

"Yes."

"Did you have sex with Trey?"

She stared at him. "I *beg* your pardon?"

"Did you sleep with Trey when you were dating him?"

"I heard you, for God's sake! That's absolutely none of your business."

"I'm making it my business."

Her heart leapt. "Why is it that you're suddenly all over my life? Who the hell opened the door and let *you* in?"

He paused. "Henry."

Uh-ha. "Well, when I see him, I'll tell *him* to tell *you* that I'm none of your damn business."

"Fine."

"Fine," she said through gritted teeth.

Behind her the coffee pot spluttered and hissed in its final throes. If he didn't watch out he'd be wearing the boiling liquid instead of drinking it.

"Congratulations on winning the first Test." He raised his voice as he wandered to the far side of the room. "Smart of you to cut to the chase like that."

She wasn't going to let him know how close she'd been to chickening out. "Thanks. I'm sure you enjoyed challenging those fire creatures to a boxing match almost as much as I enjoyed beating your butt," Serena taunted, because it was what they did. But her heart really wasn't in it today.

"It was certainly . . . interesting," he said dryly. "No ill effects?" He went to the window, turning his back to gaze down at the park. Serena couldn't help taking in the sheer size of him when his back was turned. He looked deceptively urbane. Dark, slightly curling hair brushed his collar, and the width of his broad shoulders straining at the pink Egyptian cotton of his shirt hinted at something not quite civilized, despite the color.

"No. You?"

"How's the arm?"

Which didn't answer her question. Typical Duncan. She flexed her arm. With everything else that had been going on she'd almost forgotten the bullet graze. "Okay." That seemed to be the extent of their small talk. She moved the coffee carafe off the burner and put it on the tray. She couldn't stay in the kitchen all day.

"Would you like to come with me to see Henry this afternoon?" She didn't particularly want to share Henry with Duncan, especially today, but she needed the connection of seeing her godfather. Now. She missed his counsel desperately. Even with Henry in a coma, he was a wizard. There was a chance he'd find an alternate way to communicate with her as he had with Duncan. Serena hoped so. She wanted to tell him about Hugh and Paul.

And that Duncan was blaming him for suddenly butting into her personal life.

And, she had to tell him that she was running for Head of Council. He'd be so proud that she'd won the first Test.

The Council stuff and the progress of the suit filed by Ian's sons were easy. But it would be nearly impossible to verbalize her concerns about Duncan with him standing in the room. Better to leave any Duncan discussion for another day, she decided. A day when she had a modicum of sense about him and a little distance from that last kiss.

"Yeah. I want to see him. We'll go in an hour or so when you've had a little time to regain your equilibrium." He picked up a framed photograph of Ian and herself taken on their honeymoon in Switzerland three years ago. Instead of responding to his autocratic pronouncement, she wondered what he saw in the picture. A couple in love? A laughing old man and too young woman on a skilift? Did he believe the things Ian's sons had told the court?

"My equilibrium is fine and dandy, thank you." She felt as though fire ants were crawling through her veins, eating her from the inside out. Producing a cool waterfall to immerse herself in, followed by a couple of hours spent quietly with Henry, would do a lot to restore her peace of mind. Even though Henry couldn't speak, she had to believe that he could hear her. That he was just waiting for the right moment to wake up.

And while she trusted Joanna implicitly to keep the team on track in Schpotistan, she wished Henry was back overseeing the project now that they were so close to having the thermal blanket work. It had originally been his brain child, and he should be there to see it come to fruition.

Emotions bubbled far too close to the surface, causing Serena's eyes to sting. "The coffee at the hospital isn't bad. Let's go now." She had a list of Foundation-related things that needed doing, but until her internal gyroscope was back to normal she'd be better off in Germany. The business calls and faxes could wait until tomorrow.

Duncan turned away from the window, his eyes meeting hers through the open pass-through between living room and kitchen. "I could convince those two assholes to drop their case."

Now *that* would be worth the price of a front row seat. Not that she'd take him up on such an inappropriate way of resolving her personal issues. Or any issues for that matter. Which just showed how differently they each approached conflict resolution.

But, pacifist that she was, given the way Paul and Hugh had humiliated her in court that morning, she allowed herself a few seconds fantasizing about Duncan drawing them into a game of dodgeball. Played with blazing fireballs.

Oddly, Duncan's defense of her also gave Serena a ridiculous sense of pleasure—she was touched by the idea that he would even offer to protect her. Not many people considered her the type of woman who might need it. Running a multimillion-dollar Foundation, she was considered self-sufficient and competent, and few people tried to take on the task of coming to her defense when they knew she could do it herself.

She swallowed a lump in her throat. She was losing her mind if the idea of Duncan making a threat of physical harm sounded like a romantic overture. "By doing what?" she asked, trying to get a grip on reality. "Beating them up? No thanks."

He put the frame back on the table exactly where he'd found it. "By talking to them."

Her laugh felt raw. "You're half their age. Leave them alone. My lawyer promises me we'll prevail no matter what they try to do."

"Have they always talked to, and about, you that way?"

"Not around their father, but yes. Pretty much. Those were only words, Duncan. None of them true." Obviously they weren't leaving pronto, so she carried the tray she'd been holding for a long freaking time into the living room. Sometimes the most simple tasks, done without magic, soothed her.

She didn't feel soothed at the moment. The Test,

followed by hours in the courtroom, where she had to control her temper to prevent a manifestation of her powers, had taken their toll. She was embarrassingly aware of what he'd done for her this morning. Without his help putting the brakes on her telekinetic power, things would certainly have gone haywire.

Getting shot at felt like a lifetime ago.

She was so wired she wanted to run a marathon, and so tired she could sleep for a week. "Did you find out who was shooting at you at the warehouse?"

"No. But I will."

She believed him. She placed the tray on the coffee table and sat down in her favorite corner of the plush, cinnamon-colored sofa. She didn't kick off her shoes as she usually did, nor did she curl her legs under her and get comfortable.

Duncan came and sat down on the opposite end of the sofa. Three feet away didn't feel like enough space between them to Serena, but she couldn't very well get up and move when she'd just sat down herself.

He picked up the photograph from the end table beside him. It was a twenty-five-year-old image of her and her parents. She wanted to tell him to put it down. That part of her life was none of his damn business.

She poured coffee into the waiting mugs. Without thinking, she added two sugars to Duncan's and passed it to him. Their fingers touched in the transfer, and she felt that inexplicable zing shoot through her body from the brief contact.

No! she told herself firmly. No. No. No.

"Cute kid." His lone dimple flashed. "I remember you wore these braces all the way through fifth grade."

"And I remember you had to magically extricate the gum from those braces after you dared me to chew a disgustingly large wad of it."

"Double Bubble." So he remembered. So what? She materialized a fudge cake, plates, and utensils because she was suddenly dying for chocolate. Or sex. No, *chocolate*. "Want a slice?"

He shook his head. "You never could resist a dare." His smile broadened. "Worth the punishment to see how long it could keep your mouth glued shut. When was this taken?" he asked, without missing a beat.

Serena glanced up from transferring a slice of cake to a plate. He was the king of the non sequitur. "It was a family vacation." Their *last* family vacation. She met his eyes, burning and deep, suddenly not wanting the cake after all. She thought it away.

"Do you ever talk about what happened?"

No. "Look, I appreciate you coming to the court-house, and the support, but it's been a hellish couple of days, and I really want to be alone now. You go and see Henry. I'll visit him later."

"I'll take that as a no."

The problem with Duncan was that he looked as though he could take on the world single-handedly. Most of the time that was freaking annoying. Conversely, his strength, his apparent invincibility, was seductive and incredibly appealing.

Serena didn't need a white knight. She'd always fought her own battles. But sometimes, like now, she thought, it would be wonderful to just let someone else take over. Just for a little while.

But letting that someone be *Duncan Edge* was insane.

She gave him a steady look. "I killed my parents, so no, Duncan, it's not something I bring up in casual conversation."

His scarred brow rose. "Explain to me how a child could possibly be responsible for the deaths of two adults?" He was relentless, exasperating, pushy.

Serena closed her eyes and tried to breathe in deeply. Cool green grass. Breathe. Blue sky. Breathe. Fluffy white clouds. Breathe. Slow. Deep. In. Out. In. Out.

She looked at him without seeing him. "I couldn't control my telekinetic powers. Just like today," she said bitterly. "I know you put a restraining spell on me in the courtroom so my anger didn't manifest. I couldn't control my telekinesis today, and I couldn't control it then."

"I thought they'd drowned."

The hard pounding of her heart sounded unbearably loud in her ears, and her mind's eye filled with the memory of sunlight sparkling on the water as the family yacht cut through the calm, turquoise Caribbean waters. "They did."

"Did Ian know you felt this way?"

"Of course." It hadn't been easy, but she'd managed to give him the bare bones. He'd never pressed for more detail, knowing how painful the recollection was for her. Even now the memory of their deaths made her throat tighten.

"How about Henry and Martha?"

They'd come for her at the hospital. Terrified, she'd been unable to speak about what had happened for months afterward. Then it was a wonder they'd been able to understand half of her hysterical, sobbing account. None of them had ever brought it up again. "Obviously."

"Did they believe it was your fault?"

"Not in so many words." The familiar weight pressed down on her chest, and her palms grew damp as her heart began to race. "But it *was*."

"Bullshit." Duncan said flatly. "You're trying to tell me *Henry Morgan* blamed an eight-year-old for killing her parents? I don't bel—"

"I don't talk about it." Several framed pictures fell off the bookcase. Serena glared at them, and then at him. "I don't want to talk about it."

Reaching out, Duncan touched her clenched fist where it lay on the sofa cushion between them. "Concentrate on what you're saying." Unfurling her fingers with his, he slid his palm against hers as things in the kitchen started flying off the shelves. "Focus on me."

Another dangerous path for her mind to take. She pulled her hand out of his, because touching him, being comforted by him, was seductive. "I'd rather not." She closed her eyes tightly, and visualized . . . It wasn't the memory of the past that had her emotions out of whack so much as it was Duncan.

Before the kiss, their relationship, for want of a better word, was clear, black and white. They snipped and teased each other. But now . . . God, now just looking at this man with his flame-hot blue eyes and serious expression, made her heart thud, and her senses swim. She wanted to kiss him again. She wanted—

Her head examined.

Edge. Edge. Edge.

"You're going to leave me with that cliff-hanger?"

"Apparently so." She'd already blurted out too much. Martha and Henry had insisted on therapy, and it had helped enormously. But Serena still wasn't ready to bare her soul. Especially to Duncan. Especially since she felt like a tuning fork vibrating to his signal.

"Can't you look without touching?" she demanded. Careful to avoid touching him again, she took the picture from him, placing it face down on the coffee table.

"I always like to touch what I'm looking at," he said, voice husky. She glanced up at the altered tone.

He was looking right at her, his eyes blazing hot, his face taut.

Their gazes locked.

She couldn't move. She couldn't breathe. The warning in her head became fainter and fainter and Serena met fire with fire of her own. "That's a very provocative statement," she said coolly, while her blood raced and her heart took up a jungle beat at her audacity. "Are you going to back it up?"

She looked so delectably prim sitting there in her trim skirt and blouse, her coppery hair twisted in some mystifyingly intricate coil at her nape. Daring him. Oh, yeah. This was Serena at her poker-faced best. If he wasn't keeping tabs on the jittery pulse at the base of her throat he could—almost—believe that she was unaffected. Almost.

Without moving, Duncan mentally slid the hem

of Serena's skirt a few inches up her thighs. "Is that a dare, Fury?"

She pressed her knees together primly, but seeing her nipples pressed against the thin silk of her blouse spiked his fever. He skimmed the fabric up another inch. And then another.

"We're way too sensible to dare each other into doing something stupid." She zapped open the top three buttons of his shirt as she leaned back against the soft cushions, crossing her long legs with a glide of smooth, bare skin.

He inched down the zipper at her hip. Forget the *dare* part. He cut to the chase. "We're way too sensible to do anything stupid."

"Exactly." Shooting him a gleaming, innocent glance from guileless gray eyes, the mirrors to her soul, she retaliated.

S-l-o-w-l-y.

His jaw ached as the zipper of his slacks opened. One. Tooth. At. A—Jesus! she was killing him— Time. Hard as a rock, he was grateful she'd taken the pressure off his fly.

Ah, Jesus. She was a delight. Sexy. Dangerous as hell, but she brought an unexpected lightness to his—

This was dangerous. Imprudent. Insane. But Christ, it felt good.

He wanted her more than he wanted his next breath.

"I've always wondered—" His shirt disappeared. Her gaze felt as hot as a touch on his skin. "If your chest was hairy or smooth. Hmm." Her lips tilted and her eyes glowed devilishly. "Just right."

He wanted her hands on him. On his chest. On his cock. Everywhere. Shit. She could pluck every hair on his body if he could touch her. "We've seen each other in swimsuits."

Serena in a sleek black one-piece had aroused him to the point that on many occasions he'd had to chill out in the school locker room way past first bell.

"Not for a long t—oh—time." The throb at the base of her creamy throat sped up as he got rid of the skirt. Leaving her lower half clothed in nothing more than strappy, fuck-me high heels, and a gossamer wisp of a barely-there thong.

Duncan's tongue stuck to the roof of his mouth. He tried to clear the sensual fog from his pea brain. "I don't do involvement," he said out loud. A reminder to himself.

"Fortunate," Serena told him smoothly, vanishing his shoes, socks, and watch without moving. "I'd never be insane enough to get involved with a man who had such a powerful Curse on his head."

A timely reminder of the oath he and his brothers had taken, he thought, stripping away her silk blouse and feasting his eyes on the pale mounds of her breasts pressed against her apricot-colored lace bra. Her nipples were hard little points, deep coral with arousal through the thin lace. He was going to turn to stone and fucking die here if he didn't touch her soon. "Duty over love."

She uncrossed her long legs, then crossed them the other way. Just, he was positive, to drive him mad enough to make a grab for her. "Did I say anything about love?" she asked sweetly as his boxers vanished from beneath his slacks, leaving him commando.

Duncan made whatever was holding her hair up vanish. The silken, fiery mass unfurled slowly, then tumbled down her back. One long strand slid forward over her bare shoulder to curl lovingly around her barely covered left breast. He'd never seen anything more erotic in his life than Serena in nothing more than sheer lace, high heels, and pearls. He reluctantly got rid of the choker and pearl earrings. For good measure, he nixed her watch and shoes, too. He went deaf with lust as those few accessories bared even more skin for him to feast on. Oh, Jesus. He wanted her naked, and under him now. Now. *Now.*

"'*Duty o'er love was the choice you did make,*'" she quoted. "'*My love you did spurn, my heart you did break—*'"

"You remember?" he said thickly. In a mad moment, he'd confided to her about the Curse when they'd been teens. It stunned him that, half a lifetime later, Serena recalled Nairne's Curse verbatim. A Curse that had affected every aspect of his life for as long as he could remember. The five-hundred-year-old Curse that would end—he, Caleb, and Gabriel had agreed—once and for all with the last three Edge brothers. Being here with Serena, making love to her, he was playing with fire. And while fire was his power to call, this time he was in way over his head, and burning up fast.

He stripped away the wisp of a bra. The sight of the pale globes of her breasts topped with the stiff peaks of her nipples made his body throb and his desperate brain ache. He salivated, imagining sucking one of those ripe points into his mouth.

"'*Your penance to pay, no pride you shall gain,*'" Serena continued. "'*Three sons on three sons find nothing but pain/I gift you my powers in memory of me/The joy of love no son shall ever see/When a Lifemate is chosen by the heart of a son/No protection can be given, again I have won/His pain will be deep, her death will be swift/Inside his heart a terrible rift/Only freely given will this curse be done/To break the spell, three must work as one.*' I remember."

"Right now I'm trying to forget," he whispered roughly, every nerve, muscle, and joint in his body throbbing and pulsing. He was this close to detonation. "Christ, Fury. Are you ever going to get rid of my fucking pants?"

She smiled. "I want to take those off with my own two hands."

He shuddered. "Great minds . . ."

CHAPTER TEN

Serena found herself lying on a soft, wide bed under a flowering vine-covered lattice roof, Duncan leaning over her. The hot look in his eyes affected her like an aphrodisiac. White diaphanous fabrics fluttered in the soft, warm tropical evening breeze. A susurrus came from the ocean, foaming onto white sand a few feet away. The fragrance of flowers, mixed with the briny scent of the sea, and the intoxicating clean, masculine smell of Duncan's skin made her dizzy with lust.

Marginally aware that they were on a beach— *somewhere*—she only had eyes for him. His face was close enough to see the dark outer rim of his iris, and to count, if she had the urge, which she didn't, his inky black lashes. He curled a long strand of her hair around his finger and seemed to be memorizing her features.

Vaguely, Serena hoped she didn't look as besotted as she felt. "Where are we?" She didn't care. She was here. In his arms. And at that instant in time, he was all that mattered. She brought one hand up, tracing his mouth with the pad of her thumb. Slowly, deliberately, she increased the pressure as she watched the effect of her touch reflected in his darkening eyes.

Fever burned in her body like a windblown forest fire. Her breasts ached for his touch. She was already wet and ready for him, and the too-light brush of his bare chest against her breasts made her breath falter and her heart race. The tension, as taut as the strings on a bow, ratcheted up a notch as his knuckles lightly skimmed her cheek.

"Paradise Island," he murmured, brailing the shape of her eyebrow with the tip of one finger.

"Apt."

He was sprawled partially across her body, his arousal hard and ready, pressed against her hip. The wool of his dark slacks abraded her skin where he had his leg thrown over hers. His heart pounded an exaggerated beat against her breast, mimicking the tempo of her own. They'd barely moved, but their skin was damp with the sweat of restraint.

The sun was setting quietly over the horizon in a splash of turquoise, pale orange, and pinks against the deepening blue of the sky. Sheer white drapes billowed and drifted from the corners of the overhead canopy, releasing the fragrance of jasmine and roses.

Feeling like an overripe peach, Serena ran her fingers gently through Duncan's hair. Soft, silky. So at odds with his intense masculinity.

He'd brought her here to Paradise, yet she knew that he, like herself, wanted to draw out the moment. Draw out the anticipation. She could outwait him if she absolutely had to, but if this was the slow race of postponement, she might end up coming without him. She glanced over his shoulder. She could see across the gently lapping waves, all the way to the horizon. He'd found the perfect place.

"You're a romantic."

He slipped his fingers free of her hair to cup her cheek. His hand felt hot against her face. His thumb gently traced the shape of her mouth. "Horny."

"I can fix that."

"I'm banking on it happening before my head blows off and my balls explode," he said dryly.

She grinned. "Ditto." Sliding her bare leg up his pants-covered calf, she shuddered as he drew her fingers into the warm cavern of his mouth. "Except the balls p-part." The slippery glide of his tongue made her even wetter. She retracted her fingers before she embarrassed herself, and ran them over the satin curve of his broad shoulder.

He was going to be very heavy. She couldn't wait. She skimmed one hand down his back and into the loose waistband of his pants. The taut muscles of his butt flexed under her marauding exploration. It was getting increasingly harder to catch her breath, and her heart was beating so fast and loudly it covered the sound of the surf.

"Condom?" she asked desperately, pushing his slacks over his hips. He rolled to help. But that took him too many inches away from her and she pulled him back against her, her ankle hooked around his thigh. Then pinned his hips against her side.

"As many as—Christ, Serena, do it faster would you please?—we need, he finished, then brushed his mouth over hers. "Or foam if you prefer?" He nibbled her lower lip. "IUD? Diaphr—Are you laughing at me?"

She was. As ridiculously, intensely aroused as she was, Serena felt euphoric, giddy, foolishly in love. "I've never had a lover offer me a contraceptive menu before." Magically she rolled a condom down his length, knowing if she touched him now it would be over before it started.

"I'm still wearing my pants, sweetheart. Could we perhaps postpone the chatting, and do the whole take my pants off slowly with your teeth thing later?"

Stripping him manually was going to be fun—some other time. But right now she needed his pants gone with expedience. Magic had its strong points.

"Not teeth. I said my own two *hands*," she reminded him primly, making his pants vanish. She stroked her palm down his very, *very* fine bare ass. "Not that I'm in any way opposed to nibbling you—later."

He nudged her knees apart, and slid over her body to settle into the cradle of her damp thighs. "We'll be lucky if I last ten seconds."

She wrapped her arms around his neck, and her legs around his waist as he positioned himself at the heart of her desperate need. Sweat trickled down his temples, and the muscles in his arms, braced on either side of her head, flexed. Observing the taut tendons in his neck, and the tempo of his heart, she knew he was using every ounce of control in his body not to end this erotic dance that had them both on a razor's edge.

Serena tilted her hips, locking her ankles around his waist. With merely the press of his penis against her entrance she could already feel powerful ripples surging deep inside. She clenched her teeth against the powerful internal clenching and stopped moving. "We'll be lucky if *I* last *f-five*."

"*Four.*" The cords in his neck strained as he held them both still, their breathing ragged, their hearts manic.

"*Thr—*"

He drove hard and deep, at the same time crushing her mouth beneath his. Before he could begin a rhythmic thrust, her body went rigid and she tightened around him. Her orgasm speared through her, sharp and unbearably sweet. A hot rush of blinding pleasure that had her shuddering and sobbing as her entire body clenched beneath his. Every muscle and tendon, every nerve ending participated.

He shifted, and she moaned a protest, but he just made soothing noises as he placed her knees over his shoulders and shifted his weight. Serena cried out as he started thrusting. Harder and faster in a rhythm guaranteed to drive her mindless.

Her head thrashed on the pillow.

"Look at me," he rasped, his body moving faster and faster. "See what you do to me."

Mesmerized by the tension in his face, Serena's eyes met his. God he looked fierce, almost feral as his dark blue eyes locked on hers as he continued that frantic rhythm. She couldn't look away. His cheekbones seemed carved of stone, his jaw rigid. The tendons in his neck stood out in sharp relief.

Impossibly she felt the clawing need building again.

"Yes," he said, his voice a growl. "Come with me."

She couldn't tell where his body started and hers ended. Vision blurred, heart beating like a jackhammer, she cried out his name as she came hard.

Arching back, he made a raw sound as his hips jerked and thrust with his own powerful climax. He collapsed on top of her.

Completely spent, Duncan heavy between her thighs, Serena lay gasping for air, incapable of moving. Every muscle in her boneless body felt like sunheated liquid.

When she woke later it was fully dark, and the enormous velvety bowl of the sky was filled with a scattering of brilliant white stars. Beautiful. The sound of the waves on the beach was louder, and the breeze a little cooler. She nuzzled her face into the crisp hair on Duncan's warm chest. He was lightly stroking her hip.

If she could bottle the smell of him, she'd be a billionaire. She'd usually never even *noticed* one way or the other how a man smelled. But with Duncan there was some pheromone thing going, and just the masculine scent of his skin made her hot.

She yawned. "Did I sleep long?"

His fingers traced the crease between her torso and thigh. "About an hour."

"Hmm." She explored the hard planes of his chest with her mouth. His skin was warm, and tasted deliciously salty. "Did *you?*"

"Too busy."

She smiled as her lips encountered his nipple. "Doing what?" Gently she ran her tongue over the hard bud.

"Counting your freckles."

"Hmm."

"Three thousand, two hundred—"

Serena closed her teeth not so gently around his aroused nipple. His body went rigid.

"Jesus. Do you always wake up horny?"

"I don't know," she kissed her way up his throat. "I've never woken up with you before. Complaining?" she whispered against his mouth.

"I was thinking about a swim."

"Liar. Besides, I can't swim."

"Of course you can. I used to lust after you every Wednesday afternoon in the summer when we had swim practice."

"You lusted after me? Really?"

"Oh, yeah."

"Did you ever see me wet?"

"Now?"

She smacked his traveling hand. Not too hard. She was very wet. "At *school*. No, you didn't, because I can't swim. I'd change with the others and then hang back. I can't stand deep water. Have a phobia in fact."

He sat up on his elbow. "Your power to call is water."

She rolled aside, pulling her hair out from beneath her shoulders. "Which certainly makes my aversion to it problematic at times," she told him dryly.

"Tell me about that day. And as I know how much you enjoy confrontation, it'll be easier for you to tell me if you're not trying to read every nuance of my expression."

Her eyes widened slightly, because she was thinking the same thing.

"All families have skeletons," he said against her hair. "But opening the closet doors and letting them out is usually the best way to exorcise the ghosts. There's nothing you could say that would shock or repel me, I promise."

"Stop feeling sorry for me, damn it."

"I feel that eight-year-old's pain. Finish it," he instructed.

Duncan pulled her against his chest and closed his arms around her. Serena found herself surrounded by him. She didn't even bother trying to resist. God, it felt good secured against the hard pack of his chest, listening to the even rhythm of his breathing. His hold felt safe, unthreatening, and the steady beat of his heart helped her own slow down a little. So much easier to talk without looking at the accusation and pity she knew would be clear in his eyes as she told the story.

She closed her eyes. "That whole vacation I kept telling them I was excited about going away to boarding school because I—I knew that's what they wanted to hear. But I was scared. I'd never been away from them for more than a couple of nights. And the thought of being separated from them terrified me.

"I didn't want to leave my friends. I didn't want to be away from my parents for months at a time. We were very close, and I didn't understand why they needed to be free to travel for the Foundation."

"You were just a kid. It's hard for kids to understand when a parent disappears for months at a time." His voice reverberated through her body. "Believe me, I know. My father lived in Scotland, my mother in Montana. We hardly ever saw him. Hell, we barely saw *her*. Even though we lived under the same roof, she was mentally in Scotland with my father most of the time. Keep going until you're finished."

Easier said than done. "The summer cruise was Henry and Martha's idea. They knew how much I loved the yacht, they also knew I hadn't learned to swim yet. They had no children of their own, and besides spoiling me rotten, they were caring godparents and knew how much I loved being with my parents. So the vacation was cleverly multipurpose."

"Then they also knew Ian Campbell," he murmured noncommittally.

"And Rita. And before you ask, or make a snide comment, I didn't meet Ian until years after his wife's death. Not until Henry introduced us, when I went to work for the Foundation."

"I wasn't going to ask."

"Yes you were. Everybody does."

Duncan knew she was right. She stiffened against him, braced for ugliness. His chest ached for her pain. Ached for his own, realizing that she expected the worst of him. Shit. The years of antagonism were coming back to bite him in the ass.

He knew the hostile press her May/December romance with Campbell had generated. And that was before the sons had their own vicious go at her. Ian Campbell was dead, and interrogating Serena would serve absolutely no purpose.

"You loved him."

She lifted her head to look up at him, eyes narrowed as if she expected the words to be a trick. "Yes I did. Very much."

"Then use that as a shield against the bullshit accusations," he told her quietly. "Finish telling me about that last day. All of it." When she hesitated, almost straining to extricate herself from his arms, Duncan said softly. "Don't fight me, Fury."

He'd seen Serena in a temper. He'd seen her pissed off. He'd seen her laugh until she cried. But he'd never seen her *cry*. Everything in him knew she was on the verge of breaking down, but she was hanging on by her fingernails.

She'd hate herself for crying in front of him. She'd consider that a weakness. She didn't know that if she cried, she'd realize that she was *his* weakness. He tangled his fingers in the silk of her hair, and exerted just enough pressure to bring her head back to his chest. He knew damn well that if she didn't want to be right where she was, he'd be doused with water, and she'd be across the bed pointing the fire hose.

He stroked her bright hair, enjoying the fragrant strands sifting between his fingers. "What happened next?"

"For the entire trip I alternated between begging and bargaining. I wanted them to want to be with me." After a moment she relaxed enough to slip her arms about his waist and fist the back of his shirt as she rested her head in the curve of his shoulder. Her fiery hair brushed his lips and smelled of wild jasmine.

"We'd been sailing around with no particular ports in mind, just the three of us, for two weeks. I knew, and dreaded, that eventually the vacation would end, and I'd be sent away.

"We still had one more day and night before we had to head back in. My mother was doing everything she could to make every moment special. But to me they were our last moments, and I was getting more and more resentful that they were going to ship me off," she said, a poignant hitch in her voice.

"That last day was perfect. Not a cloud in the sky. My dad dropped anchor in a little cove, and the three of us went snorkeling and had a picnic on the beach. I knew I was being a brat, but I kept begging them to let me stay with them. I could get a tutor. I could go to local schools. I could—God. I offered them bargains and blackmail and tears.

"I remember that sunset. Pinks and lavender and soft orange streaked the sky, without a hint of a breeze. When we climbed back on board later that night, we were all too upset to enjoy it. My mother had strung little twinkle lights in the rigging, and they r-reflected in the almost mirror-calm water as we set sail back to our port." Serena's voice hitched, and she held her breath for a few heartbeats until she could marshal her emotions.

"She prepared my favorite foods to eat out on deck under the stars. The last supper. I was too upset to eat. By that point, I was all bargained out. I begged and cried. My mom—my mom hated seeing me that upset. But they weren't going to relent. Finally my father started yelling back. Told me to stop spoiling our last evening together with my attitude. That they knew what was best for me and it was about time for me to stop pouting and accept their decision. It was nonnegotiable. The decision was made. They weren't going to change their minds, and that was final.

"I'd been carrying on for days. But that last night it sank in. Knowing that *nothing* was going to sway them—I went—" She lifted her head, and pulled away to look at him, one hand spread on his chest for balance.

"Oh, God, Duncan," she whispered starkly. "I went *ballistic*. Totally out of control. My powers were strong even at that age, and in the space of a second, a storm erupted, a blinding sheet of rain poured from the sky. Then a hurricane-force wind ripped through the sails and an enormous rogue wave swamped us. The boat capsized. They drowned. I didn't. My—my *temper* killed them."

He cradled her hot face in his hands, hurting for her. "It was a tragic accident. You were just a kid." He tilted her chin up, forcing her to meet his gaze. "Nobody could ever blame a child for not understanding the strength of her powers. C'mon, Serena. You're an incredibly bright woman. With all the interaction you've had with kids over the years, kids in the worst possible human condition, you know they aren't mini-adults. Impulse control takes years to develop in a normal child. Someone with your strong powers probably had an even harder time trying to harness your abilities. It was an accident, sweetheart. You'd never intentionally harm another person. It isn't part of who you are."

Closing his eyes against her pain, Duncan brushed her trembling mouth with his. Her lips clung, and he stroked his tongue across the seam. Serena's hands slid up his chest, the cadence of breath changed subtly to a sigh as she circled his neck with her arms and welcomed him inside.

He kissed her tenderly, loving the way she participated without shyness. Loving the taste of her. The texture of the inside of her mouth. Hot and sweet and Serena. Not vulnerable, but strong and confident, despite reliving the childhood horror.

He lifted his head, brushing his thumb across her cheek. "Let me help you forget." He offered a small memory loss. A magical patch to her pain. "Or let me at least help lessen it."

Her fingers tightened on the back of his neck, drawing his mouth back to hers. "I don't want to f-forget."

"Then tell me what I can do to take away the pain."

Ah, Jesus. He recognized the challenge in her beautiful eyes. He was so screwed.

"Make love to me, Duncan." Openmouthed, she kissed him. She was glad she'd told him, but she didn't want to talk anymore.

The taste of him was intoxicating. Apparently it didn't matter how many times they kissed, Serena had the same reaction. He set her blood on fire, and made her breathless with wanting him.

He started to pull away, but she made soothing noises and twisted her fingers in his hair, drawing him back again to her eager mouth. He wanted to talk. She didn't. She traced the smile on his lips with the tip of her tongue while she slid her hand down his belly. Wrapping her fingers around the hard, satiny length of him, she thrilled when he shuddered at her touch.

He slid his hand up the inside of her thigh, and she parted her legs for him as he reciprocated. "God, you're perfect," he murmured against her lips.

She was also wet and exquisitely tender, but his touch was gentle as he explored the slick folds. Serena murmured her pleasure, tightening her hold around his penis as her own pleasure mounted.

Would she ever get enough of him? She didn't want to answer that question. Not even in her wildest fantasies had she conjured up this level of need. She'd never imagined this kind of saturating pleasure, this high tension level of pure damn-the-world, all-encompassing *lust*. Not even in her most carnal, erotic fantasies.

Her brain disengaged as Duncan slid two fingers inside her. It felt like heaven and ratcheted up her desire several more, impossible, notches. "Don't. Don't. Don't," she chanted against his mouth, not wanting to come without him. Her body tightened inexorably. And so did her fingers.

Duncan chuckled against her lips. "Don't break that off, sweetheart. We're going to need it. I need to be inside you."

She moaned as he withdrew his hand, she was *so* close . . .

The next minute she found herself straddling his hips. "You're in charge," he said smiling up at her, his fingers tightening on her hips.

Serena sucked in a quivering breath and braced her hands on his chest. "As it should be." She impaled herself on his stiffened length. "My turn to drive you mad." She rose a little, then slid back down. The sensation was breath-stealingly exquisite.

"What a way to—Jesus, Fury—go."

She wanted it to last and last, but the waves of pleasure were impossible to resist, and they crashed together in a mind-blowing orgasm that left them both limp, sweaty, and satiated.

Serena collapsed on his chest, burying her face against his damp neck. She felt the manic pounding of his heart against her breast. It matched the pounding of her own rapid heartbeat perfectly.

Duncan smoothed his hand down her back. "Had enough?"

God. Yes. Exhausted, out of breath, and boneless, it took energy, but she managed to put some bite in her voice. "Nuh-uh. You?"

He started to laugh. "You know, if we keep this one-upmanship thing going, we're going to kill each other, don't you?"

Satiated, she pushed his damp hair off his forehead, surprised that she still had enough strength to lift her hand. "Hmm. But what a way to g—"

Still smiling, Duncan waited for her to finish the sentence. Instead he heard a faint—he chuckled—snore. "Serena?" When she didn't answer, he materialized a light cotton sheet, covering their sweat-dampened bodies. Shifting her into a more comfortable position against him, Duncan rested his face against her silky hair.

Oh, yeah. He was *so* screwed.

"I hate hospitals, don't you?" Serena said as they walked down the long corridor to Henry's room, her heels clicking on the linoleum floor. The soft fragrance of jasmine drifted from her swinging hair, blocking out the stink of antiseptic and illness.

"I've been in too many to care one way or the other." He repositioned the coat he was carrying over what was becoming a permanent condition caused by her nearness, her fragrance, and the soft curve of her cheek. Christ, this *thing* was powerful. And at the moment, damned inconvenient.

"I'll bet you have. If you insist on beating people up and shooting at them, it's only logical they'd retaliate," she told him unsympathetically.

His lips twitched at her prissy tone. "Well, there is that." The memory of her naked superimposed itself over the Serena the Morning After. Her hair, in a ponytail that swung against her back as she walked, was both seductive and sweetly innocent. She was casually dressed in jeans, boots, and a fluffy, mango-colored sweater, a thick brown coat over her arm. She was going directly from Germany to Schpotistan. And despite her being covered practically from head to toe, Duncan wanted her again, with an urgency that was starting to scare the crap out of him. He'd never craved a woman as he craved Serena. His brain was consumed with her.

He reminded himself that they weren't kids anymore. They were thirty-three now. Single. Available. And God only knew—willing. But every instinct in his body urged him to run, as far and fast as possible.

If he could fool himself into believing that what he felt was purely physical, it would make him feel a damn sight better. But he was a realist, there was nothing laid-back about the intensity of his emotions for Serena.

Be that as it may, he needed to address the problem

of how he felt, and what the hell he could do about it, soon. Very soon. The longer he put off the inevitable, the harder it was going to be. For both of them.

By tacit agreement they hadn't discussed Paradise Island since they'd left it the night before. Duncan had teleported her home, then gone back to his London flat where his sheets still smelled of her.

He'd always been honest with the women he dated. Any other woman, and by now he would have already told her up front that nothing could come of a relationship between them. Some walked away, some stuck around, some hoped for the best.

Perhaps that was part of his incredibly strong draw to Serena. She didn't need any explanations, she didn't have to be convinced. Not only could he tell her about the ancient Curse, he actually had told her, and she understood it. And its ramifications.

"You've been shot four times, had surgery on your kidneys, had your appendix removed, and I counted at least five knife wounds. Did I miss anything?"

She'd had a damn good look at his body last night.

He'd had a crush on her since first grade. He'd lusted after her by the time they were sixteen. He'd wanted to kill Trey when the two of them had started dating. Jealousy didn't even come into it. He'd felt feral seeing his friend with the woman he l—*lusted* after.

Thinking about how he felt—hell—wallowing in his . . . *feelings* was a useless endeavor. Last night had been an aberration. A lowering of his shields.

He realized they'd stopped walking, and Serena was looking up at him, a frown between her brows. "Hello?"

"Yeah, you missed something." He touched a hand to the back of his head, remembering her fingers tangled in his hair as he pressed his head to her breasts.

"I was hit on the head a couple of years ago." In Libya. Tango's bomb had detonated twenty-two seconds early, jettisoning shrapnel all over hell and gone. The percussion had thrown him, head first, into a truck parked nearby. He'd been unconscious for a week. "That one required twenty-seven staples."

Want to kiss all my old war wounds better? Want to touch me? Make love until we can't move again? Christ, he had it bad. His emotional shields weren't just lowered. They were down, and blown to shit, just like that tango's bomb two years ago.

"That explains the brain damage," Serena said lightly, pushing open a door. "This is Henry's roo— Oh," she said, surprised to see Henry already had a visitor. "Hi, Trey."

Trey's head jerked around when he heard them come in. For a second he didn't look any more pleased to see them than Duncan was to see him. What the hell was Trey doing here? After his initial surprise, Trey immediately rose from the straight-backed chair beside the bed, smiling his relaxed, easygoing smile as he walked toward them. "Hey, guys. Fancy meeting you here."

Yeah whatever, Duncan thought instinctively. *She's mine, asshole.* He tried to ignore his flare of irritation as they shook hands briefly. Focusing beyond Trey, he got his first look at Henry.

Ah, Christ. His friend was hooked up to tubes, monitors, drips, and looked more dead than alive.

Duncan had known Henry was in a coma, but seeing him like this made him confront the possibility of Henry's mortality.

Serena slipped her cold hand into his. Duncan tightened his fingers around hers, drawing her closer to his body. If it bothered him seeing Henry like this, it must scare her a helluva lot worse.

"Hey beautiful. No ill effects from the fire?"

Fuck you, Duncan thought with unexpected savagery. *Back off.*

"No." She smiled at Trey. "I am woman, hear me roar. Winning trumps *losing* every time. Better luck next time, boys. Oh. No." Her eyes went wide and wicked with humor. "Sorry. *I'm* going to win that one, too. Just to put you both out of your misery."

"Competitive as always, Fury." Trey shook his head. "If you win you'll shock the Council by being the first woman Head in hundreds of years. Give me a kiss hello, before you're my boss."

It pleased Duncan that, when Trey tried to kiss her, she turned her head in time for his mouth to miss hers. He bussed her cheek instead. "The Head of Council isn't your boss, Sparky. It's an *arbitrator* position."

"What are you doing here?" Duncan demanded before their friendly fucking repartee made him puke. As far as he knew, Trey hadn't see Henry since the other man had taught part-time at wizard school some fifteen years ago. Trey wasn't the sentimental sort.

"Serena told me about Henry. I liked—*like* the old guy. It's not a crime to come visit him, is it?"

"Of course not," Serena assured him. She let go of

Duncan's hand, and crossed to sit in the chair Trey had just vacated. Scooting closer to the bed, she lifted the old man's hand, slipping her own beneath it. Her fingers trembled as she curled them around Henry's. "Hi Poppy, it's Serena," she said cheerfully. "Duncan and Trey came to visit you, too.

"Did Trey tell you the three of us are all finalists for your job on the Council?"

Duncan caught Trey's eye, and jerked his head toward the door. "Let's give them a minute."

Trey nodded, following him out into the hall, letting the door swing shut behind him. He gave Duncan a curious look. "What's the deal between you and Fury? Every time I see you lately, you're together."

Duncan leaned against the wall, most of his attention on Serena agonizing over the only family she had left. He gave Trey a mild look. "We're all Testing for the same position, remember?"

Trey grinned as he took up a position against the wall. "If you think you're going to get lucky, forget it. Unless she's changed for the better, she won't put out."

Duncan thought of Serena's cool hair spread across his stomach and thighs as her mouth drove him mindless. "Is that so?"

"I dated her twice, remember? That year in tenth grade. And for a couple of months again, several years ago. She might be hotter than hell, but I had blue balls both times. Too bad the gift wrap is nothing short of spectacular, but there's no prize inside." Trey materialized a Coke. In a glass. With ice. He lifted it to his mouth.

"Anything new on the killer?"

"Not yet. It would help if we could pin down a motive."

Trey drank from his glass. "Maybe the two men had a common enemy?"

"Could be," Duncan muttered noncommittally. It was frustrating to have so little to work with. "Any word on the streets?"

Trey laughed. "I told you I don't do *streets*, Edge. And I'm not likely to learn anything about a serial killer in the circles I *do* move in. My acquaintances are more likely to dabble in insurance fraud than murder."

Which just proved, Duncan thought dryly, that bad guys moved in every socioeconomic level. He wasn't going to waste his breath debating that with Culver. "Nose around anyway."

"Like James Bond?"

"Yeah. Exactly like double-o-seven."

"I'll start with all the women I've screwed," Trey said with a lascivious smile. "Pillow talk garners the most intimate, delicious information."

"I just want to know who knows what about the deaths of these wizards." Duncan leaned against the wall, and stuck his hands in his pockets. He wondered if he should go inside and see how Serena was doing. "Pillow talks," he told Trey, annoyed, "unless you're counting wizards in that number, are useless."

Trey winked as two young nurse aides walked past them. "I've fucked plenty of female wizards, Edge," he bragged, turning his head to watch the giggling duo disappear around a corner. "Plenty. I'll start with them. See if I can help you do your job. Make you look good. That work for you?"

"I'd appreciate you doing whatever you can to help," Duncan said mildly.

As tempting as it was to shoot his fist into Trey's teeth for being such an asshole, he wasn't prepared to leave any stone unturned. Still, Trey was in the right place to have reconstructive surgery done after he was pounded to a fucking pulp. It surprised him how intensely he disliked Culver today. "Catching this guy before he kills again is imperative." He could hear the soft sound of Serena's voice behind the closed door as she did a monologue for Henry. He wasn't totally sure if he believed that Henry could hear her, but he understood Serena's need to try to reach him. This must be ripping out her heart. He'd seen her at Martha's funeral—almost inconsolable. Serena didn't accept death well. Why would she?

The dead people in Duncan's life deserved to die, but Serena didn't live in his world. Ice chinked as Trey twirled his glass between his fingers, and he also turned his attention to the closed hospital door. "At first I thought she was a lesbo, you know? Then I finally realized that she's just one of those unfortunate women who have absolutely no sex drive. Probably why she married Campbell. For *her* a match made in heaven. No sex and a shitload of money. For him a hot bit of eye candy to show off to his associates. At his age I doubt he could get it up even if he had a splint taped around it."

"Probably," Duncan agreed blandly, before he changed the topic. Trey was the last person he'd talk to about Serena's sexuality. "What do you do for a living?" He'd never been interested enough to do a background check. He knew Trey came from money. But maybe he'd wanted to make something of himself, instead of riding on his family's coattails.

"Import/export." Trey pushed away from the wall, getting rid of his drink at the same time. "Tchotchkes from China, electronics from Japan. There's a shitload of money in *crap*." He glanced at his watch. "I have a lunch date, gotta go. Tell Serena I hope Henry recovers. I'll see you guys at the next Test."

Trey waited until a nurse, walking toward them with a tray, slipped into a room. Then he vanished.

Duncan frowned. Had Trey always had such disregard for women? If he had, Duncan hadn't noticed it over the years. Or was he just especially attuned to it because of what he and Serena had shared last night?

He was profoundly pleased that Serena had never had sex with the other man. He'd hated the two of them dating, imagining . . . Imagining Trey doing what he and Serena had done last night had just about killed him.

Years ago, he'd agonized, for an embarrassingly long time, about stepping up to the plate. Telling her how he felt—fuck—breaking the two of them up so he could have her. The problem had been that Serena had been fully engaged in her relationship with Trey. And Duncan, even back then when he'd been a randy teenager, had respected that she'd made her choice.

And maybe, he thought, absently watching a woman emerge into the corridor wheeling an IV stand, followed by what appeared to be several members of her family. Maybe he'd known even then just how dangerous to his future Serena could be.

Duty o'er love was the choice you did make.

He, Gabriel, and Caleb had all agreed to stop the Curse from continuing for different reasons. His main reason was, and had always been, that if somehow, the Curse *were* broken, he might lose his powers. And while his brothers seemed capable of having lives without magic, to Duncan that was who he *was*. A wizard.

He wasn't willing to take the chance that he'd lose his powers. And if the Tests played out as he expected them to do, Serena having won Test One notwithstanding, he'd become Head of the Wizard Council. And the most powerful wizard of all. The only way for him to control his own destiny.

He wanted that. He'd always wanted that. And by God, he was going to have it.

CHAPTER ELEVEN

Serena went to Schpotistan while Duncan shimmered directly to T-FLAC's HQ in Montana. The underground command center took up a footprint the equivalent of five city blocks, and was four stories deep underground.

The bottom floor housed the nerve center of the organization. Direct satellite feed to triple-mounted plasma screens. Fiber optic connections between a wall of surveillance screens from two dozen simultaneous live shots, 3-D infrared imaging superimposed over the topographical map of the Middle East. Wireless and Bluetooth keyboards, voice-recognition-capable phones on every desk.

"Patch into the T-FLAC radar sat." Duncan stood behind Juanita Salazar, the specialist assigned to his team, as her nimble fingers plugged in the coordinates he'd just given her. He had a hunch on the recent suspect movements of the Korean satellite. And a few other things. But first things first. "Hey," he greeted Gary Landis as he joined them.

"Hey back. What'cha got for me?" Landis asked Salazar.

Without looking up, Salazar, who rarely talked

unless it was to make a specific point, handed him a thick file folder of satellite images while still typing like a one-handed maniac. She was a heavyset, rather plain young woman, with frizzy black hair and a permanent frown. She was cranky, insubordinate, and brilliant at what she did. She had surprisingly pretty hands, and was as talented on the keyboard as a grand pianist on a Steinway. She could also be counted on to locate the tangos just by analyzing the aerial views of the Earth's hot spots. Juanita was so good, in fact, that she could practically tell you what the tangos had for breakfast.

But the best thing about her was that she anticipated everything. Knew what to report to who, and when the information would be needed most.

"Just looked at that." Duncan nodded at the file in the other man's hand. "When Lark alerted us to the slight anomaly of the Korean satellite, it was starting to shift. Supposed to be a communications satellite, which means it should be doing a twenty-four-hour rotation, making it practically stationary in respect to Earth. Right now it should be over the Yeongi-Gongju region of Korea."

He indicated the printout. "But look where it is now. Way the hell off its orbit. Way too fucking close to Russia. And check this out." He indicated two more satellites, each marked by Juanita on the computer as off its original orbit. Hovering in the same vicinity as the Korean one. "No way is that a coincidence."

Duncan gripped the back of Salazar's chair. "You got the projected new orbit?" He knew where those three satellites were headed.

She put the graphs and schematics on the screen. Eyes narrowed and chest tight, he cursed.

God damn it. He was right.

Russia.

"Overlay it in the optical feed, please, Juanita. Closer. Yeah, right over Schpotistan, close in on the coordinates. That's good. Hold it right there." He had an aerial view of the roof of the warehouse.

"What's the building?" Landis fished in his pocket for his glasses, put them on, and moved beside Duncan to see better. "Looks like an old warehouse of some sort. Middle of nowhere. Not that I don't trust your instincts, Edge. But I'm having a hard time connecting the dots."

"Serena Campbell has some of the Foundation's top scientists working on a project that's in that warehouse right now."

Where she'd been shot. Was there a correlation between the two incidents?

"Okay," the other man said doubtfully. "What makes you think the satellites have anything to do with the Campbell Foundation and a do-good project?" He glanced from the Interactive Global Geostationary Weather Satellite Images back to Duncan.

"When I think Russia, Siberia, et cetera, I think Red Mantis," Salazar said in her quiet, serious voice. "I don't see a tango group wanting to solve world hunger. Do you?"

No. Of course he didn't. "Show me the Foundation location."

Salazar switched views without comment.

Duncan kept his attention on the aerial shot of Serena's building. The Campbell Foundation logo was painted on the roof of a small hangar housing the Foundation's helicopter. "I agree with you about Red Mantis. The analysis department is already ascertaining if, as well as their altered orbit pattern, there've been any changes to the Korean satellite. Some fucking onboard device that would change the velocity vector."

"I just sent the new intel to Analysis," Juanita inserted, tapping her keyboard to bring up an official-looking notice. "And here's what North Korea wants us to know. They claim that satellite is operating for NOAA, as well as weather, streaming news, and music radio."

"Bullshit," Duncan said succinctly. Unless the NKs had no idea someone was using their satellite for something more nefarious than streaming the news, but that was highly unlikely. "Sergei Konanykhine and his Red Mantis don't have a history of blowing things up."

The reminder was unnecessary, as Red Mantis was on T-FLAC's Most Wanted list and every operative, from junior level on up, dreamed of being the one to catch the bastards. Konanykhine manufactured cheap, synthetic narcotics by the ton, distributing them all over the world. In the last two years, there'd been a concentrated dump in the United States. Red Mantis ruled the Russian underworld by intimidation, murder, blackmail, and drugs. The baddest of the bad guys.

"Perhaps he's blackmailing some small European country," Landis offered. "You know, give us X billion, and we won't kill every man, woman, and child in your country? He was detained in Switzerland three days ago—"

"And as of yesterday he was out, back home in the protective arms of Mother Russia."

Frustrated, he lightly tapped the back of Salazar's chair with a curled fist. "We'll explore every angle, just like always," Duncan said shortly.

Was he overreacting? Hell, just the thought that he might be alarmed him. He was good at his job because he wasn't an alarmist. Contrary to Serena's opinion of him, he thought through and analyzed situations before taking action. He might do that faster than most. But he did it.

Now, he suspected because Serena was in the mix, he was second-guessing himself, and seeing danger where there might be none.

Red Mantis was obviously the better suspect for satellite rearrangement, but the attack on the warehouse didn't fit their modus operandi.

This, he thought, annoyed with himself, was why it was complicated bringing a woman into his world. Everything was suspect. No matter how illogical. His knee-jerk reaction to the intel was that somehow the satellites were closing in on Serena. While it was not logical in the grand scheme of things, Siberia was where she'd been shot. Duncan didn't believe in coincidence.

Three satellites out of orbit. Three satellites heading for Russia. Three satellites that could be carrying weapons of mass destruction right now. If that was the plan, then Europe as they knew it could be destroyed at the press of a remote control button.

His cell phone vibrated from the holder on his belt. *Serena.* He flipped it open. *Lark.* "Now?"

As soon as he'd ID'd the caller, he instantly went into mental battle mode. This wasn't the best time for a Wizard Council Test, but nobody was asking him. Test Two. Although it surprised him that Lark would give him a heads up.

"That'd be cheating. Don't be so eager, Hot Edge," she said lightly. "Test Two will be here before you know it. Where are you?"

"T-FLAC HQ."

"Ah, a hop and a skip away then. Gabriel wants to see you. Twenty-thirty sharp. He's convened an emergency, psi/spec ops meeting. Levels one and two. See you there in an hour." She disconnected as she always did when she was done giving instructions.

"Problems," Landis guessed as Duncan put the phone away.

"Sounds like. My brother Gabriel just convened a level one and two meeting." Landis was a three.

"Schpotistan is up," Juanita told Duncan. Their own satellite was now in orbit thirty-six thousand kilometers above Siberia, and would reveal millimeter-scale elevation shifts across a wide area of land. What *hadn't* Serena told him about what the Foundation was doing there?

"What now?" Frowning with worry, Landis slid off the edge of the desk. "Fuck! Think *another* one of us was killed?"

One emergency at a time, Duncan thought as he held up a hand for the other man to hold that thought. "Juanita? Hand off whatever else you were working on. Concentrate on this. I want to know if any other sats are out of their regular orbits. See if we have any more moving into place where they don't belong. Everybody. No matter who or what their affiliation, we've got to identify it and track them.

"*Everybody* up there," he repeated. "Including the U.S. Air Force's DSP and SEWS." The Air Force's Defense Support Program, and their Satellite Early Warning System were the United States's early warning against attacks from the bad guys, but he was leaving no stone unturned.

She didn't glance up, nor did her fingers stop tapping on the keyboard as she absorbed the info. "There are twenty-five hundred satellites currently orbiting the Earth. Not to mention thousands of other artificial objects."

"Only two thousand, four hundred, and ninety-seven satellites to go, then," he told her dryly. "And put this infrared sat com view up on another screen. Closely monitor the Foundation building twenty-four/seven."

"But I thought we agreed that Red Mantis wasn't behind the attack on the two of you at the warehouse," Landis said.

"My gut is telling me something different."

Serena was one of those heat sources moving about inside that building. He might be wrong in thinking the movements of the satellites had any correlation to her project. Nevertheless, he was going to keep an eye on what was happening in Schpotistan until he was sure it *wasn't*.

"I'll need five people on my team," Salazar agreed without expression. "Starting immediately."

"Done. Keep me posted on even the *smallest* anomaly."

"You got it."

Duncan motioned Landis to accompany him to the elevators. "What makes you think that Gabriel's meeting might have something to do with the wizard killings? Have you heard from Hart and Brown?" Each had formed a team and were assigned to the wizard murders. All in all T-FLAC, as well as T-FLAC/psi, had upward of fifty people searching for clues, gathering information, and bringing it back to HQ to their analysts and profilers. The fact that someone was strong enough to get past not just one, but two high-level wizards to kill them was chilling.

"Haven't found anything yet. But we *will*. I guarantee you that. This feels like more than a rogue wizard gone bad to me. You?"

"Yeah," Landis said as they entered the elevator. They could've teleported to the surface. But they couldn't talk while shimmering. "We're missing something big here. A *motive* would help."

Duncan pressed the up button, and the doors slid closed, blocking out the bright lights and low hum of Op/Tech Support. "Slayings were grisly and graphic. Some sick son of a bitch is enjoying his work too fucking much. See if you can give me anything new in"— he glanced at his watch, "forty minutes."

Thirty-five of which he'd use to pay Serena a visit in Siberia.

Serena shut the common room door behind her and stepped into the frigid hall. She immediately missed the warmth and camaraderie within and was just glad that she'd remembered her coat for the short walk to where Joanna was busy working in the computer lab, too busy to even meet them all for food. It felt good to stretch her legs, she thought as her breath plumed in front of her.

Her skin prickled and she slowed her steps.

There'd been no noise, but she knew Duncan was behind her. And it wasn't her wizard "radar" alone that alerted her to his presence, but an acute sensitivity to the man himself. Her body tensed with immediate desire. Anyone walking out of one of the doors leading off this corridor could see them. She didn't care.

She turned her head and felt her smile bloom from deep inside seeing Duncan a few feet away. God, he looked wonderful. He'd changed into jeans and a T-shirt that showed off his masculine torso and turned casual into deliciously sexy.

A puff of white air escaped from her mouth and it amused her no end. It was too freaking cold in the unheated corridor to be this hot. But just looking at this man made her feel hot and shivery all over.

He probably wasn't even chilled without a coat, and she enjoyed the view. They'd only parted in Germany a few hours ago, yet seeing him now made her heart knock, and an aching longing well up deep inside her.

How foolish to feel tongue-tied after all these years. Especially after, or perhaps because of, what they'd recently shared. It was wrong, and she knew it, which would explain her incredible response to him. If Nairne had felt this way about Magnus five hundred years ago it was no wonder she'd cursed the man after he'd dumped her.

"Hi," she managed in a husky voice, vividly remembering the feel of his hands on her skin.

Unsmiling, Duncan had no problem with communication. His eyes, despite the brilliant overhead lighting, were pools of shadow as he closed the space between them and thrust his fingers into her hair. Cupping her skull, he tilted her face up to his.

"What's in there?" He jerked his chin toward a nearby door.

"Janit—"

The supply closet smelled faintly of industrial-strength cleaner, and was cool and dark. Duncan's lips were hot and hungry. Her immediate response was a sigh of pure pleasure as his mouth opened over hers. Wrapping her arms around his neck, she stood up on her toes to get even closer to the delicious heat of him. Vaguely she noticed the disappearance of her thick coat, but she wasn't cold. Not in Duncan's arms. Sweet shivers rippled across her skin as he made love to her mouth with a ferocity that felt almost like desperation. Serena knew the feeling.

He sucked on her tongue, mimicking a far more intimate act. Her pulse hammered through her veins as he palmed her breast through her cashmere sweater. Her nipples were already hard and aching for his touch, and when he gently squeezed one between his fingers, she moaned. She felt a tremor of intense desire going through his large body as her tongue glided around his. *More. More. More.* She rubbed her hips against the hardness of his erection as she sampled the fascinating textures inside his mouth, the serrations of his teeth, the slick wetness of his tongue, the sensual softness on the other side of his lips.

Serena feasted on his mouth like a starving woman, while Duncan slid his hands down her hips and around to cup her behind in the hard grip of his fingers. He lifted her slightly, rubbing her against his erection a lot harder than she'd been doing moments before.

Wet, dizzy with lust, she whimpered. The taste, the texture, the smell of him, made her want to climb his body and beg him to take her right there in the janitor's closet. Standing up. In the pitch dark. Without a lock on the door. In a room anyone could walk into at any moment. She didn't care. Her body was melting like hot honey and he was all she could think about. She wanted Duncan to back her against a wall, dematerialize her clothes, and ram into her body. *Hard.* Over and over and over until they melted to the floor in a puddle of lust. And then she wanted to climb on top of him, and do it all over again. And even then she knew she'd never get enough of him.

Feeling the staccato beat of his heart against her breast, Serena came up for a gasp of air. Every cell in her body pulsed and throbbed with need. "I want you," she whispered roughly against his damp mouth. "Here. Now."

"Hold that thought, sweetheart," he said regretfully, his voice thick. "I'm not taking you in a broom closet."

She moved her lips just far enough away to speak. His body, hard and aroused, was flush against hers. She liked it that way. "What *are* you doing here?"

she whispered in the darkness. Arms still around his neck, she ran her fingers gently over his ear, learning the shape and texture.

He nibbled her chin. "I was just in the neighborhood."

"On the way to where?" She smiled as his mouth trailed like a promise up her cheek. "The Arctic Circle?" She tilted her head so he could kiss the cords in her neck.

He used his teeth to scrape a sensual path up to her ear, making her shudder. "Gabriel's."

She could hardly breathe, let alone speak or think. "W-weren't you already *in* Montana?" That was where he'd told her the headquarters of the counterterrorist organization he worked for was located.

"Had forty-five minutes to kill. Want to use them all chatting?"

Not just no. But *hell* no. Hard. Fast. Now. Apparently that was her new mantra. "I hope you don't expect to just show up for a quickie whenever you feel like it," she told him coolly, nipping his lip.

His eyebrows went up. "You mean that was an *option*?"

Serena kissed him before answering. *Yes.* "No." She loved teasing him. She loved the repartee. She loved the challenge. She loved—having sex with him, she thought, shying away from a word that could never, *ever*, be in her vocabulary in the same sentence as the name Duncan Edge.

"Damn. That's disappointing." He brushed a lingering kiss on her mouth before withdrawing his hands. He stepped away, leaving her chilled and lost in the darkness and once again wanting his coat.

"Gabriel just called a level one and two meeting," he told her briskly.

Banking the sensual fire that was blazing inside her body, just so she could think, Serena knew that if Duncan's older brother had called a meeting, he had good cause.

As a level one wizard, she was expected to attend. Damn. This couldn't have come at a more inconvenient time. Something was going on with Joanna, and Serena couldn't ignore it. The woman had lost weight, and developed circles beneath her eyes. If Joanna was on her way to a meltdown, then it was Serena's job to stop her, no matter what. Joanna was too important to this project. As in key.

Especially since the other woman had explained how they could harness energy from a satellite to power the thermal blanket. Things were finally moving forward again. The panels of thermal material were at this moment loaded, and en route on the Siberian railroad headed for the test location ten miles away.

Serena rubbed her thumb pad over the crisp hair on Duncan's forearm. "This isn't a good time for me to be away, the thermal blanket will be here in a couple of hours, and there are a million things my team needs my help with. Won't there be enough wizards in attendance to make my being there irrelevant? Could you ask him to excuse me, this once?"

Duncan touched her shoulder. "You want to be Master Wizard, don't you? That means showing up at all the meetings. Unless you want to concede your position."

The sensual fire snuffed out. "I didn't say I wanted

to concede. But this project is at a serious cross-roads. Making this work will mean the difference between life and death for millions of people." A mop flew off the wall. Damn it.

"I'm not belittling that, Serena." He caught the mop in midair and sent it back to the rack on the wall. "I know how important what you're doing is—but this meeting is important, too. Gabriel wouldn't call it if it wasn't. I'd like you to come. It'll just take an hour, and I'd feel better knowing . . ."

Her bullshit-o-meter made a faint mental clink. "Knowing?"

"I'd just like you to come."

This had nothing to do with sex. Nothing to do with Duncan feeling lovey-dovey and wanting her by his side. He was up to something. What?

"I wish I could." She tried to figure his angle. Because, knowing Duncan, there was one. Either he wanted her in Montana for—? Or he wanted her away from Schpotistan. Why? Or he wanted to keep an eye on her—because? She had no clue. She magically turned on the light, wanting to read the expression on his handsome, conniving face.

She blinked into the sudden brightness. "But I can't. I have to pick the millions over the few, and I hope the Council will understand. Send my regrets."

"Damn it, Fury, I—"

"Have an important meeting to attend," Lark finished for him as she suddenly materialized between them, making the small janitorial space even smaller. "Hello, Serena."

The other woman was dressed all in black, the soft fabric of her skirts fluttering around long, black, patent leather boots with impossibly high heels. She didn't look surprised to find them in a closet.

"Hi," Serena shifted to give Lark a little more room. "I was just—"

"Telling Hot Edge that you couldn't make the meeting. Totally cool." Lark glanced at Duncan through kohl-rimmed eyes. "Let's go."

Duncan's mouth tightened. "Don't interfere, Lark. Serena needs to stick close to me."

"How sweet. But not at the moment." Lark took his upper arm in a firm grip and they vanished.

Serena shook her head and smiled, grateful for the reprieve. "Thanks for coming, y'all," she said mockingly. Pushing open the door, she headed in the direction she'd been going before she'd been so warmly interrupted.

CHAPTER TWELVE

She was a selfish, horrible mother, Joanna knew. Her beloved son was God only knew where, and yet here she was, plain, responsible, save-the-world Joanna, lying in bed with her lover instead of being out there herself, searching under every rock until she found her baby.

She was a poor excuse as a colleague as well. Henry was a man she respected enormously. He'd been her mentor. He was brilliant and kind, and had given her the opportunity to be an integral part of the Campbell Foundation straight out of MIT. He'd also introduced her to Serena, a woman Joanna considered a friend as well as a boss.

Yet she couldn't even conjure up enough emotion to feel terrified for the safety of Casey, or guilty for not going to see Henry. She frowned. She didn't even really have the enthusiasm to *care* that she didn't care.

Maybe she was beyond clinical depression and the only thing to do was have more sex with Grant.

"Have you been to see your boss yet?" Grant's question came out in a laid-back way, as satiated-sounding as she felt. He lay beside her, smoking a thin, smelly French cigarette, with the saucer he used as an ashtray balanced on his flat stomach. Joanna wanted to tell him to put the cigarette out, but it was just too much effort.

She'd had more sex in the last few months than she'd had in her entire life. "He's in Germany," she pointed out lazily, stroking his calf with her foot. It was early afternoon, and instead of being downstairs diligently working to pull this project together, she was up in her room. Drinking wine and having sex with her lover. Her lips curled down. What was her world coming to?

"We could teleport together," he offered, taking a drag and blowing out a cloud of thick smoke. "I don't want you to go alone, darling."

If she went alone, and somehow another wizard discovered that she'd teleported, there would be a lot of questions asked, Joanna knew. Grant would get into a great deal of trouble with the Council if it was discovered that he'd gifted her with extra powers. Halves couldn't teleport. Besides being nervous that someone would catch her doing it, shimmering gave her a headache. It was an acquired skill.

The fact that Grant had given her the power was sweet and loving. And was another small sign of how much they loved one another. The trust they shared.

Her stomach tensed as she remembered going back in to speak with Henry, once she'd realized that she didn't have a vital bit of technical information for the thermal blanket. Henry frequently forgot to document his work, and it was common for one of them to have to ask him for something they needed.

Just as she'd been asking Henry for the information, he'd collapsed. It had frightened her on more than one level.

The kidnappers wanted the technology for the thermal blanket in exchange for her son's life. And by God she was going to give them what they wanted. A rare surge of emotion made her lightheaded, or maybe it was the stink of the cigarette.

"There's nothing I can do for Henry." She swung her legs over the side of the bed and slipped on a flannel robe. "The person I want to see is *Casey.*"

Grant blew out a smoke ring. "I know. Believe me, I want your son to be safe, just as much as you do."

Her heart ached as she heard the sincerity in his voice. "The thermal blanket will be here first thing in the morning." She crossed to a small table to pour herself another half glass of wine. Grant's dark suit hung on the outside of her closet door. He was very particular about his clothing. She picked a speck of lint off his pale yellow shirt and said over her shoulder, "Henry would want me to be here to oversee the placement. More important, I don't want to take the chance of missing a call."

She held up the almost empty bottle of wine. Grant nodded, grinding out his cigarette on the plate before placing it on the bedside table. He was ready to make love again, she saw. As much as she loved him, kissing him after he smoked those vile things was like licking an ashtray. Besides, she was already sore in embarrassing places.

"I'm sorry I asked about him. You're stressed out enough without feeling guilty over not visiting your mentor." He held out his hand. "Come here, baby.

I'll give you a massage, just the way you like it. That will relax you."

And maybe, she thought, padding back to bed, glass and bottle in hand, it didn't matter *what* he tasted like. He loved her more than any man ever had. They would do anything for one another. She knew that. God. She was so, so lucky to have him.

She handed Grant the bottle, left her glass on the side table, and slid across the tangled sheets beside him. As it always did when she was near him, her irritability dissolved within seconds. She remembered that it had been there, but only on a cerebral level. It was as if there was a barrier between herself and her emotions.

Whatever it was. Love. Stress. Insanity for all she knew, Grant kept her on an even keel, and right now she *needed* him.

Tucking her against his body, he sipped his wine. "Do you think a person in a comatose state can hear someone talking to them?" he mused, stroking her arm.

His touch was hypnotic, and the glass of wine she'd drunk earlier had made her sleepy. "I don't know." She didn't want to think of Henry Morgan trapped inside his body, able to hear, but not capable of responding. It would be like being buried alive.

Was this her way to cope with depression? Had she somehow learned to disconnect from her emotions? Joanna wondered about it, not terribly worried one way or another. As Grant petted her, she rested her head in the hollow of his shoulder, and closed her eyes. Then laid her hand on his smooth, sleek chest and stroked his cool skin. No worries, she thought. Grant will take care of everything.

Grant's hand moved off her arm and onto her breast. He played with her nipple, bringing it to an aroused peak. "I've read studies that claim coma patients can hear. That frequently listening to someone talking to them in a normal voice, about things that interest them, could bring them back. I wonder if that's true. Interesting, isn't it?"

"I suppose so." If she didn't know better, she'd think Grant was trying to manipulate her into feeling guilty. Which was insane. He'd been to see her *twice* today. The first time, thank God, right after she'd received her noon video conference call from Casey's kidnappers.

If he hadn't been with her, Joanna might never have stopped crying. He calmed her. He soothed her as no one else could. He was trying *everything* he knew to find her son. He was doing everything he could to help hold her together.

"I'm so grateful I have you," Joanna eyes welled as she leaned over and kissed his chest. "I love you so much."

Grant's fingers gently tugged the back of her hair. "Mm, and I love you. Show me how much, darling, I only have half an hour before I go to my meeting." He pushed her head down his body.

Duncan materialized at Edridge Castle without fanfare. Despite teleporting together, Lark managed to get there before he did. Because the formality of the room required something more than jeans, he'd replaced his casual attire with black slacks and an open-necked white dress shirt en route. Lounging in the big leather easy chair beside the fireplace, Duncan absently juggled three fist-sized spheres of fire. He sat far enough away from the group in the center of the room to give him a few moments to observe everyone before they noticed him.

His brother Gabriel sent a quick glance at the woman huddled on the sofa across the room, then continued talking to Lark and the others. Duncan presumed the woman was Gabriel's mission, the scientist Dr. Eden Cahill. Interesting that his brother had brought her here. He and his brothers had never brought women home.

What an odd group, he thought. Lark looked like a sexy Goth princess, Upton Fitzgerald was an old-fashioned cowboy, and Simon Parrish looked like freaking double-o-seven in a tux, the bow tie loosened. Alex Stone, who should have been in Geneva right now, had arrived wearing a hotel bath towel, and was being magically dressed by an amused Lark.

The only thing this bunch of mismatched people had in common was that they were all high-level wizards. There were several people missing who should have been here. Serena was one. His brother Caleb another. He supposed Trey should be here, too, but was just as glad he wasn't.

Serena had never been to Edridge Castle. She'd find it a kick, Duncan thought. She'd love MacBain, and God only knew, MacBain would adore her.

Jesus. He pulled himself up short.

Was he losing his ever-loving mind? He could never bring Serena here. What they'd already shared was dangerous enough to his future. To his peace of mind. To his sanity.

Damn it. He was not going to bring her home to meet the family so he could get their blessing. Not going to happen.

Ever.

Nairne's Curse felt stronger here. Even more powerful.

He'd be an idiot if he ignored five hundred years of Edge family history. What the hell was he going to do about her? Just thinking about Serena in the most abstract terms had his blood surging, and his heart beating faster. This . . . *thing* they were doing had no future. Was there any point in pursuing a merely physical relationship?

Sex between them was incendiary.

And while Duncan could imagine staying in bed with Serena 24/7, that wasn't the reality.

They had no future.

That decision had been made for them five hundred years ago.

Dragging his mind away from Serena, he scanned the book-lined walls, the heavy leather furniture, the faded, muted carpet underfoot. On the rare occasions when their father had come from Scotland to visit, this had been his office. It was Gabriel's now. And his older brother fit the massive chair behind the desk just fine. Duncan was proud of him. Gabriel had had to become both brother and father figure to his two younger siblings when their parents had died.

Duncan loved Edridge Castle. He'd grown up here. There was a comfort, a feeling of continuity, knowing that the place would always look the same. And that was thanks to MacPain in the ass, who kept things running to his high, exacting standards. He'd go and see the old guy as soon as the meeting adjourned.

Watching everyone through a convenient veil of fire, he looked at the wizards his brother had assembled. He knew everyone in the room, except Dr. Cahill huddled under a blanket on the sofa. He could tell she wasn't a wizard. He doubted she was even a Half. She looked about as out of her element as a hooker at a church social.

His older brother, standing in a group at the center of the room, glanced up and suddenly saw him. "Duncan." His tight expression eased, and he strode across the room.

Duncan rose to slap his brother on the back.

"Caleb?" Gabriel asked, his eyes dark and haunted.

Christ. His brother was *scared*. Gabriel wasn't fucking afraid of *anything*. Wishing he could contact their younger brother, Duncan shook his head. "He's hunting for Shaw, and he warned me that he'd be deep undercover. I left a coded message on his cell."

"Me, too."

Leaning closer, Duncan lowered his voice. "Don't go there, bro. If we haven't heard from him, it's probably because he had to go back in time, following a lead. Chill. If something," he implied the wizards' deaths, "had happened, we'd know." Duncan tapped his chest, right above his heart.

"You're right. I know you are, but I'd feel better if I was sure."

"Ditto. I'll see what I can find out when we're done here."

Lark knew where Caleb was. Duncan would figure out a way to get the woman to tell him. She was a phenomenal control and a powerful wizard in her own right, but the last time he'd needed info it had taken a signed first edition Anne Rice novel to pry it out of her. What next? Bauhaus's classic Goth single about Bela Lugosi?

It would be easier if the woman liked chocolate or jewelry.

Not happy, but accepting that there was nothing else to be done, Gabriel nodded, then went to stand with his back to the massive stone fireplace. "Blaine can catch up when he gets here." He glanced at the wizards. "In the past thirty-seven days, three wizards have been killed."

"*Three?*" Simon Parrish asked, sitting forward.

"Thom Lindley's body was discovered early this morning. The sweepers confirmed ID. Vaporized. Same MO as Townsend and Jamison." Gabriel searched the faces of the people in the room. "We have a rogue wizard. Either one of ours, or an outsider."

"Man," Alex Stone muttered. "What we have here, ladies and gentlemen, is a major clusterfuck. And, Jesus. Look at the timing. Isn't the Council sitting right now to install a new Master Wizard as leader?"

"They are. I'll go talk to them." Duncan juggled five larger balls of naked flame. They were moving so fast they were nothing more than a constantly shifting arc of orange, red, and yellow. The pattern reminded him of Serena's hair.

"Can't get anywhere near them until a new leader has been chosen. Caleb first," Gabriel instructed.

Duncan shook his head meaningfully. If they had any hope of vanquishing this rogue wizard, they couldn't do it if the three of them were together. When he, Gabriel, and Caleb were within visual range, they cancelled out each other's major powers. The thought sent a chill down Duncan's spine.

Losing his powers was his biggest fucking fear.

So while he and Gabriel wanted to make sure Caleb was okay, they couldn't have him with them now anyway.

"One more thing—" Gabriel said grimly. "Tremayne and I are currently working on replicating a robot stolen from Dr. Cahill's lab. Until half an hour ago we didn't connect the deaths of three wizards to our current op. That changed when a man morphing as the Homeland Security agent tried to kill Eden while shimmering."

"Impossible!" Lark slid off the arm of the chair she'd been perched on. "If there'd been anyone but us in this house, palace, castle, *whatever,* in the last twenty-four hours, I would have *felt* him. There's not a particle of residue indicating the presence of an unfamiliar wizard."

"Cloaked," Duncan murmured, adding a gleaming silver dagger to his fireballs. It caught and reflected both the lights and the orange of the fire as it flipped and wheeled high in the air above his head.

"Impossible," Simon inserted. "Okay. Not impossible with the right device, but pretty damn improbable."

"Improbable or not," Gabriel told him, "it's fact. He was here. Which means he wants what we want. Intel on this bot."

"No," the woman on the sofa said flatly. "He didn't want anything to do with the robot. He wanted me *dead*."

The chill skimming Duncan's spine turned to ice. If the rogue wizard had attempted to kill this woman, then it was feasible that he was also responsible for trying to kill Serena.

If the two attacks were connected.

He wasn't the target. *Serena* was.

Or was he getting soft? There didn't seem to be any correlation between the op Gabriel was working on, Artificial Intelligence, and what he was working on, wandering satellites.

"He wanted to frighten you enough to lower your guard so he could extract the data for Rex," Gabriel told the doctor. Duncan looked at his brother's face as he spoke to her. He sounded casual, like his usual controlled self. But his eyes . . . Duncan had never seen that heated look in Gabriel's eyes before. Not ever.

"Excuse me? *I* was the one struggling to breathe as he squeezed the life out of me. You didn't see his eyes." She rubbed her upper arms. "He was . . . *shimmering* so you couldn't catch him."

"What *kind* of device?" Yancy asked. "What kind of device would be capable of cloaking him from *us*?"

"Something ancient," Lark offered, her expression guarded. "An amulet of some sort?" She glanced at the other woman. "Was he wearing anything out of the ordinary? Jewelry of some kind?"

Dr. Cahill frowned. "Nothing I could see."

"Something in his pocket?" Peter Blaine moved to the center of the semicircle. Short and muscular, he was dressed in a slightly too-tight dark suit, and conservative tie that made the pale skin on his neck roll over his yellow collar.

"You're late," Lark snapped, sounding cranky and very unlike her Goth persona.

"Sorry. I've been here long enough to get the gist."

"The *gist*," Gabriel said in a hard voice, "is that we now know that the missing bot and our mysterious intruder are inextricably linked. We know that this person is capable of cloaking himself and blending right in. We know that he's capable of murder. And we know—" He looked from face to face.

"We know, *unequivocally*, that he's assimilating the powers of the wizards he kills."

Joanna poked her head around the door of Serena's small office. "Hi. Do you have a minute?"

"Of course! I was looking for you earlier. Sal mentioned you'd gone upstairs with a headache." Serena rose. "Are you feeling any better?" At Joanna's nod she smiled. "Good. How about a nice hot cup of tea? I just made it."

She'd taken one of the smaller rooms on the ground floor as an office because it was one of the few spaces in the old building that had a working fireplace. The little fire was blazing nicely, and she crossed to the electric kettle to pour water into a waiting teapot.

Serena frowned slightly as her friend walked past her to get to the seating area. Had Joanna suddenly taken up smoking? It seemed unlikely. But her clothing smelled strongly of French cigarettes. A smell Serena distinctly remembered because she'd had a boyfriend in college who'd smoked the things.

"Sure," Joanna blushed and said hurriedly. "Why were you looking for me?"

The blush was interesting, Serena thought, amused as she glanced at her friend just in time to see her cheeks turn bright pink. Had Joanna's "headache" been Denny? She certainly deserved all the joy she could get. She'd wondered if the two of them were having an affair. She'd heard a man's voice late one night as she'd passed Joanna's bedroom door.

"Just a visit, actually," Serena told her easily, fixing the tea. "Sit over there by the fire, I'll bring it to you. Milk, one sugar, right?"

Joanna nodded.

Serena carried two mugs over to the chairs she'd pulled up to the fire. Thank God Joanna had finally come to her. Whatever was putting those dark circles under her friend's eyes needed to be resolved. And Serena had a pretty good idea what the problem was. But how to approach it? Usually she didn't have a problem being confrontational. She preferred things out in the open, and under a bright spotlight. But in this instance she needed to take a gentler approach. Joanna looked ready to collapse.

Handing one of the mugs to her friend, Serena sat on the opposite chair curling her legs under her and leaning against the soft cushions. "After a while it feels a little like a bad reality show out here, doesn't it?"

Were the isolation and loneliness getting to Joanna? Serena came and went as she liked, but the team only took one week off in three. It must feel interminable to have to wait three weeks to be with family and friends.

"I don't mind it." She lowered her eyes.

"You're a stronger person than I am, then." Serena glanced toward her cell phone.

"Are you expecting a call?" Joanna asked, almost hopefully. "I can come back later."

"No, stay. I'm just waiting for a call back from my attorney; we've been playing phone tag."

Joanna sighed, and it had a desperate sound to it. "I hate that game."

Inhaling the calming scent of chamomile wasn't helping Serena's stomach unknot as she wondered what the brothers Grimm were planning now. Which made her think of Duncan, and the real reason he'd shown up here earlier. Taking a sip of her tea, she was grateful for the break Joanna provided. Someone else's problems were usually easier to solve than her own.

"You must miss Casey," she said easily, trying to keep her distraction out of her voice. "How's he liking the new school?"

Joanna's eyes grew damp. "I m-miss him terribly."

Serena leaned over and touched Joanna's cold hand. "Take a few days off. Go and see him."

"I—I can't."

"Of course you can. I'll cover the unloading in the morning. When you get back we'll have the blanket in place."

"Can we talk about something else?" Joanna asked almost desperately.

This was a first. Joanna *always* wanted to talk about her son. "Sure. What would you like to talk about?" Had the boy gotten in trouble at boarding school?

Joanna set her mug down on a nearby table, and stood. "Never mind. This was just—it doesn't matter."

"Of course it matters," Serena said gently, even though her emotional radar was suddenly picking up a huge distress signal. "Please sit down and drink your tea. If you don't want to talk about what's bothering you, we'll talk about something else." She shot the other woman a teasing grin. "We can talk about your new boyfriend."

Joanna, having picked up the mug again, almost choked on a sip of tea, and her eyes went wide. "Boyfriend? What makes you think I have a boyfriend?"

Serena lifted one shoulder slightly. She wasn't going to embarrass Joanna by telling her she'd heard a man in her room the other night. "Nobody here smokes, and unless you've started puffing on Gauloises, I'm guessing it's your friend. I must admit, I do wish you'd talked to me before bringing someone here. Until we can show the world at large that we have a practical way to produce crops, this is still a top-secret project. Which is why Henry and I handpicked everyone on the team.

"But since I know how important this blanket is to you, too, and your judgment has always been sound, it shouldn't be a problem."

Joanna bit her lip as her eyes welled. "I love him,

Serena. I know I should have asked permission to bring him here, but I was scared you'd say no."

Joanna was right. She would have said no to having any unauthorized person on the premises at this time. Still, she was pleased her friend had met someone she cared about, and no harm had been done. "Frankly, I'm thrilled. Nobody deserves a man who loves them to distraction more than you do. I was kind of hoping you and Denny would hook up," she laughed and waved her hand dismissively, "but as long as this guy worships at your feet, I'm ecstatic. Tell me about him. Who is he? Do I know him?"

"He's a full wizard," Joanna said almost shyly as her cheeks pinked. "His name is Grant Cooper, and I'm crazy about him. And yes, before you ask, he's just as crazy about me, and Case."

"He's a full? Well, that explains his mode of transportation, then. He can shimmer in and out. I'm happy for you."

Suddenly animated with sparkling eyes, Joanna smiled. "I've never had a relationship like this. Oh, Serena! He's so handsome, and he's as nice inside as he is outside, but—"

Ah. The *but* was the problem, and probably what had created the dark circles. "But?"

Joanna's shoulders slumped and knuckles went white as she clutched the mug in both hands. "When I'm with him it's almost as though—I don't know. I can't think of anything else. Nothing else is important, or relevant. Not even things that I know are important or relevant. Am I losing my mind?"

"I can relate," Serena told her dryly, feeling the exact same way about Duncan. "And the answer is: you're in love—Uh—"

"—Oh." Serena suddenly found herself standing alone, somewhere cold and dark.

CHAPTER THIRTEEN

The average depth of a stair tread was about twelve inches. The ledge Duncan suddenly found himself standing on was barely eight. Limited visibility was sufficient to orient himself without moving. Taking a minute to let his eyes adjust to the near dark, he realized that he was in some sort of large cavern. A wall of rough hewn rock scraped his back through his shirt, and the air held a chill.

Stalactites hung from the domed ceiling like the serrated teeth of some gigantic fossilized creature. Interestingly, they cast no shadows, despite the illumination. Scant though it was, the light had no visible origin.

The air smelled a little stale, and a lot damp. The sound of water lapping unevenly against stone echoed through the vast space. Echoing, then fading, only to be replaced by the next wash of water.

Turning his head, he observed the way each end of the uneven, rock-strewn ledge curved slightly to disappear into darkness. Casting his eyes down, he took note that the toes of his shoes projected over the sheer drop. Far below, distant slices of light caught ripples on the surface of the opaque black water, the source of the sound.

Long spears of jagged stalagmites protruded at varying heights from the inky, slightly choppy surface. Impossible to judge the depth of the water, not that it mattered. If he jumped from here, he had an 85 percent chance of being impaled on one of the dozens of cement-like formations.

Interesting that the Elders had chosen first fire, and now water as Tests. Fire was his power to call, and water was Serena's. What next? Something applicable to Trey? Pestilence? Duncan thought drolly.

Cautiously, he dislodged a small stone with the side of his foot, then counted the seconds until it splashed into the water below. He calculated it was roughly a twenty-five-foot drop.

He wasn't going to fall, he had good balance, but standing in this spot forever wasn't an option. He wasn't going down, not with those stalagmites so damned close together. The only option was a left or right strategy.

He knew Trey was here, and Serena arrived just as he was wondering where the hell she was. He heard her surprised intake of air. "Serena, get your bearings before you move," he cautioned.

There was a long pause and he imagined her slender fingers familiarizing themselves with the rock wall at her back before she answered. "Did you just throw down a stone?" She sounded breathless. Duncan doubted she'd been running at the time the Council had taken her. Running had never been Serena's thing. What was it? Excitement? Nerves? Stress? Hell. It was the *water*.

"Yeah." *Are you okay?* Christ. Wanting to ask, but knowing he had to keep his concern to himself was hard. "Heads up." He filled her in on what he'd learned about their surroundings. She let out little groans of displeasure when he ran down the trifecta—the size of the ledge, the dangers inherent with the stalagmites and stalactites, and his rough estimates on their position against the water. The latter elicited the loudest reaction.

"Great," she muttered under her breath.

He smiled at her pithy tone, but hoped she hadn't developed a sudden fear of heights to go along with her paralyzing issues with water. He figured that this wasn't the time to ask. She wouldn't be here if she wasn't more than competent to handle whatever was dished out.

She was below him, maybe six feet down and to the left, if her voice was anything to go by. But he knew, too, that the acoustics of a cavern such as this could easily skew his mental calculations. The rocks started to vibrate. Instantly alert, he braced his body in preparation as the walls around him continued to shake and he got a strange feeling at the back of his neck. "Serena?"

The water below suddenly churned like the mysterious insides of a witch's cauldron, a sure sign Serena was experiencing emotions she couldn't control. She wouldn't answer. Not until she got her emotions under lock and key.

Damn. His knee-jerk reaction was to teleport her away from the impending danger. He dared not act on those feelings. He'd disqualify them both if he chose to interfere, and she'd literally dump rain on his parade for being a controlling jerk. No. He wouldn't voice his concerns for her, but that didn't prevent him from experiencing a knot in his gut at what she was about to face.

What they were all about to face.

"Rein that in, Fury." His warning was curt as the ledge beneath his feet started to crumble like a stale cookie. Jesus.

"Hey! Don't blame me. I'm not doing anything."

Duncan tried to levitate. No go. Tried to shimmer. That didn't work either. Apparently the Council had banned the two powers that would have come in damned handy right now.

"Trey?" He sensed the other man was above him somewhere, but it was impossible to get an accurate read with the walls of the cave shaking and hunks of the ledge raining down into the water.

"What is this?" Trey's amused voice came from above, his voice vibrating in sync with the shaking of the walls and ledge. "Roll cal—"

A green phosphorescent glow appeared directly in front of Duncan. The instructions floated out of the envelope and hovered two feet away, weightless over the black abyss.

> *An ancient scroll is the goal of this quest*
> *Four pieces are torn and that is the Test*
> *One fragment protected by water within*
> *Retrieve the prize and you might win.*

Ah, shit. Protected by water. Duncan imagined Serena's nervousness.

The green glow blinked out, taking the instructions

with it. Trey's laugh echoed off the shimmying walls. "Start your engines, folks. May the best man win."

"Best *woman*," Serena taunted. But the bite was gone from her voice.

Duncan was edging to his right, moving as quickly as made sense. A chunk of the ledge was gone, and he almost vaulted headlong into the chessboard of rock and stone protruding from the water. He did a quick step, and crossed to more solid footing.

"Fuck! Try teleporting, Edge."

Duncan already knew he didn't currently have that ability. "We were told we'd only be able to use the 'powers allocated' to us, remember?" Keeping his arms spread and braced against the rough wall, palms skimming the damp stone, he shifted his feet, moving right. He had no idea which way the scroll was, but he had a 50 percent chance of being right. Bits of rock and small stones splashed into the water as he cautiously and deliberately slid each foot along the edge, ignoring the movement around him.

"Don't look down, Serena," Trey said quietly, moving in the opposite direction from Duncan. "The footing is treacherous, and that water down there looks really deep. I'd hate for you to fall."

"Shut up, Culver." Trey knew Serena couldn't swim. Duncan would bet his next paycheck on that piece of info. Did Culver know the intimate truth about her parents? That she was terrified of water in general? And if he knew, was it because he'd been told, or was he mining in Serena memories for something that would throw her off her stride? Son of a bitch. Was the win so important that Trey would use Serena's terror against her, even if it meant she'd die?

How could Trey be such an ass? Duncan banked his anger and concentrated.

The shaking and vibrating movement stopped as rapidly as it had started, leaving a throbbing silence interspersed with the clink and rattle of small stones tumbling in the aftermath.

Not one to let the grass grow under her feet, Serena started moving in the same direction as Duncan. "I'm not going to fall," she told Trey. "Balance is my middle name. I was top of my class in gymnastics, remember?"

Yeah. Duncan did, now that she mentioned it. She'd been awesome on the balance beam. A balance beam that rose to the ceiling of the school gym at will. Yeah. Awesome. He felt marginally better as all three of them started moving in small, cautious increments.

The auditory enhancements in the cave were as good as at the Met. He could hear every step, every gasp, of both Serena and Trey as they all moved along their respective shelves of rock. At some point the ledges would either lead somewhere, Duncan speculated, or there'd be an opening in the rock that they'd need to explore. It was a humongous place. It could take days. Weeks. Months. Time was irrelevant to the Council.

He'd like to get to wherever the hell he needed to be before the place started rocking and rolling again. He didn't like the look or number of those sharp rocks down below.

Too bad he and Serena didn't have a psychic connection. He wanted to talk to her, make sure she was doing okay.

"Smells like seawater in here to me, how about you guys?"

"What difference does water salinity make?" Serena asked, tone clipped. "Think the scroll disintegrates in saltwater?"

"Just making conversation," Trey said easily. "The sound of all that water sloshing around down there makes my teeth stand on edge. As bad as fingernails down a chalkboard. I'm just trying to block it out."

"Talk quietly to yourself then," Serena snapped, just as the ledge started shifting under Duncan's feet. Serena's too, since her voice cracked under the weight of her fear. Thankfully, it was mere seconds before the walls stopped shaking.

"We're probably in some cave off the ocean, don't you guys think? What with all that wave action down there?" Trey asked, sounding cheerful. "You don't like the ocean, do you, Fury?"

"How—"

"It's only logical. You were with your folks when they drowned, so I'm guessing the ocean isn't your fav—"

"Jesus, Culver. Shut the fuck up. Some of us are concentrating here." The son of a bitch was going out of his way to demoralize Serena. He'd zeroed in on the one sore point that could do the damned job, too. Duncan tried for a small bolt of lightning to shoot up Trey's ass. Nada. Damn. "No more talking. This isn't a group effort."

"You know," Trey continued despite Duncan's warning. "When you came to wizard school, every-one said it was your fault your folks drowned. I never believed that. Did you, Edge?"

This was not a pissing match Duncan wanted to participate in. But by the same token he was damned if he'd let Trey get away with jerking her chain. Not here and not now. Not ever again. Especially when he knew how sensitive Serena was on the subject. "She was eight fucking years old, and nobody with an IQ over seven believed that crap."

Had Serena told *Trey* about her parents? No, Duncan thought savagely, he knew damn well she hadn't. She'd told him that she'd talked to her godparents about the incident, and she'd said she'd told Campbell. If she'd shared anything of the sort with Trey, she would have said so the other night.

Duncan, like the rest of the kids at school, had been told that Serena's parents had died in a terrible drowning accident, and Henry and his wife, her godparents, had taken her in. They'd all been more sympathetic that she was stuck living with the most demanding teacher at school than they were about her being an orphan.

As far as he knew, *nobody* knew she'd been with her parents at the time they'd drowned.

Trey let out a loud and dramatic sigh. "Tough break, Fury. Just awful. You must've needed years of therapy."

"I did. And you can damn well stop trying to freak me out. It won't work." Her voice was cool and even.

"Good girl," Duncan said proudly.

"I'm the *woman* who's going to beat both of you," Serena said briskly, managing, God only knew *how,* not to let her fear bleed into her voice.

"Both of you be quiet so I can concentrate." *God. How far down was that water?*

Worse, how deep *was it?*

Cold sweat prickled across her skin, and her heart was knocking so hard it almost drowned out the threatening whisper of the waves beating against the rocks so far below her. *Don't think about it,* she told herself, as she inched along the ridiculously narrow ledge an inch at a time.

She knew what Trey was trying to do, and it wasn't going to work. While it had been almost half a decade since they'd dated, briefly, she wondered what she'd seen in him. Surely a man didn't change this drastically in five years? Trey had always been charming, and fun to be around. He'd been careful never to show her this unattractive side of his personality.

It was almost shocking to discover how manipulative and self-centered he was. What a jer—Oh, my God, Serena thought with dawning realization. She almost slipped, and had to dig her nails onto the rough wall behind her for balance. She swore under her breath. *This* was the real Trey Culver. The reality of him didn't match the man she'd known for years. He was freaking Jeckyll and Hyde.

He'd *Charmed* her. For years he'd used Charm on her to make her believe he was who and what she wanted him to be. Why? He was good looking, wealthy, and gave every appearance of being suave and intelligent. He could have, and had, dated some of the prettiest, most popular girls in school. He'd dated drop-dead gorgeous women over the years as well. Why had he needed to use Charm on *her* when he could have any woman he wanted?

The ledge shook, and she had to press her back hard against the rock face. Focus. Trey was a puzzle to solve—or not—later.

First things first.

She couldn't look down, knew she *shouldn't* look down. It was almost as though the black water was taunting her with a whispered siren's song. *Look. Closer. Jump.* "Fuck you!" she whispered to the voice in her head, her words echoing through the chamber. The rise in her temper created an avalanche of pebbles and debris, sending it clattering and bouncing down the sheer rock face before splashing down into the waiting water below.

She gritted her teeth. The cave was doing its own thing without any help from her, damn it. If she had any hope of success, she had to get her emotions under control.

Deep breaths. Think clouds. Blue sky. Grass.

Somewhere above her Trey chuckled. "There goes that priceless temper of yours, Fury. Better get a grip on that or we'll *all* go shooting off our perches. Man. I wonder how deep that water is? Fifty, seventy-five feet at least, don't you think, Edge? Good thing I was diving champion three years in a row. It won't be a problem for me."

"Unless you're wrong, and it's only a *foot* deep," Serena said sweetly. "And just as a btw—you were diving champion *two* years in a row. It was Duncan who won that particular trophy three times." It was interesting to note that Trey wasn't making any attempt at Charm now. Either that, or because she'd realized what he was doing, it no longer worked on her, Serena thought, feeling her way along at a frustratingly slow pace.

"Culver," Duncan said tightly, his voice echoing in the space. "One more word and you won't dive off that ledge, I'll toss your sorry self down and shove a stalagmite up your ass, got it?"

"Keep your chivalry to yourself," she told Duncan smartly. "Keep screwing with me, Culver, and when this is over, I'll give you incontinence that'll have you wearing Depends into your golden years. Consider that a promise, not a threat."

Glancing over the ledge, she shivered. Walking sideways wasn't easy, but she found that if she slid her feet instead of stepping, she could push the loose debris out of the way as she went. One problem down, with more to go. The narrow ledge appeared to not only be getting more narrow, but there was a subtle decline, making it a real challenge to keep her balance—balance beam experience or not.

"Anything your way?" Trey called, not seeming to care that his companions were pissed.

"No," Serena and Duncan shouted in unison. Trey, being Trey, immediately changed direction. Fine with her. There really wasn't anyt—

Trey's shout was almost lost amid the thunder and crash of rocks—*big rocks*—ripping loose from the ceiling high above their heads to splash into the water below with the impact of missiles.

Ridiculously, Serena sucked in her stomach as if, by doing so, she'd be a smaller target as huge chunks of stone and debris crashed and thundered past her precarious position, sending up sprays of water. The sound of rock hitting rock made a god-awful noise as stalagmites were shattered by the falling debris.

With an inhuman scream, Trey's body went cart-wheeling over Serena's head and into the water below.

Oh God, oh God. "Trey?" Serena pressed her back against the wall, digging her short nails into the uneven surface as the increasingly narrower ledge shook, dislodging more bits of stone and shale.

"Brace yourself as best you can," Duncan yelled over the cacophony, a moment before the ledge gave way under her right foot. Teetering, heart in her throat, Serena fought for balance. She held her breath, not daring to move so much as a muscle. When she was almost positive she wouldn't fall, she very, very carefully pulled her leg back to safety.

Forget finding the scroll. She wanted out of here. Duncan deserved to be Head of Council, he really did. Just like the first challenge, he was handling the situation calmly and proactively. He didn't have the handicaps of abject fear and inability to control the special powers he'd been allocated. He definitely was better suited for the job. She'd be very happy to go back to her work at the Foundation, and leave him to it.

Lark had told them that one of them might die, but Serena hadn't really believed it. Was Trey dead? God. She hoped not. She had many reasons not to want him to be dead, not the least of which was wanting to ask him why he'd Charmed her.

Rocks splashed into the water twenty-five feet below. The walls shook more violently, the sound deafening. Her stomach clenched. Who was going to be dislodged next?

"Serena?"

"I'm okay," she managed to call back. "This is part of the Test. Nothing to do with me." She hoped. If this was her uncontrollable telekinetic meltdown, she'd end up killing them all. Duncan was a strong swimmer, but that wouldn't matter if he was impaled on one of the stalagmites, she thought with a shudder of horror. And she couldn't swim at all. Something she really had to rectify if she ever got out of here alive. It was time to overcome the debilitating fear once and for all.

"It's *not* you, sweetheart," Duncan sounded his usual cool, rational self. "Just stay as calm as you can. I know, not easy under the circumstances, but hang in there. Don't get shaken off."

"Gee, ya think?" Cautiously Serena started moving again. "I'm hanging on by my fingertips like a terrified bat. What do you think happened to Trey?" This wasn't the time to discuss Trey with Duncan, but Serena made a mental note to do so later. If they *had* a later.

"He's down there in the water."

"Is he . . . ?"

"No. I heard him kicking and paddling after he hit the surface. We aren't allowed to help each other, so focus on yourself."

Concentrating on herself was all well and good, Serena thought, scared out of her mind. Duncan might have heard Trey thrashing about down there, but all she could hear was the hard pounding of her terrified heart. If she was going to die here, she'd vote for a rock to the head, rather than fall from this damned shelf she was trying to balance on, eventually ending up swallowed by the black, choppy water. The ledge seemed to be shrinking at an alarming rate, and the more scared she became and the stronger her emotions, the better chance she had of losing control of her telekinesis. If that happened, the avalanche was going to get a whole lot worse.

And just as she'd been responsible for killing her parents, she was going to be responsible for killing Duncan as well.

Stop it. Just damn well stop being a defeatist! I can do this. I can. Calm down. Just calm down. Think clouds. Think calm. Grass—

Thunder boomed, like a harbinger of bad tidings. "Shit, shit, shit!" Windswept rain pelted her, the sudden downpour a result of the palpable dread gnawing at her from the inside out. "That *was* me."

The rush of water down the wall made the already precarious ledge slick. The violent storm conjured by her fear was eroding the stone beneath her feet. Deep breaths were impossible given the volume of water pouring down on her. Thunder shook the walls. Lightning crackled. Golfball-sized hail pelted them, pinging off the walls, ricocheting off the rocks and splashing into the water like bullets.

"Think *calm*, God damn it!" Her self-made storm worsened, picking up strength by the second, which fed her fear, which in turn fed the raging storm. Her skin stung from the icy bullets of striking hail. "Duncan!" she screamed.

* * *

The force of hitting the cement-like stalagmite knocked the air from Duncan's lungs, and he sank beneath the water like a fucking stone before he clawed his way back to the inky surface. The second he could draw a breath again, he yelled Serena's name.

She wasn't going to hear him over the ruckus of the rockslide, or the incessant noise of thunder and lightning produced by her fear. Still trying to suck in air, he scrabbled his way to the backside of the stone formation for protection from the shit splashing into the water all around him.

His only consolation was that as long as the unexpected hailstorm continued, Serena was still scared. And if she was still scared, she was alive.

Two hours later, Duncan wasn't sure about anything. Much to his gut-wrenching fear, Serena's storm had stopped some time ago. As had the rock-slides and earthquakes. The cave was eerily quiet except for the sound of his limbs cutting through water that was an unpleasant body temperature.

No matter which direction he swam, he couldn't get out of the fucking maze of stalagmites to find an exit. He was a strong swimmer, but after hours of swimming against a tide that had no rhyme or reason, and water so deep that he had yet to find bottom, his limbs felt weighted, and his lungs and sore ribs ached.

When he'd struck the stalagmite on the way into the water he'd hit it back first and bruised a couple of ribs. He'd had worse. He'd participated in missions where he'd been shot, or stabbed, or beat to shit. Hell, sometimes all three. But there'd always been an end in sight.

Not so Test Two. He'd done every maneuver he knew, and some he'd invented to get the fuck out of the water so he could mount a more thorough search for Serena. Because unless he saw her lifeless body he was going to hold out hope that she was alive.

He'd yelled himself hoarse for her. Hell, he'd even shouted out for Trey. To no avail. Had Serena survived the slide?

Christ. Wouldn't he *feel* it if she were gone? He assured himself he would. He couldn't imagine his world without her in it in some capacity. Any fucking capacity. "Serena, answer me God damn—" It started to hail. *Thank God.*

"Seeereeena?!"

Ohgodohgodohgod! Golfball-sized hail morphed into solid spheres the size of a grapefruit. Serena managed to hang on when the first two hit her like fists. The third one caught her sideways, knocking her off the ledge.

She sucked in a panicked gulp of air at the same instant her fingers caught, more by accident than design, on an outcrop of rock. Flinging up her other hand, she managed to grab onto a sliver of a ledge with a death grip. Struggling against the strain and pain of supporting her body weight with her hands, she dangled panting, sobbing, and praying.

The complete absence of light made this a thousand times worse, Serena thought as she hung there, too scared to move. How close was she to the water? Thirty feet? An inch?

The rock face felt cold and slimy against her body, but she pressed her cheek to the rough stone ledge in the darkness, too terrified to move. She could barely breathe, her heart was pounding so hard. "Duncan?"

The cave was eerily, preternaturally silent. She opened her eyes to total darkness. A darkness with an absence of sound, smell, or sensation. Her blood froze. "Duncan! Damn you. Answer me!"

There was no answer. This time she controlled the surge of emotion and threat of tears by biting her lip until she tasted blood. "Duncan? Duncan! What did I d—" The sliver of rock that was her only anchor gave way. Without anything to hang on to, her body was flung into the unimaginable. Space.

Weightless, she spiraled down. Head over heels, legs and arms cartwheeling uselessly, her upper body tangled in the long skeins of her wet hair.

She body-slammed the hard surface of the water. The painful belly flop cut off her scream by knocking the air out of her lungs like a hard fist to her chest.

Terrified, she sank under the oily black water like a rock.

Dark.

Cold.

But not silent. Every erratic, frantic beat of her heart sounded loudly against Serena's eardrums. Something slithery curled around her upper arm. Her eyes flew open. Oh, God. Oh, God. She jerked backward. Slammed into something hard and unyielding. A stalagmite?

Her lungs burned. Screaming for air.

Dark.

Cold.

Up.

She had to go toward the surface. It didn't take skill to rise to the surface, she reminded herself, fighting the overwhelming panic surging through her. Her body's natural buoyancy would work for her, wouldn't it? Making a grab for the stalagmite, she encountered nothing but water.

No up. No down.

She put a hand against her mouth. Her fingers shook. *I can do this.*

No you can't! The waves will come. The waves and the wind.

I'll die.

I'll die before I tell Duncan—

There aren't any waves, she told herself fiercely, kicking her legs. This isn't the open ocean. I'm thirty-three years old, not eight. Old enough to know that even if I can't swim I can get to the surface, get to air. Float. Everybody can float.

If I don't panic.

Do. Not. Panic.

Holding her hand a few inches away from her mouth Serena braced herself, then cautiously released a precious sip of air. Bubbles tickled her fingers. She was upside down. Relaxing went against every single flight-or-fight instinct in her, but she forced her muscles to go limp, and allowed her body to rise in the inky blackness.

A sudden cone of pale yellow light, faint, but unmistakable in the blackness made her blink and falter. What the—

The illumination showed the entrance to an underwater cavern, then as suddenly as it had appeared, it winked out, leaving the water blacker than it had been minutes before.

No. Nonononono. If that was a heads-up to where the scroll was hidden, deep underwater, inside some sort of cave, she shuddered, count her out. Not just no. But hell no.

Serena turned her back, and with agonizing slowness rose to the surface, then bobbed there like a cork, sucking in great drafts of wonderful, life-giving air, her heart beating like a sledgehammer against her ribs. The hail and rain had stopped. Thank God.

Blindly she reached out and her fingertips hooked on a ledge. She hung on more by sheer will than strength.

"Duncan?" Her voice echoed. "Trey?"

She knew Trey had fallen earlier. Had Duncan? Yelling his name produced zero results.

Serena hooked her elbows over the ledge and hung there, trying to get her heartbeat and breathing back to a close proximity of normal. Resting her head against her arms she shut her eyes, weary beyond belief.

What would happen if none of them retrieved the scroll? Would they be given another chance? Could they skip one Test and try the next? She doubted it. There were only the four Tests. Duncan, Trey, or herself had to win two of them. That was it.

Would the Council select three more candidates?

Whichever damned way she looked at it, she couldn't allow different contestants to be chosen. There was a reason that she and Duncan were in this together. She might not want to think about it, she might not want to do anything about it, but Fate had intervened by putting her in direct competition with Duncan Edge for this position for a reason.

She was going to have to go back under the water to retrieve that damned scroll, whether she wanted to or not.

All her internal organs cramped at the thought. "I can't do it," she whispered against her folded arms. No matter how she tried to rationalize her terror of being in deep water, the bottom line was she could very well drown. Just because she'd escaped with her life once, didn't mean she'd do so again.

It made no damned difference if the water in question was a storm-tossed ocean, or placid cave water. She didn't like it.

"Buck up," she told her whiny self grimly as she lifted her head. "I don't have a choice. One." She braced herself. "Two."

"Three." With a deep breath, she allowed her body to slip back under the water before she could talk herself out of it.

Just because she'd never been taught to swim didn't mean she didn't know the basics. Arms and legs needed to move. Simple enough. She might not be poetry in motion, but who gave a rat's ass? She was moving. Hopefully directly to where the light had been shining.

Her lungs were already bursting. If only the water would dry up, and let her . . . Feet first, she drifted gently to the soggy, sandy bottom. Air flooded her lungs.

No way.

Way.

The water was gone.

Sucking in great drafts of air because she could, she muttered, "Flashlight," and a large flashlight materialized in her outstretched hand. Clicking it on, she shone it up to illuminate the sheer rock walls, and impressive glistening spears of the stalagmites rising above the ground like giant ragged columns. Water dripped from every surface, including herself.

The damned water had been deep. Fifty feet at least from the waterline far above her head. She shuddered. Everything was wet, of course, and the briny, fishy, musty smell was pretty damn powerful, but the water was gone. How absurd that it hadn't occurred to her sooner to simply wish it away. Fear had locked her mind.

The ground was saturated, spongy, but relatively easy to walk on. "Duncan? Trey?" she called, walking carefully, and moving the beam systematically against the shiny wet walls.

She followed the cone of light and, before she could chicken out, sucked in a breath and stepped into what had been an underwater cavern. More a long tunnel than a cave.

"Spelunking is not for me," she muttered to block out the thump-thump-thump of each individual heartbeat echoing in her ears. "But swimming lessons are definitely in order. I'll start in the baby pool and work my way u—Crap. Now what?"

The flashlight was gone. Her heartbeat slammed into her ribcage, and she braced her body for water to rush in and fill the tunnel where she stood.

Nothing happened. She opened one eye. "Maybe *I'm* dead."

"No, actually, you're very much alive." Lark's voice came out of the darkness. "But you really are going to have to work at controlling those telekinetic powers of yours as Head of Council, Serena."

"I'm not Head of Council, and this is a little melo-dramatic, isn't it?" Serena asked, her voice shaking. Chances were her heart wasn't going to stop knock-ing any time soon. Head of Council was the last damn thing on her mind. "Is Duncan all right?"

A lamp clicked on. "Sorry. I like it dark when I med-itate," Lark said cheerfully, not answering the most important question of all. Dressed all in black, she was lounging on a daybed piled high with frou-frou, ruffled pink satin pillows. Serena blinked against the soft lighting. The room was all pinks and creams, ruffles and lace, and soft romantic lighting. Very girlie and elegant and totally unlike Lark, yet the Goth young woman looked perfectly at home amongst the beribboned pillows. It took a moment for Serena to notice that the walls were made of rock, and water seeped from crevices and cracks to pool in shimmering ribbons on the stone floor. She was still in the damn cave.

The scroll was on a silver platter placed on a round, lace-draped table in the center of the room.

Serena stepped onto a deep-piled floral area rug, more intent on getting through to Lark than picking up the damn scroll. "Get Duncan out of there, please, Lark." They seemed a million miles away from *here*.

One of Lark's perfectly sculpted, pierced brows arched. "Scroll first. That's the rule. And could you dry off a bit? You're dripping on my carpet."

Serena changed herself into dry clothes, without much thought. "Screw the scroll—" The lights flickered. "End the Test—" The lights flickered again. "For God's sake, Lark! Duncan might be hurt."

"The Tests are *supposed* to be dangerous." Lark leaned back against a mound of pillows, and looked at her, eyes dark. "The object of this very important exercise is to see how you handle pressure."

"Clearly I *didn't* handle it," Serena snapped as she grabbed the tightly rolled scroll off the platter, because at this point she'd do damn near anything to see Duncan alive and well and standing right here with her. "I freaked out and may have gotten Duncan killed. So if the Test was to gauge *my* reaction to stress, I failed it miserably. End of story."

"You meant Duncan or Trey killed," Lark reminded her.

"Or Trey killed," Serena amended. Lark had a propensity to skip around the bits of conversation that didn't interest her.

Serena waved the scroll. "This is it?" she demanded, holding the blasted scroll aloft. "All I had to do was pick up the freaking thing from a silver platter? No water monsters? Fine. Got it. Can we get a move on now? Get him, er, *them* out of there. *Now.*"

Lark indicated a large ormolu clock that suddenly appeared over a fireplace that hadn't been there a second ago. The hands on the clock froze. Fire leapt in the small marble hearth. She turned her head, her kohled eyes locked on Serena. "That'll hold the status quo until we're ready." She swung her feet to the floor. "You combatted the water monster in your own way. You overcame your fear."

"Was there another option?" Serena glanced at the clock, preoccupied with Duncan's safety.

"You know you've been living on borrowed time, Serena. You've been playing with fire, literally."

Serena clenched her jaw. "I just want Duncan safe."

"And Trey?"

Serena tossed the other woman an impatient glare. "Of course. And Trey."

"I don't have to state the obvious, do I? You have no future with an Edge. No future with Duncan. You know that. Not unless you tell him the truth. And we both know what will happen if you do."

Each word stabbed Serena through the heart. "Don't worry, Duncan's whole life is dictated by the Curse. Happily Ever After isn't an option."

"Especially now," Lark said. "If you break your promise and tell Duncan the truth, you can't be Head of Council. If you're responsible for breaking the Curse, you can't even be *you*. You'd be stripped of your powers. You'd be *mortal*."

"I know." Serena felt a shiver of foreboding travel up and down her spine. "Duncan won't risk breaking the Curse. His powers are too important to him. I know that only too well." Serena met Lark's eyes. "When did everything get so freaking complicated?"

Lark materialized a full silver tea service replete with steaming teapot and flowered cups. She picked up the pot. "Five hundred years ago when your great, great, *ridiculously* many greats, grandmother, Nairne, foolish girl that she was, put a Curse on Duncan's great, great, et cetera, grandfather, Magnus. Tea?"

CHAPTER FOURTEEN

Duncan fell through space to land on all fours. He was in a narrow, dimly-lit hallway. The space smelled faintly of jasmine. His heart leapt. *Serena.*

He'd been teleported to her New York City apartment. Convenient, because she was the only person he wanted to see right now.

Two Tests and he hadn't won either of them, he thought with disgust. He had one more shot at it. It had never occurred to Duncan, not once, that he wouldn't win the Master Wizard's Medallion. Not that he was out of the running, but the fact that Trey and Serena had each won one was a grim reminder that he couldn't always win just because he wanted to.

And that applied to both the Tests *and* Serena.

Water from his saturated clothing pooled around him. Cold all the way through to his marrow, adrenaline still racing through his system, he started to get to his feet to look for her.

Tying the belt of a long silk robe, Serena suddenly appeared in an open doorway. Her eyes went wide. "Duncan. Thank God!" She fell to her knees beside him, wrapping her arms around him tightly, her rapid breath hot against his cold skin.

"Where are you hurt?" she demanded. Her soft gray eyes darkened with worry as she searched his face, and her hand shook visibly as she stroked his face. "Thank God you're alive. I've been out of my *mind* terrified. Where did you disappear to—" Her words tumbled one over the other, interspersed with frantic kisses that landed on his head, face, or shoulder. Her slender hands skimmed his body looking for injury.

Duncan grabbed her hands, doing his own visual inspection. She looked breathtakingly lovely with her cheeks flushed by emotion, and her fiery hair like a mantle around her shoulders. An intense, almost overwhelming emotion grabbed him by the throat as he looked at her.

"I'm fine," he told her thickly, skating his thumb along the petal softness of her lower lip. "Were you hurt?"

She shook her head. "I was so damn scared that I'd—" Her eyes welled. "God. I thought I'd k-killed you."

He bracketed her face with both hands, and kissed her. Her mouth was sweet and hot, eager beneath his. Trey must've won the damned Test. But right now Duncan didn't give a shit. Serena was safe, and here, where she belonged. In his arms.

"I'm so sor—"

He pressed a finger against her trembling mouth. "Don't." He caught her upper arms to steady her as they staggered to their feet in the narrow hallway. "The only thing I give a flying fuck about is that you weren't injured in any way. We need to talk, but first I need a hot shower. How about y—"

Grabbing the front of his shirt, she twisted the wet fabric in her fists, pushing him against the wall. "This," nipping his shoulder with sharp, white teeth, "will warm us up." She pulled his shirt up his body and over his head. "Twice as fast." The shirt plopped onto the carpet. "Right." Leaning forward she licked his nipple. He jolted with pleasure as her lips closed over the cold peak. "Here."

"I'm soaking wet—" It was a half-assed protest. There was nowhere else he'd rather be than with Serena. He didn't care where or how. This was another memory he could store.

Not realizing what intense emotion was feeding his hunger, her smile was wicked. She ran the flat of her hand down his abs, following the line of hair to his waistband. "And I'm getting there," she murmured against his throat. "I love how you taste," she teased his skin with her teeth. "I love how you smell. I want to absorb you. I want—I want you inside me. Now."

Hell. This insanity with her was so going to bite him in the ass sooner than later. He knew it was. But until then, until that last second when he had to tell her good-bye—

Unbuttoning his pants, she brushed cool fingers beneath the fabric. His penis pulsed and came to attention as Serena pushed the fabric out of her way. Duncan grabbed her wrist.

"Audience participation?" he asked, his breath strangled. "Or do you want to take this one?"

She cast him a sassy glance. "If you can keep up, participate by all means."

He slid his hands beneath the thin silk of her robe

to cup the globes of her breasts. Her nipples responded instantly to his touch. Duncan skimmed his hands down her midriff, over her hips, and down to grip her bottom. Lifting her, he carried her to the narrow table against one wall.

Serena wrapped her arms about his neck and drew him closer, her long legs wrapped around his waist. "How many seconds this time, do you think?" she murmured against his mouth as her robe glided off her shoulders to pool around her hips on the table.

"We have all the time in the world," he lied, lowering his head to trail a string of kisses down the long, elegant line of her throat. Serena combed her fingers through his hair as his mouth traced the satin smooth skin of her left breast. His lips closed over the hard peak of her nipple, and she sighed, tightening her legs around him.

Aroused to the point of madness, he wanted nothing more than to plunge into her welcoming body. But he wanted to make a lasting memory, and to do that he needed to take his sweet time.

"I have to tell—Oh, God, I love when you do that. Do it again."

Closing his teeth gently around the aroused bud, a little harder this time, Duncan caressed the smooth skin of her inner thigh, loving her wholehearted response to his lovemaking.

Sliding his hands over the cool silken skin of her hips, he cupped her rounded ass and slid her forward, impaling her on his shaft. Her slick heat made him shudder, and when her internal muscles closed around him like a fist he groaned against her throat.

Serena whimpered, tightening her strong legs around his waist. "Duncan. I won. The. Position."

They cried out their release at the same time.

Instead of collapsing against him, Serena took his face in her hands. "Did you hear what I said?"

"You love when I suck your nipples?"

"Yes, I do. But that wasn't what I meant." Her eyes were serious as she searched his face. "Duncan, I won the Council position."

"Good for you," he said mildly, pushing her long hair over her shoulder, then dropping a kiss to the silky skin he'd bared. There'd always been the possibility that he wouldn't win. But amazingly, Duncan was fine with not winning the coveted position. "You'll make a superb Head."

She frowned. "You're *pleased* for me? But this is something *you've* wanted your entire life."

"There'll be other opportunities. I'm only thirty-three, sweetheart." It stunned him that he was not only okay with her winning, he was pleased and proud. Was this what love did to a man? Made him want was what best for the woman he loved, no matter what the cost to himself?

Apparently so.

"Thank you for that. I was so worried that you'd be—"

"What?" He smiled, loving the twin lines of concern between her eyes. "I'd freak out?"

"I'm not sure. I guess because it's always been such a big deal, I was afraid that you'd be . . . strongly disappointed."

He smiled. "Strongly disappointed, huh? Mildly disappointed, maybe, but damn pleased and proud that you got in. You're exceptionally well qualified. I also know that you're smart, resourceful, and fair. I have complete confidence in you, sweetheart. The Council will be better with you in charge. Really, Serena, you'll do a fabulous job and if it couldn't be me, then I'm completely thrilled that it's you. Honestly."

"Wow. How mature of you." She grinned. "Thank you. I'm certainly going to do my best. Now I want a shower, and then I want us to make love *slowly*. In a bed." Her voice was throaty as she trailed kisses across his jaw. "How's that sound to you?"

Duncan slid his hands up her back, drawing her against his chest. He dropped a kiss on top of her head. "Give me five minutes to recover." His breath was still ragged. "I'll see what I can do."

"You're going to have to carry me, I can't move— Your pocket is ringing."

Grinning at her put-upon tone, Duncan shimmered the ringing phone out of the pocket of his wet pants, which were on the floor, to a convenient position between his shoulder and ear as he lifted Serena and whisked her into the bedroom.

Lark, he mouthed. "What do we have?" Serena motioned to be put down. He complied. He wouldn't put it past Lark to have freaking X-ray eyes.

Lark didn't bother with a greeting either. "They just discovered Peter Blaine's body in Mexico City. Same MO as the others. From what was left of him, our forensic people guesstimate he's been dead for at least forty-eight hours.

"Blaine managed an upscale art gallery in the Boston area. He might have been in Mexico looking at artists, but if that was the case we've seen no evidence of it. Nor was he booked into any of the hotels."

"Don't tell me." He watched Serena straighten her robe and tie the sash around her slender waist. Her skin shone through the thin material, making it look like mother of pearl—

Jesus. When he started waxing poetic about a woman it was time to . . . Time to what? he thought blankly. It had never happened before.

"No airline ticket either." He dragged his attention away from the way the thin fabric clung to the slopes of Serena's breasts, and the long length of her legs as she indicated she was going into the bathroom to give him some privacy. He held up a hand for her to wait, but she shook her head, sending him a Mona Lisa smile.

"Teleported before or after he was murdered." While he was talking to Lark, he was admiring the rounded curves of Serena's rear as she slipped into the adjoining room. She closed the door behind her. He frowned. When the fuck had he ever been distracted by anyone or anything while in mission mode?

Never.

He needed to address the Serena problem. And soon. Instead of diminishing with propinquity, his attraction to her was growing until he could barely think of anything else. Before this veered off into uncharted and forbidden territory, he was going to have to—to . . . *do* something.

"Dumped there in the hopes that it would be a while before his body was found," he hypothesized, forcibly dragging his mind back into the game. "Family?"

"Two exes. No kids."

"Christ. He was *that* close to all of us at Gabriel's yesterday, and we didn't know it."

"It would appear so. Watch your back, Hot Edge. Nobody is who they appear to be." The line went dead.

No shit, Duncan thought with annoyance. Culver for one.

Add to that that they now had *four* dead wizards, and no fucking clues. He put in a quick call to Juanita to have her contact the rest of his team to fill them in on the latest murder. One thing at a time.

"What's the satellite situation?"

"All of them are lined up like ants at a picnic," she told him. "China shifted into a new orbit to join them."

China's satellite too? What in God's name was everyone gathering for? Duncan's radar was on red alert. "Any closer to Schpotistan?"

"No. But not further away either. And no activity at the warehouse or the factory," Salazar added before he could ask.

"Call me if anyone so much as takes a leak."

"You got it."

Duncan snapped his phone closed and placed it on the bedside table, then hesitated. Things were heating up. Another wizard murdered, another satellite added to the odd mix of shifting orbits. And while he doubted the two had any correlation, he needed to keep ever vigilant on both. This was no time to be thinking with his dick.

And he'd keep believing his dick was what he was thinking with, he thought, striding toward the closed bathroom door. Because if this *wasn't* just about sex, he was in way the fuck over his head. Nairne's Curse played in his head. Like watching a damned car wreck, he knew he was heading toward disaster. Knew it with every cell in his body. Loving her wasn't a possibility. He could deal with his known emotional flotsam and jetsam, but he was damned if he'd allow Serena to be hurt. The fucking Curse had nothing to do with her.

He was going to have to start backing off. Easing the path for her. Duncan's gut clenched. He'd rather rip out his own heart out than hurt Serena.

He pushed open the door and strode into the steam-filled bathroom. The shower stall was disappointingly empty. Fortunately the enormous bathtub across the room was full. Of a mountain of fragrant bubbles. And Serena.

He groaned. "I'm going to smell like a sissy girl."

Her face lit up when she looked up and saw him standing in the doorway. The pressure inside him felt as though someone were stabbing him through the heart.

Serena laughed. "You could never smell like anything but a man, trust me." She held up an arm encased in white foam, and wiggled her fingers. "Come and get warm."

"I'm plenty warm."

"And happy to see me." She shot him a provocative glance from under black spiky lashes, and dropped her arm back into the water with a little splash. "Fine. Wait for me then. I shouldn't be too long."

"Have to do the environmentally correct thing, right? I mean, you're the humanitarian." He stepped into the hot, jasmine-scented water. "This tub's too big for one person. Conservationists would be horrified that you're wasting water by bathing alone." He settled his knees on either side of her hips.

"Horrified?"

He nodded. "Appalled."

"Can't have that."

"Nope."

Protected in the circle of Duncan's arms, Serena closed her eyes, her cheek resting on his chest, an arm and one leg flung over his body. Duncan had conjured up soft jazz and candlelight, and her bedroom was cool and dim. Neither of them had any desire to talk, and Serena was enjoying the aftermath of some spectacular lovemaking. Duncan was lazily playing with her hair, his breathing deep and even beneath her ear, his large body relaxed. She should also be feeling relaxed and well-loved; instead, it was almost as though she were waiting for another shoe to drop. Silly really. She knew what that shoe would be. This crazy interlude with Duncan had to draw to a close. And soon. She knew that with every fiber of her being. As much as she'd always wanted it, there was absolutely no chance of any kind of meaningful relationship with Duncan Edge.

Either she took the initiative, or he would. It wasn't a case of if they would part, but when.

Serena would prefer to be the one to walk away.

It would be wonderful to forget everything. Just for a few more hours. To pretend that she was the woman he loved instead of the woman who'd deceived him from the get-go. To forget everything but the magic of being with him. But that wasn't reality.

Nairne and her Curse stood between them.

Nothing was going to change that.

She might have taken the Council position away from him, even by winning it fairly. But she refused to be the one responsible for lifting the Curse and making him lose something he prized even more than the job of Head of Council.

His powers.

She wasn't sure how she felt about his calm acceptance that she'd won. The Council position was something she knew he'd wanted all his life. Serena wasn't sure what kind of response she'd expected, but that hadn't been it. She'd known him long enough to believe that his congratulations had been heartfelt and genuine. But would he feel the same way days and weeks from now, when the postcoital glow was a distant memory?

Once her appointment was official, would his loss pierce him deeply? Would her beating him hurt him on a deep, fundamental, masculine level? To think that she'd thought him too hard, too violent . . . She breathed in the scent of his skin, feeling his chest rise and fall as he rested. It killed her knowing that she was going to bring him pain. He'd been the one who had wanted it, not her.

She'd be a good Master Wizard, she was sure. But in her heart of hearts she knew that Duncan would've been just as good. He'd be great. Exceptional, actually. They were fairly evenly matched in every area save one—Duncan didn't conjure rain, hail, thunder, or lightning when his emotions were taxed. Serena cringed, imagining the Council chamber flooding in mid session because a person or issue made her lose control. It wouldn't be the first time.

The first time she'd met Ian's sons, she'd drenched them and everyone else in the restaurant and had been forced to call on Caleb Edge to reverse time. But that memory paled in comparison to knowing that her time with Duncan was limited. *Had* to be limited.

Lying here in his arms, anticipating how he was going to feel, and how *she* was going to feel—afterward—was damn stupid. They had *now*. She dropped a kiss to his very nice chest. "Who was that on the phone earlier?"

Duncan could almost hear Serena's brain working a mile a minute. What was going through her mind? She was only pretending to be relaxed. "Lark."

He sifted her damp hair through his fingers. Christ. He couldn't get enough of her. It didn't matter what the hell part of his anatomy was in charge. "She called to tell me Peter Blaine was killed."

Serena tilted her head to look up at him, her gray eyes sympathetic. "I'm sorry. Who was he?"

"A level two." He stroked her arm with the pads of his fingers. Her skin was incredibly smooth and soft. "He wasn't that likable a guy, but he didn't deserve to die.

"Blaine makes the fourth wizard murdered in less than two months. I don't know the extent of his special powers, Lark's checking into that, but whatever they were, the killer has assimilated them. Speculation is that Blaine was killed before yesterday's meeting.

The killer morphed into Blaine in order to attend the meeting, blending in seamlessly with the rest of us." Duncan frowned. "We had no fucking clue."

Serena shifted to sit up, casually pulling the sheet to cover herself. She wasn't shy, so Duncan had to presume that the gesture was symbolic. "A serial killer is frightening enough. But a *wizard* serial killer?" Serena tucked the sheet under her arms. "That's terrifying. And knowing that with every murder he's assimilating new powers and gathering strength—God, it's chilling."

"Yeah. It is. If we don't find him soon, he's going to be unstoppable. He'll be too powerful to kill. Even by magic."

Serena rose with the sheet wrapped around her body toga-style, then materialized jeans and a purple tank top before dropping the bed coverings into a pool around her feet. "Is there anything I can do?"

Disappointed, but knowing that it was time, Duncan got out of the other side of her bed, and materialized his own clothing. "If I asked you to stay with me twenty-four/seven until the killer is caught, would you get pissed off because I was telling you what to do?"

Serena's arms were raised behind her head as she did some knot thing with her hair. "I'm not the stupid girl in some cheesy slasher flick, Duncan. If we stick together, at least we'll know that *we* aren't the Morpher. But it's going to be complicated as hell. We both have demanding jobs and now I have the whole Council thing, which, thank God, isn't official just yet. How on earth are we going to be able to do our jobs if we're living in each other's pockets?"

"Inconvenient, but not impossible."

"I'm willing to give it a shot. We'll work out a viable schedule and take it from the—" This time it was her phone that rang. Shimmering the phone into her hand, she checked the caller ID. "Hi, Rhonda. No, that's fine." She listened for several more minutes, then smiled. "Yes, Ian would have. Thanks."

"We should have left our phones down in that god-awful cave," he told her when she was off the phone.

"No, that was good news from my attorney. The resolution of my court case. Paul and Hugh agreed to each accept an additional five million dollars if they'd waive any and all claims, present and future, to any money or other assets of their father's. They agreed and signed this afternoon—it's over."

"That's a large chunk of change."

"Yes, it is. But Ian and I were prepared to give each of them up to ten million after his death, knowing his sons would make a huge stink at the reading of the will. Ian bequeathed them one million each. So the Foundation just saved itself eight million dollars. Not bad for a day's work."

"Beautiful and smart."

"And sexy." This time her smile didn't quite reach her eyes.

Christ, Duncan thought, observing Serena's subtle withdrawal, was he telegraphing the last good-bye?

CHAPTER FIFTEEN

Because Duncan had an itch about it, they agreed to go to Siberia first. Sticking together, while it made sense, was also going to test his self-control to the limit. But until he could assure himself that nothing going on in, around, or above Siberia had a damn thing to do with Serena, he'd bite the bullet and stick to her like white on rice.

When they arrived at the factory building it was almost empty. Everyone had gone outside to assist in the assembly of the blanket.

They teleported close enough not to have to walk the two miles in the icy cold, but far enough away not to arouse suspicion with their instantaneous arrival.

Everyone was bundled up to their eyeballs in the freezing cold. Duncan was already aware of who these people were and their backgrounds. Juanita had done thorough background checks on everyone for him several weeks ago when this persistent goddamned itch on the back of his neck had intensified.

He'd been so caught up in his personal musings that the cold had yet to permeate his system. The hum of idling snowmobile engines nearly drowned out the sound of snow crunching beneath their boots as they walked. Christ it was cold. The air was crisp; each breath condensed into a swirl of white crystals before dissipating on the stiff, westerly breeze.

There were two dozen workers threading heavy wires through the grommets at the seams of the thermal blanket. Duncan supposed this crazy idea could work, but he was leaving the jury out on it.

"Where's Joanna?" Serena asked Dennis Cole. How she knew who was missing was a mystery to Duncan, since everyone was dressed in heavy outerwear to combat the brutal cold.

Dennis frowned. "She was waiting for an important call. I was just about to go back inside to check on her. She shouldn't miss witnessing the first stage of this."

"I'll go and talk to h—"

"Would you mind if I went inside first?" Dennis interrupted. "I'm kinda worried about her."

"She might—" Serena started, then changed her mind. "Sure. Go ahead." She waited until the other man had walked away before saying quietly, "I'm worried about her, too. She hasn't been herself for weeks."

Duncan was only half listening as he watched the men working in unison to roll out the heavy material across the snow-covered ground. The fabric weighed hundreds of pounds and the men's heavy breathing was visible as they worked tirelessly to position each enormous square. Magic would have been quicker, but he didn't offer.

"Are those two an item?" he asked, turning to Serena. Anything that might have an effect on her was grounds for inquiry as far as Duncan was concerned.

"Joanna and Denny? No. Although I suspect with very little encouragement he'd be interested. But she already has a guy she's seeing."

"Someone possessive," Duncan observed absently as he returned to watching the fruition of Serena's plan to bring food to the world. She just might do it, too, he thought, proud of her amazing humanitarian accomplishments. He admired her enormously. Serena was a woman who put her money, and her actions, where her mouth was.

She gave him a curious glance. "Why possessive?"

"Because he gave her hickies, remember? Something teenage boys do to their girlfriends to show ownership. "

Neither mentioned that Trey had given Serena several of the damn things way back when. Duncan had known even then that Trey had marked Serena to prove to everyone at school that Serena was his. At the time Duncan had been relieved that Trey hadn't known how strongly that incident had pissed him off.

"Trey used Charm on me, you know."

Christ. The bastard. Duncan had suspected. But his jealousy of Trey and Serena's relationship had made him doubt his instincts, and made him imagine that his suspicion was just a case of sour grapes. "Are you telling me you only dated Trey because he Charmed you?"

"I'm not sure. But in retrospect? Probably." Serena shrugged. "To tell the truth, I only realized that he'd used Charm when we were in the cave. *That* Trey was nothing like the man I thought I knew. It suddenly dawned on me then that he must've Charmed me. But even with that," she said dryly, "my attention was short-lived."

"Happy to hear it." They shared an intimate smile.

"Duncan, I—"

"We need to—" They spoke simultaneously. "One thing at a time, okay?"

She nodded, then turned back to watch the workers. "God. Look at this, isn't this amazing?" Her gray eyes glowed, and her nose was pink from the cold. She glanced up at him, and his heart melted to see the excitement on her beautiful face. Her beauty struck him every time he saw her. Whether it had been five seconds ago, five hours, or five years. He needed to store up her every expression for After. After he reminded her that the Curse made any relationship between them impossible. After he could no longer see her. After he could no longer touch her.

Looking at the purity of her profile, Duncan wondered if he would always think of Serena when he caught a drift of jasmine scent on a summer's breeze.

Yeah. Probably.

She watched the men dragging the heavy netting into position. The brown material stood out against the stark, barren, snow-covered tundra in a crosshatch pattern taking up a footprint the size of a football field.

"Once the crops start growing," Serena snugged her fur-lined hood more tightly around her throat, "no one will even see the thermal blanket. But it'll be there, carrying water and nutrition to the plants. We believe we'll be able to harvest at least three wheat crops before we need to replenish the fertilizers. This is an incredible breakthrough, and as soon as we finish our negotiations we'll have a power source and really get to see how this baby works."

A theory slammed into him with chilling clarity. "What kind of power source?"

"Oh, we're negotiating right now with a Spanish company to be able to use their satellite—"

"Christ! That's it!" Duncan looked toward the sky as he worked the hypothesis in his head. It was possible. It explained the repositioning of the satellites. It was a fucking disaster waiting to happen.

"What am I missing?"

Duncan grabbed her arm. "Let's get inside. I have some calls to make."

But the moment they raced inside, they bumped into Denny. "What's the matter?" Serena demanded, seeing his pale, worried face.

"I don't freaking *know*," Dennis combed his fingers through his hair in a gesture of frustration. "But Joanna is in her office crying hysterically. She won't tell me what happened, and she won't let me comfort her. Go and help her, Serena. Please."

Serena glanced at Duncan. "Let's see what she has to say," he told her. "My calls can wait a few more minutes."

"She'd not going to talk to me with you there," Serena told him as they hurried down the hallway, leaving a concerned Dennis behind.

"Yeah," Duncan told her grimly, "she will. Especially if I suspect that she's very much involved in one of my operations."

"Joanna isn't involved in one of your operations." Serena wasn't sure whether she should be amused at

the very idea, or horrified that Duncan would suspect Joanna of being a terrorist. "She's a scientist, and
a damn good one. She loves working for the
Foundation. She'd never do anything to jeopardize
or compromise her work here."

"Let's see what she's so upset about and go from
there, all right?"

Since her day had somehow taken a left turn into
uncharted territory, Serena wasn't sure about anything. She pushed open Joanna's office door without
knocking.

"Joanna?" she said, moving over to where the
woman sat on the floor, head in her hands, and her
back against the cold brick wall.

The low, desperate sounds of her raw sobs echoed,
as did the hiccups. Joanna made no attempt to control her sobs. She didn't even seem to be aware that
Serena and Duncan were in the room.

"Hey," Serena crouched beside her friend, wrapping her arms about her heaving shoulders. "Shhh,
shhh," she crooned, rocking Joanna while she continued sobbing as if her heart were breaking.
"Whatever it is, we can fix it, okay? Can you get
up? Let me help you. There you go. Come and sit in
the chair and tell me what's going on." Serena
helped Joanna to her feet and led her to a nearby
chair.

Out of the corner of her eye she saw that Duncan
had materialized a bottle of Scotch. She nodded,
and he poured a few fingers into a glass and handed
it to her. "Here, sip this slowly, and try to stop crying. What's the matter? You should be thrilled. All
your hard work for the last few years is about to

become reality. Is it Henry?" Serena asked, reasoning that Joanna might be feeling melancholy because their friend and mentor wasn't there to see the thermal blanket come to fruition. But there was a vast difference between feeling melancholy and this kind of desperate sobbing.

Serena got a sick feeling. Oh, God. "Has something happened to Casey?"

Joanna gulped down the Scotch, her eyes red and puffy. Finding a box of tissues floating within reach, Serena shot Duncan a grateful look. Pulling out a handful, she gave them to Joanna who dabbed at her streaming eyes, then blew her nose.

"Lord save me," her voice broke. "Yes. He—"

Concerned, Serena rubbed her back. "Is he hurt? What hospital is he in? I'll teleport you—"

"He's been ki-kidnapped."

"When?" Duncan demanded from his position leaning against the closed door. He looked deceptively relaxed unless one saw his eyes. He was watching Joanna intently.

"A little over three weeks a-ago."

"Oh my God! Why didn't you say anything?" Serena asked, as a mental slideshow of Joanna's recent behavior played in her mind. The moodiness. The way Joanna had stopped interacting with the rest of the group. She'd known something was wrong for ages and wished she'd nudged her friend weeks ago to tell her what was wrong.

"I couldn't. They threatened to kill him if I said anything to anyone."

"I'm not anyone," Serena told her quietly, relieved that the wrenching sobs had petered down to an occasional hiccup. "I can help. Duncan can help. Tell us what you need. Ransom money?"

Serena's mind was going a mile a minute, but Joanna shook her head. Her eyes welled again. "It was never about money."

"The thermal blanket?" Duncan pushed away from the door.

Serena felt a chill even as his warm hand came to rest at the small of her back.

Joanna looked up at him, hollow-eyed, and nodded. "They want the final codes for manufacturing the thermal blanket. I d-didn't have all the damned codes! Henry forgot to document them. I went to him, and he was going to give them to me but then he . . . he . . . he collapsed. Then I didn't know what to do. I've been working day and night to decipher his notes all while my poor baby is suffering God knows what."

"Not all your days and nights," Serena reminded her gently. "Unless you made up that fabulous new boyfriend?"

"You started a relationship knowing your son had been kidnapped?" Duncan asked, clearly surprised, but his tone conveyed something else that Serena couldn't decipher.

Joanna combed shaky fingers through her short salt-and-pepper hair. "Yes. No. Not started. Grant and I had been together for a while before—" Her eyes squeezed shut. "I know, God, I know what you're thinking. Believe me, I feel horrible, but Grant promised he'd help me find my son, and whenever he was around I . . . I don't know how to explain it. A sense of calm came over me, and I knew Casey would be okay, and e-everything would work out."

"Who is this Grant?" Duncan asked.

Serena heard the censure in his tone and discreetly elbowed him. Joanna was already in meltdown mode. The last thing she needed was Duncan's disapproval.

"We were neighbors," Joanna explained. "We ran into one another in our local branch of the bank. He asked me to lunch. Strangely, I didn't even hesitate in saying yes. One minute we were ordering sushi, and the next thing I knew, we were in a hotel room."

Joanna bit her lip. "Serena, you know I don't normally do that sort of thing. But Grant, well, he just has this way of making me feel—I don't know—*special*. Cherished. We started dating, then a few weeks later I came to Schpotistan. He's been visiting me on a fairly regular basis ever since." Her face was pink. "And he was horrified when I told him that Case had been kidnapped. Grant runs some sort of communications company, and he's had his techs reviewing the disks of Casey for some clue as to where he's being held."

"Disks?" Serena asked.

"The kidnappers have been sending videos to me via e-mail every day, and I've been copying them onto disks and giving them to Grant. Today was only the second time in three weeks that they haven't contacted me." She finished the sentence on a hiccup.

"What changed?" Duncan asked briskly.

"Nothing—I don't know! I *gave* them what they wanted." Joanna's fingers went white around the empty glass she was holding. "I finally put the last piece of the schematic together. Grant thought it was too dangerous for me to meet with the kidnappers, so he went on my behalf. But that was more than six hours ago and I haven't heard a thing. What if they did something to Case? Grant walked into a trap set for me. What if they—"

"What exactly did you give them?" Duncan cut her off. Which was probably a good thing, Serena thought. Joanna was getting more and more hysterical.

"They wanted to know all about the power source. I gave them the coordinate codes for satellite positioning on the thermal blanket."

"Shit," Duncan muttered as he hit speed dial with his thumb. "Have Chapman and Brown here ASAP. And have that data ready when I get there," he said briskly into the phone. "I'm on my way."

Joanna shot out of her chair, grabbing Duncan's arm. "What? No! I *swore* I wouldn't tell anyone. I won't risk Casey's safety."

"Calm down, Joanna," Serena said as soothingly as possible, tugging the other woman back to her seat and out of reach of Duncan, who was rattling off instructions to someone on the other end of the phone. "He knows what he's doing. Have you tried contacting Grant again?"

"He isn't answering his cell phone and I tried teleporting to him but—"

"Teleporting?" Duncan repeated. "You're a Half. You don't have that kind of power."

Joanna blushed. "Grant gave it to me."

"Double shit," Duncan met Serena's eyes. "Grant's a wizard?"

A wizard who was gifting powers. A big no-no. Dread pooled in the pit of Serena's stomach. She'd known the man was a wizard, but hadn't thought much about it. Now it was starting to ominously add up.

"Grant made me promise not to tell anyone." Joanna rubbed her face. "He told me a lot of things and at the time, it all seemed to make sense. But ever since I gave him the codes, I haven't felt the same. It's like, I don't know. Like someone turned on a light and I'm standing in an empty room."

"Charm," Serena said softly.

Duncan's jaw clenched. "Culver."

"Yes," Serena said flatly. "Joanna, is Grant tall, with light brownish blond hair, and brown eyes?"

"No." She started to look relieved. "He's medium height, and very blond, with hazel eyes."

"Does he look familiar to you?" Serena asked. "Perhaps like someone you knew? Someone else you were fond of?"

"No. He—" Joanna glanced from Serena to Duncan and then back again. She took in a harsh shuddering breath as reality seeped into her consciousness. "Yes. He looks exactly like Casey's father. My God. No wonder I was instantly attracted to him, he looked so familiar. Why didn't I see that?"

"He's morphed into someone you'd instantly be comfortable with," Duncan said grimly. "He's our killer."

Joanna went bone white, clutching Serena's fingers tightly enough to cut off her circulation. "Killer?"

"We have a serial killer. Four full wizards so far."

Joanna's mouth moved as she tried to speak.

Finally she managed, "He's going to kill Casey. Oh, my God. He's going to kill my baby! What have I done?"

She covered her face and started crying again.

"We'll try to undo it," Serena told her. And prayed that would be possible.

"How?"

Serena told Joanna about her impending position on the Council. "In accordance with tradition, I get the Medallion and a power boost sometime in the next forty-eight hours. I'll help you, I promise."

"Casey might not *have* forty-eight hours!" Joanna cried, rising from her chair to start compulsively neatening her already tidy desk.

Two men shimmered into the room, making the already small office even smaller.

"What are you doing?" Serena demanded of Duncan as she stepped protectively in front of Joanna.

"My job. Serena, Brown, and Chapman." Curt introductions out of the way, Duncan quickly ran down the situation with his men. "Question Dr. Rossiter," he finished. "Get what info you can from her, then meet me in Montana. I'll copy the e-mail videos and send them to Juanita to enhance and analyze. We'll find your son, Joanna. I promise." He lifted the phone he was still holding to his ear. "Still there?" Duncan asked Juanita. "Assemble the team. ASAP."

"Consider it done. What's your ETA?"

"On my way," he answered as he gripped Serena's arm through the thick layers of her parka.

The instant she lifted her beautiful face to his, she

must have sensed something was wrong. *Very wrong.* "What? Another wizard murder?"

He shook his head. "You're coming with me."

"To whe—?"

In a flash, Duncan teleported them both to Montana, and then dispatched their tundra-appropriate clothing. Once they were both more suitably dressed for T-FLAC's underground facility, he took her by the hand and led her through the maze of desks and hi-tech equipment. Ushering her inside the conference room, he shut the door.

Con Jordan rose as he was introduced to Serena, as did Noah Hart. Duncan kept moving, tugging Serena along behind him to the other end of the table. The men returned to their seats.

"Serena Campbell." He pulled out a chair for her, and nodded to Juanita. "Juanita Salazar. Okay," he sat down at the head of the koa table. "Let's see what we're dealing with."

Liquid crystal screens hummed as they lowered from the ceiling, surrounding the group with images collected over the past few days.

"We know all this," Con pointed out as he slouched back in his chair. "The satellites have shifted to convergent orbits."

Again Duncan spoke to Juanita. "Did you finish the projections?"

A keyboard appeared on the table in front of her. "Before you finished asking." Her fingers flew across the keyboard, morphing the images into an animated film short.

They all watched in silence as the satellites moved into a circular position around the dedicated communications satellite owned by a private Russian communications conglomerate.

Then, like some high level on a video game, signals passed from the soldier satellites to the center one. In a matter of seconds, a single lightning-like beam shot down to earth.

"We were right," Noah Hart said. "They are aiming at a specific target. So, someone has managed to get all the orbit codes and is about to blow up a target?" There wasn't any sense of urgency in his tone. "So we have our friends at Lillenfield Aeronautics launch a counter drone to knock it out."

"Not enough time," Duncan countered. "It would take a drone almost seventeen hours to launch, intercept, and destroy."

Landis suggested Duncan simply send up some fireballs of his own to destroy them all.

"Can't." Duncan glanced at Serena. "Four of the feeder satellites control electronic banking. Destroy them all at once and the economies of most developing companies will collapse. Hell, we'd knock out every ATM in the world."

"Well, shit." Stan Brown tapped his pen on the table. "Though I've got to say, it's a brilliant plan. Control the money, control the world. So which one of the terrorist groups thought this up? Because the target isn't disrupting international banking. That would only buy the terrorists a few weeks of success before the world's economists and aerospace engineers fixed the problem. It's too short-term."

"But they would have enough time to amass a decent chunk of change. That'd cover their expenses for six months at least."

Juanita sighed heavily. "Think bigger. Why settle for a few months of bonus cash when you can corner the market on commodities and untold amounts of natural resources?"

"Oh my God," Serena said with dawning horror. "The thermal blanket."

"Yeah. The thermal blanket." Duncan acknowledged, placing his hand on her shoulder and giving a little squeeze. Quickly, he filled his team in on the Foundation's latest project, including the secret testing location.

"Has to be Red Mantis," Hart offered. "Someone in that group has been eating their Wheaties. All our intel indicates they're violent as shit, but did we know they had someone with this kind of hi-tech expertise?"

"Wait!" Serena half rose. "Someone is going to steal my blanket and use it to do—" She fell back into her chair and frowned. "What exactly?"

"Red Mantis will use their satellite to superheat your thermal blanket. Once they warm the frozen tundra, they'll have access to huge, untapped oil reserves. They'll make what OPEC has to sell look like a fruit stand. Juanita, pull up the aerial images." The screen changed to a series of still photographs. "Those drilling rigs are a hundred miles south of Serena's test site."

"How did they move that shit into place without us knowing?" Con Jordan demanded, sitting up to glare at the screen. "We haven't figured that out yet and they aren't on the latest images."

"Protective spell?" Noah asked.

Duncan nodded. "Serena's not the only one with a

mole. We've got a traitor, too. That hiccup in the protective spell happened at the same time Blaine was being murdered. My theory is that when the wizard was assimilating the powers of his latest kill, he couldn't maintain the protective shield hiding the drilling equipment."

"Then there's the gold." Juanita switched screens again. This time a 3-D geological map just north of Schpotistan hovered in the room.

"Gold?" Serena asked, eyes wide.

"Enough to fund Red Mantis into the next millennium," Duncan added. "With unlimited access to crude oil and gold, they'll be virtually impossible to stop."

Serena looked blank. "But there are half a dozen satellites orbiting. The thermal blanket only needs one as a power source."

"I suspect Culver has got a bidding war going on as we speak." Duncan spun his chair to look at the monitor behind him. "Someone else is going to be sharing some of the wealth. And doing most of the labor-intensive work, I imagine, knowing Culver."

"I don't get it." Serena tried to decipher the markings up on the screen, but gave up. "How did Trey get involved in this?"

"We now suspect Culver's been pulling the strings of Sergei Konanykhine." Duncan turned back to the group. "Konanykhine is the head of a terrorist group called Red Mantis. Red Mantis is comprised mainly of Halves.

"Culver has most likely been controlling them by giving the terrorists additional powers. Like he gave

Dr. Rossiter. Not enough to threaten him, but just enough to keep them happy and motivated."

Noah Hart looked as skeptical as Serena felt.

"Trey Culver is our wizard killer."

"That dickhead playboy Trey Culver?" Con Jordan demanded. "He couldn't mastermind something like this, for God's sake. He's dumber than a stump."

"He's been using Charm."

"Fuck!" Hart said flatly. "Are you serious? *Culver* is head of Red Mantis?"

Duncan nodded. "Yeah." He glanced at Juanita. "How much time do we have to get those satellites out of orbit?"

"Not enough," Juanita said, frustration knitting her brow as her fingers continued tapping. "By my calculations, the satellites will be in position in less than four and a half hours."

"Get me everything you can. Serena and I are going back there."

Duncan took Serena's hand and teleported them back to Siberia. After materializing their heavy outerwear, Serena took Duncan's hand as they walked briskly down the corridor at the Foundation building.

"Mind if I ask why we came back here and where the hell we're going at warp speed?"

"We have to get the thermal blanket broken down ASAP, *before* one of those satellites activates it."

"Can't be done," Serena panted, running to catch up with his long strides. He cast her an incredulous glance. "Not even with magic." She flushed. "Henry and I used a powerful binding spell to ensure all the components stayed together. No matter what. Without him, I can't undo it. We can't even re-roll the sections. That was part of the spell. Once that puppy is down and fully assembled, it's *down*."

"Christ, Serena, why the hell did you and Henry put such a powerful spell on it?"

"Because in the places that we will be using the thermal blanket—Slow down, would you please? I have a stitch in my side. In the places we'll be using the blanket, people steal their own mother's . . . teeth. We had to ensure that once it was set up, no one could come in and swipe bits of it to mend their roof, or feed it to their livestock or, hell—make a hat!"

"Then we'll go with my other plan." He shoved open the outside door, feeling the razor-sharp cold bite into his lungs.

Their boots crunched across the frozen earth. "It better be a brilliant plan."

Duncan stopped. They were in the middle of nowhere. The completely assembled blanket was on the other side of the building. And the only witnesses to what they were about to do were the sullen clouds overhead and a spindly tree without leaves.

He turned to Serena. "Together, we are going to make the biggest mother of a storm, and blow those satellites the fuck out of the sky."

CHAPTER SIXTEEN

Between her ability to call water, and Duncan's ability to call fire, they produced a storm of biblical proportions.

Aiming their power miles above the earth, they made sure the storm was barely noticeable on the ground. But heavy winds, fierce lightning, and torrential rain propelled all the hovering satellites thousands of miles away from their intended target of Schpotistan.

Duncan turned to her with a grin. He gave her a high five. "We make a hell of a team."

"That might be how you congratulate one of your guys for a job well done, but I require a little more personalized appreciation," she told him, wrapping her arms around his neck despite the bulk of their heavy coats. Her chest ached as they silently turned to walk back to the building. Fighting the urge to clasp his hand, she glanced up at Duncan, matching her strides to his. Most of his face was covered by the fur-lined hood of his thick black coat. He looked like a giant teddy bear. No, maybe a grizzly. Duncan's power, his confidence, his masculinity—it used to scare her, but now she just wanted as much as she could handle.

Because she knew that their story didn't have a happy ending. She tried to keep her voice light, but it wasn't easy. It felt as though a tiny metronome in her head was ticking away their last minutes together. "That was fun, but only solves half the problem. Right?"

"If Trey *is* the killer, then he's assimilated the powers of all the wizards he's murdered. He's incredibly powerful now."

Duncan held the door open for her, and as she brushed by him, her body tensed as if she and Duncan were naked and on her bed rather than bundled under pounds of clothes. In a cracking voice she managed, "Yeah, I know."

Serena wanted to grab hold of him, and never let go. She wanted to bury her face against the warmth of his chest, and hear him murmur in her ear as they made love. Her throat tightened.

By nonverbal agreement they teleported up to the third floor, and her room. Neither removed their coats, although the room was toasty warm. It was over; they both knew it had to be.

"Will you be able to capture or defeat him when he has that much power?" She could give him more, not that he would ask her for it. When she had the Medallion she'd be able to gift it to him. The problem was, she wasn't sure what would happen if she did so.

Either his powers would be amplified, or, God forbid, he'd lose them altogether.

Did she dare?

Did she dare not?

Her eyes drank him in. Chances were, this was the last time they'd see one another. Once Duncan knew that she'd kept a secret for most of their lives, a secret that was about to be revealed and profoundly change his life, he'd never want to lay eyes on her again. She knew that. And was willing to risk never seeing him again to keep him alive.

How had she mistaken his confidence for arrogance? She'd been a scared fool, loving him always and knowing that he was the one she couldn't have. Maybe she'd made excuses, but she couldn't lie to herself anymore. She loved the maddening man. Loved him more than she'd ever imagined possible. It was going to rip out her heart to let him go. But first things first.

"Can you defeat Trey?" Serena repeated, knowing the answer, but praying for another.

"Certainly not on my own," he admitted tightly. "My people are top notch," he said in his typical noncommittal way. "Frankly, I'd like my chances a whole lot better if I had my brothers at my back as well, but that isn't an option."

"Because of the Curse?"

"We can't break the Curse unless all three of us work as one, but we can't work together without negating each other's powers. It's times like this that I'd like to send Caleb back in time to glue Nairne's lips shut before she could curse Magnus."

Her lips twitched, but inside, her heart was being squeezed like a vise. "Ever try that?"

Duncan gave a humorless laugh. "Yeah. Caleb

was about twelve. He traveled back and suffered a concussion when he hit Nairne's protective spell."

"Trey could kill you," she said, her voice catching.

He ran his finger along her jaw. "Not if I kill him first."

"But there's no chance of that, is there? He's too strong now." Trey had assimilated the power of four level one and two wizards.

"Don't worry. I still have a few tricks up my sleeve."

Mind made up, Serena took his hand in hers and brought it to her lips. "So do I."

The freaking bright lights of the Council chambers almost burned out Duncan's retinas. He materialized sunglasses for both himself and Serena. Probably a big no-no, but he didn't give a flying fuck. "I don't have time for this, Serena," he whispered quietly, as the Elders' robes rustled in the midnight gloom behind the massive Head of Council's desk. "I'm very proud of you, but can we try and keep this short?"

"You were not summoned," Allen told them, his voice stern. "The Medallion ceremony won't be held until tomorrow at noon."

Serena's damp fingers tightened around Duncan's; she was so tense her entire body was vibrating. "I'd like to exercise my right to forfeit." Her voice was strong and clear.

What the fuck?

"I forfeit the Medallion to Duncan Edge."

For several seconds, silence throbbed in the vast room, then someone's voice boomed from out of the darkness. "This is unprecedented."

"But possible." She lifted her chin. Stubborn little witch.

Unprecedented? That was a serious understatement. Duncan had never heard of anyone forfeiting the position. Why would they? It was the most coveted, hard to attain position in the wizard community. And it was Serena's. She'd won it fairly. "What the hell are you doing?" he demanded.

"Are you positive this is what you want to do?" Lark asked quietly. "Are you aware that once the position has been forfeited you can never again run for any position on this Council?"

"I am."

"We will convene a Council meeting, and inform you of our decision on this matter at noon tomorrow."

"No!" Serena quickly modified her tone. "No. I'm sorry. But I need this done immediately."

This time the silence was longer, and more speaking. "Very well." Lark didn't sound pleased. Fuck, Duncan thought, *he* wasn't pleased. "Read this. Take your time. Once done, this cannot be *un*done."

A glowing blue square materialized without fanfare directly in front of Serena. It cast an eerie glow on her pale face and set features. "I understand completely."

Duncan knew what she was doing. She was giving him the Head of Council position so that he would be more powerful than Culver. Clever. But he couldn't allow her to do it. "I object."

"You are merely here as a silent observer. Please refrain from interfering in Council business." Lark's tone was flat, and left no room for argument.

"I'm not going to allow Serena to give this up just to help me," Duncan informed the Council tightly, before turning to look at her. "Stop this, Serena, before it's too late."

Serena ignored him. "Do I need to sign anything?"

"You fully understand the ramifications of this act?"

"I do."

"Very well, then sign and date the terms and conditions on the last page." Lark's sigh echoed around the room.

Serena took the pen hovering beside the document, waiting as the pages flipped one over the next until the last page was exposed.

Duncan had no idea what the terms and conditions were. But he was damn sure they wouldn't be pleasant. "Don't."

Serena signed her name with a flourish. The blue glow vanished and in its place hovered the gleaming Medallion of Office, hanging from its intricate and heavy silver chain.

Duncan sucked in a breath. Jesus Christ. He'd wanted this for so long he couldn't remember not wanting it. So for Serena to give this up . . . the concept boggled his mind. "Are you su—"

Serena stood on her toes and brushed a kiss to his mouth. "I'll always love you, Duncan Edge," she whispered as she raised the heavy silver links. "Bow your head."

He did, feeling the ridiculous urge to drop to his knees before her as she settled the chain around his neck.

Duncan's heart knocked hard as a tidal wave of

euphoria tore through him. Power as old as time rocketed through his veins. The sensation of peace, of overwhelming humanity surged through his body. He'd never experienced anything like it.

The smooth links of the chain felt cool around his neck, and with the Medallion resting heavily in the middle of his chest, he raised his head.

"I—"

Serena was gone.

Cold flooded after the fire in his body. "Where," he said, ice in his voice, "is she?"

"Since she is now defenseless," Lark's voice held a hint of reproach, "we've sent her to Edridge Castle for protection until you've resolved your conflict with Trey Culver."

He deliberately slowed his racing heart, controlling the heat of his anger. "You know about Culver? Wait a damn minute. What do you mean Serena is defenseless? She's the least defenseless person I know."

"She's been rendered powerless, Duncan," Lark said quietly. "By giving up the Medallion, Serena has been stripped of all her powers."

"Bullshit! Since when has relinquishing a position on the Council meant losing one's powers? What kind of crap is this?"

"You'll have to ask Serena—"

"Oh no you don't! I want answers, damn you, and I'll take them *now*." He strode toward the empty desk, glaring into the darkness beyond, ready to jump the furniture to get to the Elders who seemed to have all the goddamned answers.

"The Medallion you wear was originally a piece of jewelry," Lark said from the darkness.

Duncan waited.

"The necklace returned by Nairne to Magnus five hundred years ago was melted down, and given to the Elders centuries ago."

"So?" Fucking what? he wanted to add, even while a cold trickle of foreboding slithered down his back. He didn't give a flying duck what the hell the Medallion was made out of. It was the symbolism of the elaborate piece that he wanted.

"Serena broke a promise by gifting it to you."

"What kind of promise?" Duncan braced his fists on the desk, peering into the veil of blackness beyond. "And to whom?"

"Those are Serena's questions to answer. For now, all you need to know is that she is no longer a wizard. Whoa," she snapped as he started to shimmer. "Hang on just a sec, Hot Edge. When you get to the Castle, ask Gabriel and Caleb if they, too, have received a gift."

"Yeah, sure." Duncan didn't give a shit if his brothers had received presents or not, all he cared about was Serena. Once he'd talked to her, he'd go to deal with Culver. Once and for all.

Serena basked in a shaft of sunlight in the beautiful sunroom of Duncan's ancestral home. The flower- and plant-filled room overlooked a small jewel of a lake. But while the view and her surroundings were lovely, she was impatient to speak to Gabriel, and let him know what Duncan had planned.

MacBain, Gabriel's ancient butler, shuffled over to the cloth-draped table. "Ye'll be wantin' a bit of a warm up on that tea then, Miss Serena."

"No thanks, MacBain, I'm fine—Okay. Sure." She smiled as the old man poured yet another cup of tea. "Will Gabriel be down soon?" She'd been here for over an hour and had consumed five cups of tea already. She was too preoccupied about Duncan and Trey to really think about her loss of power. She was sure the loss would eventually have a deep impact on her, but Duncan being safe was the best balm in the world.

"Oh, aye. He'll be down in a trice. We've had a spot of bother today, and he has to put some affairs in order." The old man lowered himself carefully into the wrought iron chair opposite Serena and pulled forward another cup. Wrapping his gnarled fingers around the handle of the teapot, he poured himself a cup, then added milk and six spoons of sugar.

"Ye're the one for Master Duncan then, are ye, lass?" He lifted the cup to his mouth with both hands and drank, his rheumy eyes watching her over the gold rim.

"He's Cursed." Serena figured this old guy must know everything about "his three boys," as he'd called the Edge brothers earlier. He hadn't been surprised to come across a strange woman wandering the entry hall of the castle without an escort. He'd shuffled her into the sunroom and plied her with tea and questions.

For some reason Serena had found herself telling MacBain far more than she would normally ever tell a stranger.

"Well, there is that," he agreed, eyeing a plate of frosted cookies with a gleam in his eye. "That bloody

Curse has been around for five hundred years now." He selected a cookie with blue frosting. "Time for it to end, don't ye think, lass?" He gave her a sly look.

"If you know your 'boys' as well as you say you do, then you know Gabriel doesn't care if it ends. Never has. Caleb pretends the Curse doesn't exist. And Duncan doesn't *want* the Curse to end." MacBain's snowy hair caught the sunlight as he tilted his head.

"We don't always know what's good and right for us, though, do we now?"

"If the Curse ended and Duncan lost his powers, he'd be devastated."

"And ye, lass? Are ye devastated by your loss of powers?"

"I haven't had enough time without them to know for sure," she told him truthfully. Right now she was more concerned about *Duncan's* powers. *Had* the Curse been broken when she'd freely given him the Medallion made from Nairne's necklace? Was that act alone enough to break such a powerful curse? She didn't know. And if it *was* broken, she thought with a frown, had he lost his powers or had they remained unaffected? Not knowing was making her crazy.

"I probably will miss the sheer convenience of having powers," she told MacBain absently. "But I don't think not having them will impact me personally. Duncan, however, believes that he's defined by his powers. So if he *were* to lose his, I think he'd be devastated." If he was no longer a wizard, the wizard Medallion wasn't going to help him. It could only amp up the power of a full, level-one or -two wizard.

His very life depended on him not losing his original powers if, and when, the Curse was broken.

"And would ye be lost without *him*?"

She already felt as though someone had ripped out her heart with a dull instrument. "*Devastated*. But I always knew he was just on loan to me."

"Yet ye gave the lad the Medallion, knowing its history. Knowing its power?"

Serena looked at him, narrow eyed. "How do *you* know the history and the Medallion's power?"

"'*Only freely given will this curse be done.*'" MacBain lifted his cup and sipped his tea.

"Quoting a line of the Curse doesn't answer my question."

"The Master Wizard's Medallion is made from Nairne's necklace. And ye gave it freely, did ye not?" He picked up a green frosted cookie. "Perhaps Gabriel and Caleb also received gifts of jewelry freely given." He bit into the cookie, his eyes alight as he chewed.

Had Duncan's brothers been given the other two pieces of jewelry by their Lifemates?

MacBain gave her an innocent glance from wise, wise eyes. Obviously he wasn't going to tell her *how* he kn—*Yes*. Gabriel and Caleb had been given the other two pieces. "The Curse is broken?!" Serena sat forward, heart pounding. "Is that it? *Is* the Curse broken?"

He wiped his hands carefully on a starched, pale green linen napkin. "Tsk. Tsk. Now how would an old man like me know something like that, Miss Serena? And why don't ye be tellin' me *why* ye gave the special gift to Duncan? Ye've known all along how to break the Curse, have ye not? Being a descendant of the witch, Nairne, as ye are."

She had no idea how he knew what he knew, but he was a wily old man, and clearly knew more than he was telling her. Serena picked up her cup in both hands, just to give herself something to do with them.

"I've always known about Nairne's Curse. Each generation has been sworn not to reveal that the Curse can be easily broken by giving the three sons a piece of the jewelry."

"Not *any* lass can give over the pieces and break the Curse, aye?"

"An Edge's *Lifemate*," Serena added hoarsely, her throat constricted by emotion.

"Aye. His *Lifemate*."

"I had to take the chance that his brothers hadn't been gifted with their jewelry, because if they had, there's a possibility that Duncan and I could both lose our powers with my actions."

"Is that so? And why would ye be believing that, lass?"

"I'm not sure that I do, but Duncan has always been worried that if the Curse were broken that's what would happen. All I *knew* was that once I gave him the means to break the Curse, I would lose *my* powers."

Serena swirled the dregs of her tea in the bottom of the cup, wishing she could read tea leaves. What would these say? She glanced up to meet MacBain's eyes. "I'm still not sure that that won't be the case," she admitted. "But without being Head of the Wizard Council and having the inherent strength that comes with the position, he couldn't hope to vanquish Trey

Culver. And Duncan, the strongest man I know, realized that. Besides which, he'll make a phenomenal Master Wizard. And it was something *he* would have won if I hadn't been nominated."

"And who is it you think nominated you? Two people, correct?"

"I'm pretty sure one of them was Trey. I imagine he thought I wouldn't be any competition. He was wrong. And he'll be wrong again if he thinks he can best Duncan."

"And ye love Duncan enough to give up everything ye are to help him gain everything he thinks he wants?"

That sounded convoluted as hell to Serena, but she got the gist of it. "Yes. I love Duncan that much and more. I'd give him anything in my power to give him. But to set the record straight, I'm not defined by my powers. There are more wonderful things in my life than the ability to create water. Frankly, sharing my power with Duncan today was the best use of my gift I've ever made. Fortunately I have other things of value to offer the Foundation."

MacBain's faded blue eyes twinkled in his craggy face, and his snowy hair shone in the sunlight. He glanced over Serena's shoulder. "What's this then?"

This was one of Duncan's men—Hart?—carrying Casey Rossiter. The moment the boy saw Serena he started crying and struggled to be put down. "Auntie Sereeenaaa!" Serena leapt out of her seat, meeting Case halfway. When she crouched down to gather him in her arms, he wrapped his arms around her neck and held on tightly.

She met Noah Hart's eyes over the head of the sobbing child. He nodded.

Serena whispered to Case for a few minutes. He'd been terribly traumatized, and was still afraid. He needed to be with his mother, and then, Serena was sure, he'd require some serious therapy. Serena was relieved to note that other than having lost weight in the past three weeks, he seemed to be okay physically. She smoothed the child's hair off his face. "Your mom is in Siberia. Would you like her to come here, or would you prefer to go to her there?"

"There."

Serena rose, one arm around Casey's shoulders. Her throat ached as she realized that she couldn't take poor Casey to Joanna herself. "Would you mind teleporting Casey to his mother in Schpotistan right away?"

"Sure."

Serena gave the boy a quick hug and a peck on the cheek. More than he normally allowed, she thought with watery amusement. "See you soon, sweetheart."

Hart and Casey disappeared.

"You didna ask him to teleport you to where Duncan is."

Was MacBain psychic? "It was more important to get Casey and Joanna reunited. Can you—?" A cold little ball of fear lodged in Serena's tummy. This was the first time in her life that she wasn't able to sense another wizard. Was MacBain even a Half? She had no idea and suddenly she decided that she didn't need to know.

Serena's phone rang in her coat pocket. For a moment she forgot that she couldn't shimmer the garment to where she was sitting across the table from it. She rose. "Wow, this is weird." She fumbled in the pocket and retrieved her cell phone. "Hello?"

As soon as she heard it was the head nurse at the facility where Henry was in Germany, Serena backed into a chair. "Is he . . . ?"

"You asked to be called as soon as Professor Morgan regained consciousness, Mrs. Campbell. He's been asking for you."

Serena closed tear-filled eyes in relief. "Thank God. Please. Put him on."

There was a loud throat clearing and then, "Serena?"

Her voice was choked. "Poppy."

There was a moment's silence, before Henry demanded, "Who is this?"

He might recognize her voice, but he wasn't sensing her. This small manifestation gave her a clue as to what her life would be like without powers. "I forfeited my powers, Poppy."

"Darling girl, why?"

She wanted to cry. "It's a long story, and I promise I'll fill you in soon. I can't wait to see you. Tell me how you're do—"

"Health's fine," he said dismissively. "Someone kidnapped Joanna's boy. Has he been found yet?"

"He was found today. He's scared, and shaken, but okay."

"Good. I tried to send Duncan Edge a mental SOS, to go find the child. Joanna was being pressured to give the kidnappers information." That explained why Duncan had interpreted Henry's request as a need to help "her." The "her" in question had been Joanna, not herself.

"That's all been resolved, Poppy." How much should she share? How strong was he?

"Get me out of here today, girl. I've had one damned meal, and it was pig slop. Oh, and by the way. Trey Culver's been visiting me, Serena. Asking me all sorts of questions about the thermal blanket and power source while I was in a coma. What did the idiot think? That I'd mumble out the damned answers to him while I was unconscious? What's he up to? No good I bet. Cheated in school. Charmed you. Get Duncan off his ass and tell him to find out what Culver is up to. And you stay far away from the son of a bitch until the matter is resolved, you hear me?"

Plenty strong, then. "It appears he was the one responsible for kidnapping Joanna's son, forcing her to give him information on the blanket," Serena told him, confirming his suspicions. She made no promises on getting him out of the hospital. Not until she'd had a chance to talk to his doctors first. "Duncan's on it."

"Damn! Well, if anybody can handle Trey, it'll be Duncan."

"Poppy?"

"Whatever it is, the answer is *yes*. You know I could never deny my girl anything."

"I'm longing to see you, but there's something I must do first. Can you please teleport me to wherever Duncan is right now?"

Apparently so, because the last thing she saw

before being teleported was MacBain's unhappy expression.

Duncan left the council chambers and teleported directly to Edridge Castle. He arrived precisely in the middle of the vast entry hall, instantly aware that several other wizards were present. Had Gabriel called another meeting? He'd find out soon enough, he thought, heading to the library which was the most likely place to find his brother. Hopefully Serena was there with him.

Christ. He was torn. He had what he'd always wanted. But at what price? Serena without powers? Just the concept boggled the mind. She'd sacrificed everything for him. Stunning. He was still reeling at her generosity.

He had to find Culver, but first he and Serena needed to lay some cards on the table. "Shit," he muttered under his breath as Tremayne, Alex Stone, Fitzgerald, and MacBain rounded a corner and intercepted him. He wasn't in the mood for a party, and by the expressions on the other men's faces, neither were they.

The butler's wizened face looked even more pinched with concern. "Och, no, lad!" he exclaimed, shooing him back with his hands. "Ye must leave right away! What are ye thinking coming here now?"

Duncan had no idea what MacPain was blathering on about, nor did he give a rat's ass. "Where's Serena?" he demanded, without greeting. There was a strange and profoundly unnatural silence in the castle, and the hair on the back of his neck rose. He glanced around for the source of the feeling, but there was nothing visible.

"For fucksake, Duncan, listen to MacBain. You have to *leave*!" Tremayne grabbed his arm in a powerful grip. "Gabriel's battling Verdine. Having you in the building will cancel his powers. He needs everything he can give to best the bastard."

Duncan shook him off. He'd leave when he had what he'd come for. Serena.

Upton Fitzgerald, all five rail-thin feet of him in his cowboy boots, intercepted. "Hold it pardner. Bad sh—"

Duncan grabbed him by the upper arms and lifted him aside, then approached MacBain in two strides. "Where's Serena, old man?"

Narrow-eyed, the butler poked him in the chest with two bony fingers. Directly beneath the Medallion. "Och! Don't ye be using that tone ta *me*, laddie. We'll talk *ootside*!" He gripped his arm in a surprisingly strong hold and marched him, as he'd done when Duncan was a kid, *ootside*. The other men grimly followed them out into the brilliant sunshine.

He glanced from face to face. "Before the rest of you tell me what the fuck's going on in there," Duncan said through his teeth, "where's Serena?" he demanded of MacBain, who today looked old, pale, and very frail. Duncan ran a hand around the back of his neck and moderated his tone. "Is she inside?"

"The lass was here for a spot of tea," MacBain said, shading his eyes against the glare. "She has now departed."

Duncan's dropped his hand. His jaw hurt from clenching his teeth. There was no point rushing MacBain. The man didn't respond well to pressure, and when MacPain didn't want to talk he was like the goddamned Sphinx. "Did she mention where she was going?" Five minutes ago he wanted her here, but if here was where his brother was in a fight to the death, Duncan would prefer she was anywhere else.

There wasn't a breath of wind on the warm, sunlit air, but he felt forces gathering about the castle that he couldn't see or hear. A strong, icy, invisible current of evil seemed almost tangible as it eddied and spilled around the ancient stones of Edridge Castle.

His senses were now stronger, more attuned than they'd ever been. His vision, he suddenly noticed, was extraordinary. He could clearly see a spider weaving its web in the stones beside an attic window, high in the eves. He could hear the faint rustle of insects in the lawn twenty feet away. And the erratic beat of MacBain's old heart. Duncan's vision and hearing had increased tenfold, yet layered over his new superpowers was the thick unnatural silence that he would be experiencing without them.

Another thing he realized as he waited for MacPain-in-his-ass to spit it out—his body was getting battle ready. Culver wasn't here. Couldn't be here. Yet Duncan was experiencing the same physical manifestations he did when he was about to go into danger.

"The lass was on the telephone earlier. Her godfather, I believe," MacBain told him, glancing around as if he expected Serena to suddenly materialize beside them. "She was teleported—Somewhere."

Two excellent bits of information. Henry had recovered, and Serena was with him in Germany. Duncan would have to be satisfied, for now, knowing she was safely out of the way. He glanced from

Fitzgerald to Tremayne to Stone. Culver, like Serena, was going to have to wait. His brother needed him *now.* "Fill me in on Gabriel's situation."

Alex Stone did so. He included the fact that Verdine had morphed into Duncan and strolled right into the castle, and the dining room where Gabriel had been waiting for him. Duncan hoped to shit his brother hadn't been fooled for a second.

When Stone was done, Duncan shook his head. "I don't know what *Verdine's* story is, but he isn't the killer. Trey Culver is."

"Culver? No way. Not according to your brother or the rest of us," Tremayne inserted flatly. "We saw him, Duncan."

What the fuck was going on? "Culver *also* has the ability to morph. Not a fucking coincidence, I'd bet." Duncan's gaze followed MacBain's to the open front door. The pervasive silence throbbed against his eardrums like an extra heartbeat. "If there's a battle going on inside, it's damned quiet."

Fitzgerald pushed back his straw Stetson with a well-practiced thumb. "I expect it'd be a damn-sight noisier inside that room."

Duncan suspected there was some sort of isolating shield preventing them from hearing whatever the hell was going on in there. A chill raced up his spine. Was it deathly quiet because the battle was *over?* Was his older brother alive? Christ—"I'm going in."

As it happened he *couldn't* go in. He teleported into what felt like a tungsten steel wall, and ended up on the wrong side of the door, unable to get inside. No matter what he tried, Duncan couldn't penetrate the shield.

Helpless, he stood outside as his brother fought for his life. There was nothing he could do. Not a damn, fucking, thing. After several minutes, the others joined him. Ready. Willing and able to help. But equally powerless to do so.

"I'll fetch refreshments," MacBain said, shuffling off down the corridor to the library, and the drinks table, before anyone could stop him. Duncan leaned against the wall opposite the sealed door, bracing a foot behind him. Good. He didn't want the old man this close to the action.

As badly as he needed to be with Serena, as urgently as he had to seek out Culver and have his own battle to the death, Duncan stayed outside the dining room with the other three T-FLAC operatives and waited. And waited. And waited.

Eventually he experienced a small . . . pop. Almost like going through an air lock. "It's over." He shoved open the door.

Chaos.

The room had been destroyed as if a hurricane had blown through it, leaving devastation in its wake. His brother was sprawled on the floor across the room. "Gabriel!"

Dead? Duncan shimmered to his side, then crouched to place two fingers beneath his chin. "Alive. Thank God," he told the others, who came at a run.

Stone called in a cleanup crew while they waited for Gabriel to come out of it. He wasn't too banged up, Duncan noticed with relief; nothing a few weeks wouldn't fix anyway.

Duncan propped up the wall, waiting for his brother

to wake up. Finally he leaned forward and snapped his fingers next to his brother's eardrum. "Hey, bro, time's a'wasting, I have people to see, and butts of my own to kick. Wake the hell up, would you?!"

Gabriel's eyes opened and he struggled to a sitting position still looking a little—okay, a lot—shell shocked.

"I should kick your lazy ass for napping on the job," Alex Stone said with a grin, giving Gabriel a hand up. "Jesus. You look like hell."

"You should see the other guy," Duncan muttered. His eyes met Gabriel's. "Scared the crap out of me when nobody could get into the room. You okay?"

"It was an . . . interesting experience. Is he dead?"

"Hell yes," Tremayne assured him. "Simon went off to do some hocus-pocus with the bastard's head. Lark and Upton took the body off for some kind of wizardly cremation."

Duncan grabbed his brother's arm as he staggered to his feet. "You okay?"

Gabriel gave a negligent half shrug and a slight, not now, shake of his head. Explanations would have to wait. Duncan released his arm, but gave his older brother a lift of his eyebrow, a look that demanded explanations. Details.

"I don't know how the hell you pulled that off, big brother." Duncan acknowledged the delay non-verbally, but he was studying Gabriel like a bug under a microscope. How had he done it? "The odds were stacked against you. Big time." He gave Gabriel a sharp, penetrating look. "How do you account for that?"

"He was twice as strong as I was. I shouldn't have

been able to get anywhere near the son of a bitch."
Gabriel rubbed the back of his neck as he glanced
around the chaos of the dining room. "Shouldn't
have been able to best him. Yet here I am."

Gabriel's power appeared to be supercharged, too.
Strange. Exciting. Inexplicable. And clearly, Duncan's
presence had not negated Gabriel's powers. To the contrary, they'd been strengthened. Meditatively he
touched the Medallion. This was a discussion for when
the dust settled.

Now that he knew Gabriel was okay, he wanted to
assure himself that Serena was, too. Then he had to
deal with Culver.

"You can give me details later. But we *are* going to
have to analyze this business with Verdine."

"There's someone higher than Verdine," Gabriel
told him flatly, his gaze straying across the room. "A
whole fucking lot higher, and more powerful."

"You read Verdine's mind? Give me a clue as to
where to look for the son of a bitch?"

"I'll have to sort through the swill."

"Make it quick, bro."

"Yeah. I hear you," Gabriel said, uncharacteristi-
cally distracted. He turned and walked off.

"Immediate debriefing at HQ," Sebastian said, at the
same time Stone yelled, "Yo! Where are you going?
The Council wants to talk to you right a—Where's he
going?"

"In the morning," Gabriel said without turning,
lifting his hand up to one of the stiffly painted por-
traits, he brought Dr. Cahill down to stand beside
him. He kissed her then swept her up in his arms.

The men parted to let them through as Gabriel carried the Doctor across the train-wreck of a room. They met MacBain half way.

"Och! This mess is unconscionable," the old man muttered, kicking aside a chunk of mahogany paneling in the middle of the water-logged, smoke damaged carpet with his highly polished black shoe.

Tsking, he picked up a glass from the floor, and placed it, just so, on the heat buckled silver tray where the drink listed to the side when he lifted it. "This will take me at least a m——Oh, aye. Now *that* is a neat trick. Is it here to stay?"

The room was completely back to normal. Nothing broken, nothing awry. No sign that anything other than a quiet candlelight dinner had ever happened there. Duncan shook his head and grinned. Hot damn. It was as if nothing had transpired.

Gabriel glanced from MacBain to his brother, and then back to the woman snuggled in his arms. "I have no freaking idea. MacBain? Politely escort our guests to the front door. Then remove the bell. I'm not at home."

They gave Gabriel a moment to get out of the room before Duncan and the other operatives grinned at one another. "Did you see his *expression*?" Fitzgerald chuckled.

Yeah, he had. Duncan knew how that expression felt from the inside, too. "Wizard Council's going to want details," he responded, more concerned than amused by his brother's lover-like demeanor. Reality was pounding on his door, and time really was a'wasting. He had his suspicions about the identity of Verdine's boss.

"Since you're apparently head honcho now," Stone

said, green eyes intent on the chain of office still around Duncan's neck, "he'll report to you, right?" He shook Duncan's hand. "Congratulations, by the way."

"Thanks. Let's go get that drink MacBain offered; then I have to make tracks."

They started filing out, Duncan in the rear. "It'll have to be a quick one, I—" The door slammed shut in his face, followed by a *pop* as if he'd been pulled from deep water before decompression.

He turned slowly. Trey Culver was lounging against the end of the dining room table. He shot Duncan an affable smile as he pushed away. "We're just going to fuck up the room all over again. What a shame."

Duncan remained by the door. "If you have a point," he said calmly. "Make it before I kill you."

"Figured it out yet?" Trey started jabbing and feinting, bobbing on the balls of his feet like a prize-fighter. As if they'd really do something as innocuous as duking it out. "You don't know the half of it, asshole."

MacBain was going to have his ass, Duncan thought as he shimmered the furniture out of the room. He had no plans for dying today. He had unfinished business to deal with.

But more important than his own mortality was the knowledge that if *Culver* won this battle, he would have unbeatable powers. More powers than any wizard had ever possessed in all of time.

No matter what the cost to himself, he couldn't allow that to happen.

"Why don't you go ahead and tell me how fucking clever you think you are?" he taunted as he shot a bolt of lightening at the other man's chest. The fiery spear bounced off Culver's protection spell, leaving him unaffected and still grinning.

Duncan had no intention of *torturing* the son of a bitch. Not that Trey didn't deserve it. It was just a waste of time. Just as Gabriel had had to kill Verdine, it was Duncan's job to exterminate Culver. It was fucking inconceivable that two rogue wizards had been preying on the wizard population right under their noses for weeks—maybe longer—without detection.

One down. One to go.

Death was the only option with Culver. Not only would it put paid to the senseless killings of wizards, but with their leader dead, Red Mantis would crumble as well. Two carrion with one stone. If Culver wasn't eliminated, he would kill again and again, gaining more and more power.

Of course, Duncan thought realistically, Culver might very well be invincible *now*. He wasn't sure if the Curse had been broken or not. At least, he thought as he circled his enemy, waiting for an opening, it appeared his brother Gabriel had come to terms with whatever it was that Fate had handed him.

Just because things had gone well so far didn't mean they'd *continue* to do so. He had no idea if or when he might suddenly be rendered powerless without warning. Christ—

Without his original wizard powers he would no longer have the amped up strength afforded him by his position as Head of the Wizard Council either. Hell, he'd no longer be Head of Council.

How long did he have one way or the other?

He had to end this thing with Culver fast.

"I've fucked you every way to Sunday, Edge. Fucked your girl. Fucked T-FLAC. Fucked with your head. I win. B-bye!" Trey lobbed an arc of electricity at his head.

Duncan shifted out of the way. The arc of silvery lightning followed his movement like a heat seeking missile. It seemed to come at him in slo-mo. This was the proof of the pudding. Either the electricity would bounce off him, or he was dead.

A split second later, the shaft hit the Medallion, making him stagger, but not touching him. In the blink of an eye it boomeranged back at Trey. This strike pierced Culver's protective shield with the sound of a cannon blast. Stunned, the other man had to fall back a few quick steps to keep his balance.

"You can't beat me, Edge," he panted, his eyes manic, his color high. "Not fucking possible. I'm *fifty* times stronger than you could ever be."

"If that were the case, I'd be dead right now." Duncan extended both hands and fired off a barrage of fireballs faster than the human eye could count. Culver quickly erected his damaged shield, but the fiery orbs cut through it like hot knives through butter. "Math was never your strong suit, asshole."

"You're only ten times stronger against the three of us together, dickhead." Gabriel appeared to Duncan's right. His brother Caleb materialized to his left. Without a word they spread out in front of Culver.

"Christ. What the hell are you two bozos doing here?" They'd cancel each other out for sure, Duncan thought grimly. He and Gabriel hadn't, but he sure as shit didn't want to test to see if his elevated powers made that bit of the Curse redundant. He'd soon find out.

"You've been in here having fun far too long," Gabriel shouted as a bombardment of small, sharp, silver knives flew through the air directly at them, so fast it was hard to see what they were. He waved a casual hand, and they turned around and aimed for Culver like a school of sardines, glinting in the sunlight pouring through the arched windows.

The tiny silver projectiles quivered in Culver's protective shield for several seconds before disappearing.

Duncan grinned as Gabriel shot a claymore sword in a spinning arc at Culver. He wished he had a couple of minutes to enjoy working together with his brothers for the first time ever. Not going to happen of course. But damn, having them at his side felt amazing.

"Curse's lifted," Caleb did a running jump, used a wing-backed chair as leverage, and somersaulted behind Culver.

Culver's manic laughter carried on the wind as he shimmered up to the ceiling, out of the way. Clearly he hadn't heard what the middle Edge had said. "I've dedicated most of my life to this moment, don't spoil it by being stupid."

He materialized a swarm of bees that circled Duncan and Gabriel in an ever buzzing, stinging mass. Duncan vanished them a second before they could do any real harm. "You think you're going to kill *us*? Are you fucking *nuts*?" Duncan said with a laugh.

"*This* is what I wanted all along," Culver shouted, sounding slightly crazed. "The three of you together. The three of you, each stronger than before because you couldn't keep your dicks in your pants! Christ. This is priceless."

And suddenly Culver's motivation over the years became crystal clear. "You waited until all three of us amped up our powers." Duncan did a roundhouse kick, surprising both himself and Culver when his booted foot connected with the other man's jaw, knocking him on his ass. Culver slid across the floor on his back. "Killed the other poor SOBs to gain their powers in the hope you could kill *us* and take ours?"

"He's not that much of an idiot," said Caleb, hauling Culver to his feet before his shield was up. Pulling him forward, he delivered a strong knee strike to the other man's face. "Is he?" He had to raise his voice over Culver's scream of pain as his nose was crushed by the force of the blow.

Culver broke Caleb's grip by jettisoning his opponent across the room without warning. Caleb went flying through the air to crash into the stone fireplace. It only took his brother a few seconds to shake himself off and come running back for more, Duncan saw with pride.

"What about Verdine?" Gabriel demanded, circling Culver with slow measured steps and animal grace. He was about to morph and pounce.

Trey wiped his bloody nose with his forearm, his eyes glittering as he kept his eye on first Gabriel, then Duncan, then Caleb. Since they had him circled, he had to keep moving, turning his body to see where they were. "The moron actually believed that we'd eventually be partners in power," Culver grinned. "Asshole was so fucking greedy, he had no idea I was using him. Double the killings, double the powers, and in half the time. You gotta admit that was fuck-ing *brilliant*." Trey bragged as he started duplicating himself.

One Trey Culver was bad enough—but ten? Fifteen?

"You found—" Trey one asked, "How many?" Trey three taunted. The fifth one added, "Four?" Another offered, "Five bodies?" The smiles on each of his identical faces were pure evil, tinged with madness.

Yet another Culver, this one perched on the heavy iron chandelier in the center of the room said matter-of-factly, "Between us we sliced and diced more than twenty-two full, class one, two, and three wizards."

A Culver seated at the other end of the long table inserted, "Assimilating their powers as we went."

"I let the prick keep the powers," the man beside the fireplace told them. "Hell," yet another Culver said with relish, "I didn't give a shit who won this last round. You, Gabriel or Verdine." The man on the chandelier dropped lightly to the floor. "I knew I was going to be the sole survivor and assimilate those powers too."

"You try to kill Serena that night at the warehouse in Schpotistan?" Duncan demanded dangerously. He kept his eye on the prize. There might be upward of twenty Trey Culver's wandering about the large room, but only one had a heat signature.

"Not me *personally*. I told you she was nothing more than a filler, Edge." Each piece of the sentence was uttered by one of his clones. Made no fucking difference to Duncan who was speaking. He knew which one he wanted, and he didn't take his eyes off the dirtwad for a second.

"The easiest way on earth was to let you win the Tests, then sit back while you almost killed yourself," he chuckled. "I get all the payoff with none of the work. And once I've dispatched the three of you, I'll assimilate your powers, too. I'll have it all."

"And what is *all* going to get you, Culver?" Duncan asked as he walked toward him. The man's insane overconfidence was going to be his undoing. That and messing with the Edge brothers!

"You're questioning my career plan, Dunc, old pal? How about this for a reason? Nobody is ever going to be able to stop me. I'm gonna rule the *world*!"

Culver levitated across to the bank of windows high above their heads. "Stupid fuckers. Thanks for making this so God damned *easy. Sayonara,* suckers!" He had to shout to be heard as he dropped a hailstorm of boulders on top of them.

His doppelgängers disappeared like soap bubbles.

Duncan, Gabriel, and Caleb instantly shimmered out of the way, then turned the huge, heavy stones back on Culver. Collectively they held the weight high in the air, bouncing them repeatedly against Culver's shield until they broke through.

With a scream of surprise and rage, Culver shimmered out of range. "That's impossible!" he cried, incensed and red in the face. "You *can't* beat me."

Gabriel morphed into a black panther, his body lean and low to the ground as he crept up on Culver's left flank. Invisible, Caleb skirted to his right.

Duncan's powers were intensified to the point that he could anticipate Trey's every action. Amazing, he thought, seeing the shadow image move seconds before Trey did. Anticipating where he'd be in the next second, Duncan blasted a powerful bolt of fire up Culver's ass. Trey shot ten feet in the air, screaming like a girl, his butt on fire. Caleb's laughter came out of thin air.

"Stop dicking around, Duncan," Gabriel growled, the muscles in his haunches tensing to spring, his sharp claws gleaming in the dusty sunlight streaming through the high windows. "Finish it."

Yeah. Got it. While flexing his newfound powers was a thrill, the bottom line was death, not entertainment.

Duncan gathered every last ounce of his powers into one intense sheet of white-hot fire. He sent it spinning, end over end, at Culver's throat. The cut was so clean that Culver's body was still prepping to send more magic their way as his decapitated head rolled on the floor. His death mask was his stunned expression.

"Finished enough for you?" Duncan asked his brothers as he incinerated what was left of Culver. Jesus. MacBain was going to have a coronary. Gabriel and Caleb came to stand beside him, looking down at the small pile of ash that had been Trey Culver.

"Good job." Gabriel slapped him on the back.

Caleb grabbed him around the neck. "Awesome."

Duncan shoved his brothers aside as he looked up to see the door standing wide open, and framing three women. "Come on, you two, there's someone you need to say hello to."

Gabriel turned his head, his face wreathed in a smile. "*Your* someone is standing over there with *my* someone."

"And mine," Caleb said, grinning from ear to ear.

"No shit?!" Duncan started running toward his future.

Duncan teleported them to his flat in London, only to find Lark lounging on the sofa waiting for them.

"Damn it. Not now, Lark."

"I'll be quick, I promise."

"Time's up," he growled.

Serena elbowed him in the side. "Duncan!" She gave the other woman an inquiring look. "What can we do for you?"

Lark spread her arms on the back of the sofa cushions looking as though she was there for the long haul. Duncan decided he'd nip that idea in the bud. Soon. "I just came to tell you that you and your brothers have broken Nairne's Curse. It's over."

"I know. And I didn't lose my powers." Thank God. From what he'd seen, Serena was handling her lack of powers with equanimity. Duncan wasn't sure *he* would have been able to under the same circumstances.

"Nobody said you would." Lark's lips twitched. "An erroneous presumption on your part, Hot Edge." She glanced at Serena standing next to him. "You, however, *are* powerless. Sorry."

Serena shrugged, not looking too concerned about the prospect. "Because I negated the Curse."

Lark played with the jet necklace at her white throat. "That, too. But Gabriel and Caleb had to do their share.

"Each of them received the gift of one of Nairne's discarded pieces of jewelry. *'Only freely given will this curse be done/To break the spell, three must work as one.'"*

"Great," Duncan said impatiently. "Got it. Thanks." While the damned Curse had been with him like another fucking appendage all his life, now that it was gone he wanted to hold Serena in his arms. He wanted to—

"Since you're here," Serena said, engaging Lark in conversation when Duncan was doing his best to get her to shut up and leave. He liked Lark. A great deal. But he wanted to be alone with Serena. *Now,* damn it. "Could you explain what earthly purpose those Tests had? As far as I could see, they didn't do a damn thing."

"The Tests served their purpose very well." Lark crossed her legs, leaning back against the plush cushions.

"Don't get comfortable," Duncan told her shortly. "You won't be staying."

"Serena overcame a debilitating fear. You, Duncan, learned to chose lo—Learned to overcome your need for violence," she corrected smoothly. "And Trey was punished for his evil deeds by death. All in all the Tests did exactly what the Elders wanted them to do. Don't you think?"

Serena hadn't moved since their arrival, but now she stepped forward, her beautiful eyes narrowed. "You *wanted* Trey to die?"

"There was no other way for it to end," Lark said simply.

"No. What you wanted was for Duncan to kill him."

"That was written. Yes."

"Written *where*?" Serena demanded so aggressively Duncan put a quick restraining spell on her telekinesis, but of course it was unnecessary. She had no powers, thanks to her gift to him.

Lark rose, her nose ring glinting in the lamplight. "Written where these things are written," she said enigmatically before disappearing.

"Well, hell. That didn't tell us much of anything, did it?"

"Oh, I think it told us a great deal," he said softly, as he started stalking her around the mammoth stone coffee table.

"Hmmm," Serena said, walking backward as she met his glare with limpid gray eyes. "Shimmer us naked."

"No." Duncan told her firmly. "Don't muddy the water because you know I want you. You may remove your *coat*."

She gave him a sultry look from heavy lidded eyes. "I can talk very well when I'm prone and naked."

"That may well be." Duncan felt his lips twitch. "But I can't concentrate when you're naked." Hell, he could barely concentrate with her sitting there fully dressed, her bright hair falling like a copper curtain around her slender shoulders.

Serena shrugged out of her coat, then went and curled up in his favorite chair. "Naked would be more fun, but if we're playing twenty questions, let me ask you this first, then. Why did you share your knowledge of the Curse with me that night after Trey's sixteenth birthday party?"

He closed his eyes for a brief second, remembering the sharpness of feeling Serena had always brought, even then. "Because I would have done anything to keep you with me for a few more minutes outside Henry's place. Because I knew I'd missed my opportunity with you, and I was just borrowing you for the evening. And I was right. The next day you went back to Trey."

"He Charmed me." She still sounded annoyed by it.

"I should have dispatched him then and saved us all a hell of a lot of freaking trouble. Except you and I are absolute trouble together, thanks to Nairne and my ancestor."

"I knew that night as you were kissing me, that you were a descendant of Magnus Edridge. I always knew. Like you, I was brought up on the story of Magnus and Nairne. Fireworks, fire and water, we create powerful energy. I'm a direct line descendant of Nairne. And I wanted you to kiss me so badly that night I wasn't going to spoil that moment, even though I knew I'd be in so much trouble if my family found out. Henry knew. Don't be mad at him for not telling you. He helped me keep a family promise passed down through generations. Even when I desperately wanted to break it, he kept me honest. I've been fighting my feelings for you ever since the night of Trey's birthday party when you kissed me."

"Jesus," he whispered dropping onto the coffee table in front of her and taking her slender hand in his. "How wild is that?"

"Pretty damn wild all right," Serena said softly, turning her palm so that their fingers could entwine. "I grew up knowing that I had the power to lift the Curse. Each generation is taught Nairne's righteous anger, and we're shown the Edges' lack of commitment throughout history."

"How can we commit when our lovers will die the second we do?"

Nodding, Serena agreed. "You have a point. But I hardly think that a five-hundred-year-old Curse is going to take in the finer points of your sensibilities."

"Curse. More like a grudge."

Lips twitching, she said, "Let's not fight about it, okay? So, each generation is told about the Curse and then we're told that if we were to help break the Curse, we'd lose our powers. As you know, Nairne was a strong witch."

"True," he said dryly.

She pulled a face. "We'd have no powers. Or worse."

"Worse?" He couldn't imagine anything worse. She'd given away her powers to help him defeat Trey. Duncan would never forget the sacrifice she'd made. "I'll never forget what you've done. Now what can I do for you?" he asked, bringing her fingers up to his mouth.

She batted her lashes. "Later. Seriously? I want you to be the best Head of Council ever, Duncan. You've always wanted it, you worked hard toward it. You'll be terrific." She put her feet on the floor so that their knees bracketed one another. He could see the darker rim around her pupils, and count the freckles across her nose. The urge to kiss her was overwhelming.

"Everyone knew," she reminded him softly. "You made no bones about it. Truthfully, I took a big risk without your permission. I risked breaking the Curse. I couldn't give you extra powers I knew you'd need to defeat Trey, unless I gave you the Medallion, and I know that by doing so I stood a good chance of also breaking the Curse. I didn't want to give you the chance to talk me out of my decision."

"How so?"

"I wasn't sure if my forfeiting the Head of Council position would work if your original powers were stripped."

"Doesn't matter now." He kissed her fingertips.

"But I couldn't let you go against Trey without the power boost afforded by the position. He had the power of at least four wizards assimilated. Even if your brothers could have helped you, the Curse prevented the three of you from working together."

"Also true." His heart swelled with love for this woman and the way she was trying so hard to qualify what she had done.

"That meant the only course I had left open to me was to give you the Medallion of Office. I've always known that Nairne had turned down the three pieces of betrothal jewelry when she Cursed Magnus.

"Family lore says that the necklace had been remelted, and cast into the Medallion worn by every Master Wizard for the past five centuries. I knew that if you had that, you would have the collective strength and power of all wizards—giving you the opportunity to beat Trey on a fairer battlefield." She stared into his eyes. "But I also knew that there was a chance that you would *lose* all your powers once the Curse was finally broken. Can you forgive me?"

"There is nothing to forgive. It worked the way you intended. I just can't get over how you chose your love for me, instead of your duty to the Council."

She didn't even blink. "Without a qualm."

"I feel like we're being given the chance to put history to rest."

"I hope so. It's time to end the fighting between our families."

"I have the strength of all the wizards. I thought I would be different, really different," he pointed out, stunned that he felt so calm about the choice he knew he would make. He never could have imagined it, not without watching how brave Serena had been.

It had taken a while, but he'd finally learned that rushing in with a hot head sometimes backfires and that taking the extra time to research all angles has its benefits.

She put her hand over his, her head bowed. "I know. But I would have done anything to prevent Trey from hurting you."

"Without the strength of the Medallion he would have killed me," Duncan acknowledged, tilting her chin up. "Thank you."

Her gray eyes grew charcoal. "What will you do if your powers are stripped, Duncan? What if the lifting of the Curse takes time to come into effect? What if you do end up losing *all* powers? Would you have chosen what I chose for you?"

He'd wondered that same question himself. Honestly, he wasn't sure he knew the answer.

"I have to report to the Elders in half an hour. And I already know that whatever happens, I will choose whatever will keep me with you. I love you, Serena."

"Duncan," she whispered, cupping his face.

"I'd choose love with you, over duty to the Council, or my country, every time. I finally get why my parents couldn't stay away from one another, even though they sure tried. You are my Lifemate. You, Serena Brightman Campbell, are my love. Without you my life is meaningless. You've had my heart from the time you scarred me with your pencil."

She laughed and traced a fingertip over his brow. "You could have had Caleb get rid of this for you at any time. Hey, if we both end up powerless, I'll even shell out the cash for a great plastic surgeon."

He tackled her back into the chair, pinning her arms over her head. "This scar is a visible reminder of you. Leave it alone."

She clasped his fingers tightly, leaning in to brush her mouth over his. "I love you, Duncan Edge. No matter *what* happens."

"No matter what," he whispered against her soft mouth. "We're in this together."

She gave him a troubled look. "Even if you lose your powers?"

"Even then," he assured her with a tender smile, using a finger to rub away the frown between her pretty eyes. He drew her into his arms, and their mouths met in a kiss filled with promise.

EPILOGUE

NINE MONTHS LATER

Lark Orela strolled into the vast kitchen of Edridge Castle, high-heeled boots clicking on the stone floor, black lace skirts swirling around her ankles. She smiled to see the white-haired old man sitting at the enormous kitchen table. He had a glass of Gabriel's best Scotch in his hand and an expectant look on his face as he rose to greet her.

"It's done, then?"

She grinned. Serena, Heather, and Eden had all just delivered their babies with the assistance of three midwives. Mothers, babies, and Edge boys were all in fine fettle, and over the moon. "Aye. Three bonnie wee lasses."

"Took you long enough," he groused. But he was smiling beneath his white moustache. Even ancient, he was still a handsome man, she thought. The white hair didn't detract from the strength in his face, or the intelligence in his blue eyes as he looked at her.

He lifted the cut-crystal decanter. When she nodded he filled the glass with three fingers and handed it to her. "Are ye gonna sit, or must ye go haring back upstairs any minute to check on your handiwork?"

"They don't need me anymore."

Duncan, of course, had never lost his powers. And he'd gifted back Serena's as an engagement present. And a good thing, too. They'd need their combined powers to deal with their first daughter, Lark thought with an inner smile.

She pulled out a chair and sat down, enjoying the swish of her taffeta-lined skirts drifting on the floor around her. She was going to miss these clothes, she thought, sipping Gabriel's fine whiskey and enjoying the smoky heat of it sliding down her throat.

"Five hundred years was a powerful long time to be bearing a grudge." MacBain scowled.

"Aye." She looked at him over the rim of her glass. "It was a powerful hurt."

He walked painfully to her side, then sank to his haunches in front of her, his bones and joints creaking. He took her hand in his. "The lesson, long and painful as it was, was learned. And learned well."

She touched his weathered cheek. "Aye. I know. 'Tis done now." Nairne morphed back into herself, half reluctant and half excited. She'd liked the clothes, and the shoes, of this century. The freedom. The energy. Still, Curse lifted, she felt lighter, freer than she had in five hundred years. "I miss my lover."

"Aye. As have I, my dearest heart." Magnus's snowy hair returned to his familiar black, the lines left his face, and his eyes, those hot Edridge blue eyes, blazed up at her. He rose, tall and straight, broad shouldered and handsome. Dressed now in his *feilidh-mhor*, his Highland belted plaid, gathered into folds and belted around his strong, young body. A white linen *leine*, and leather *trews*.

The man she'd loved for over five hundred years.

No one, in all the years since the day they'd met, had even come close to holding her heart. She'd never loved anyone else, not since that fateful day when she'd fired his love tokens at his feet, and cursed his family for all time.

Magnus held out his hand and drew Nairne to her feet beside him. He cupped her cheek, his heart overfilling with love for her. "The boys have chosen well, have they not? Their brides are fine young women. Together they will raise strong children of their own. They will have perfect lives."

"Not perfect. No." Nairne brought his hand to her mouth and kissed his palm. "There'd be no learning from perfect. No fun. No fighting. No making up. But there will be great love and joy. Many beautiful children, lads and lassies, to bless their days, and each other to bless their nights. Your descendants will live long, healthy, productive lives. Surrounded by the people they love."

Magnus threaded his fingers through her thick black curls, and, cupping the back of her head, drew her up on her toes. "Worth the journey, my darling?"

"Oh, aye. And a lesson hard learned. I punished myself as much as I punished you, my love. Five hundred years wasted."

Magnus swung her up in his arms. "Then let's not waste a moment more. I want you to myself, woman. Let's go home."

"To Scotland." She rested her head on his brawny shoulder, content. "Aye, Magnus, my love. Let us go home. I've a thing or two I've learned over the years that I want to show you."

The sound of their laughter lingered in the empty kitchen of Edridge Castle long after they were gone.

  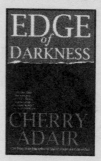